ARCANE HAVEN

ALSO BY KRISTEN MARTIN

Beyond the Stars and Shadows

THE INTERNATIONAL BESTSELLING SERIES

Shadow Crown

Renegade Cruex

Jaded Spring

Crescent Fire

Arcane Haven

Midnight Reign

THE INTERNATIONAL BESTSELLING SERIES

The Alpha Drive

The Order of Omega

Restitution

ARCANE HAVEN

BOOK FIVE

KRISTEN MARTIN

BLACK FALCON PRESS

To my fellow students of life —
may you soon discover all that is
truly possible for you.

PRONUNCIATION GUIDE

CHARACTERS

Arden: Ar-den

Rydan: Ry-den

Darius: Dare-ee-us

Aldreda: Al-dray-duh

Cerylia: Sur-lee-uh

Braxton: Brax-ten

Xerin: Zer-in

Cyfrin: Ka-frin

PLACES

Trendalath: Tren-duh-loth

Sardoria: Sar-door-ee-uh

Vaekith: Vy-kith

Orihia: Or-eye-uh

Ipcea: Ip-see

Chialka: Key-all-kuh

Miraenia: Mur-ay-nee-uh

Lonia: Lone-ee-uh

Lirath: Leer-ath

Eadrios: Ay-dree-os

OTHER

illusié: ill-oo-see-ayy

magick: ma-jik (magic)

Caldari: Kal-darr-ee

Cruex: Crew

Vaekith
Mountains
Drakken
Isle
Rovie
Volkham
Trendalath
Miraenia
Declorath
Crostan Islands
Ipcea
Athia
Sunngate
THE LAND
AERID

rath Cave
Eadrios
Sardoria
Woods
Eroesa
Chialka
Orihia
Thering Forest
Isle of Lonia
OF
on

ARCANE
HAVEN

ARDEN ELIRI

THE NEWS OF Braxton certainly comes as a shock. And Opal's assuredness in the matter?

Even more so.

Rydan and I fall back behind the others, watching as Lane ushers everyone into Midvale. Opal is the last to join them. She brushes by us without so much as a glance or a smile, and it takes everything in me not to reach out and pin her to the ground.

From the front of the group, I notice Felix glance over his shoulder at me. I give him a small nod, and I can tell he's about to smile . . . until his eyes land on who's standing next to me. With a sharp jerk of his head, he turns back around and swiftly follows Lane inside.

"I suppose we shouldn't straggle too far behind," I mutter, pulling on Rydan's arm.

He follows me without saying a word. Honestly, he doesn't have to. I know exactly what he's thinking because it's exactly what I'm thinking.

What have we done?

"We need to talk about this—"

I shake my head as if to say *"later"*, but deep down, my blood is boiling, my heart is pounding, and every inch of me feels on edge.

We shouldn't have brought Opal here.

I should have told Cerylia.

I should have delayed this as much as possible.

Because now, not only have we endangered ourselves; we've also endangered everyone in Midvale.

"Come on, you two!" Lane calls from the giant doors.

Rydan and I pick up the pace. When we finally cross the threshold, the rest of the group is standing in the center of the haven, staring up and around in awe, just as we had.

"I take it you've been here before?"

Lane directs her hazel eyes right at me. "Yes. Many times." She tilts her head, ebony ringlets falling alongside her face. "You haven't?"

"Only once." I force a smile. "Our trip here was cut short."

"An accident?"

"More or less, yes. But a happy accident, I suppose."

I follow her around the corner of an ancient-looking desk, its legs secured deep in the ground, as if they were the sturdy roots of a tree themselves. She opens a few of the drawers until whatever she's looking for floats out. A yellow orb. "Let's see," she says, referencing something I can't quite make out. "How about the northeastern wing, chambers three through seven? Once we get you all settled, we can talk about what's happened with Braxton." She nearly chokes on his name, and

I can feel the guilt that's currently gripping her as if it were my own.

I feel for her. I really do. I know what it's like to feel entirely at fault for someone else's fate. I want to say something, but words fail me. So, instead, I watch as the yellow orb closes in on itself before splaying out in what appears to be a map. "I assume you don't mind pairing up?" She moves the images of the chambers around with her hands, zooming in, then back out, checking to see what's available and what isn't.

Confused, I say, "I thought this was a school?"

"It is." She stops what she's doing as a small smile tugs at the corner of her mouth. "An *illusié* school, mind you."

"So there's housing?"

"Mmhmm."

"And there's . . . *more*? Of *us*?"

"Honestly now, you didn't believe you were the only ones, did you?"

I'm about to tell her that it'd certainly started to feel that way, what with all we've been through as a group, but I think better of it. "Believe me, I've hoped. I just figured, well, isn't that what Orihia is for?"

"Oh, don't get me wrong. Orihia is lovely. But it's more for leisure. Midvale is, how do you say, better *equipped* for illusié. To further hone our abilities."

"At a place where not even illusié *know* they have access?" My question comes out sharper than I'd intended, but I don't regret it. In fact, if I've gathered anything from this brief interaction, it's that the people here have been *hiding*. And that's infuriating.

Her answer is clipped. "They know when they need to know."

"I'm not sure I agree with that. Sure would have been nice to know about Midvale *months* ago."

Lane's gaze doesn't leave mine as she blatantly ignores my remark. "Pairs, then?" she repeats as she gestures to the glowing outlines of the open chambers floating before us.

"That should be fine." I glance over at my friends. "I assume Estelle will stay with you?"

"That would be wise. Especially if we have any late arrivals." She sizes up the group. "Will Queen Jareth prefer her own quarters?"

"Opal and I will stay together," Cerylia calls out, somehow having overheard our conversation from clear across the room.

Vira's head whips toward me then, her eyes shooting daggers. For some reason, I'm the one who's being tasked with rooming everyone. *Great.*

"So Cerylia and Opal will be in one room, Rydan and Vira in another," I say, motioning in their direction. I try to ignore the pang of discomfort hearing their names paired together, yet again. "I suppose Haskell and Avery can stay in a room."

"Which leaves you and Felix," she finishes.

I hesitate before saying, "Yes. That'll work just fine."

Lane catches my trepidation. "Will it, though?"

For someone I've only just met, the girl's sharp.

"Yes," I say curtly, readying to turn away from her.

"Don't forget your keys." She holds out two gigantic brass keys, engraved **M.V.** at the head.

Amused, I take them from her. "What, no incantation to open the door?"

"Oh, don't worry, everything here is enchanted. Once you open the door and the room recognizes you, the key essentially disappears."

"Essentially?"

"Yes, in that *you* become the key itself." She gathers the remaining keys, nearly tripping over herself as she leaves to distribute the rest to the group.

It only takes a second to catch Felix's stare from across the room. I flash the two keys at him and offer a small smile, hoping it'll lighten the mood—but from the bleak look on his face, it seems this unwelcome tension between us is here to stay.

FELIX BARLOW

AS INCLINED AS he feels to pull Opal aside for a private conversation, doing so would undoubtedly raise some eyebrows. A sinking feeling forms in the pit of Felix's stomach as he watches Lane hand Queen Jareth her room key, all the while wondering how the arrangement could possibly benefit either her or Opal.

His gaze burning a hole in the back of her head, the silver-haired Caldari turns, catching his stare. However indirectly, his eyes must communicate his rising level of urgency because she tilts her head toward a nearby pillar, to which he casually glides over.

"Can't this wait?" Opal murmurs through gritted teeth.

"That would depend on your reasoning and subsequent level of insanity," he whispers back.

Opal turns, hand hovering over her chest in mock offense. "So, it's *my* fault that *your* girlfriend chose my roommate for me?"

"She isn't my girlfriend."

Opal smirks. "Lover?"

"No."

"Play-thing?"

"Nope."

"What then?"

If her recovery hadn't been so recent, he would have strangled her right then and there. "A friend."

Opal scoffs. "She won't be once we're through with her."

He levels a steely gaze at her, despite the horrifying truth of her statement. "What good can come of this arrangement?" he asks, desperate to change the subject.

"What I've been tasked with is none of your concern."

Xerin. Felix blows out a long breath. "I think it is."

"Ask him, then. The next time you two meet."

Her laissez-faire approach to their conversation is growing old. "Who knows when that will be? Especially since we're here, in the Veil—"

"If you'd rather call attention our way by requesting that we change my—and only my—room assignment, by all means, be my guest." She waves a hand in the air to try and grab Lane's attention. "Just know *you'll* be the one answering any and all inquiries regarding said change."

Felix smacks her arm down just as Lane finishes distributing the keys and starts walking their way. He forces a smile as she strolls by them, his grip locked tightly around Opal's wrist. When she's well out of earshot, he leans in and whispers, "For the record, this is a bad idea."

Opal breaks free from his grip. "I'd hardly call it bad."

Before he can counter, Arden approaches, keys in hand. The passing glance Opal gives her is cold enough to shatter even the thickest ice, but Arden isn't focused on Opal. She's focused on him. "Your key."

It's hard to ignore the sensation that rolls over him as he reaches toward her, hand brushing hers. "Thanks."

She glances over her shoulder then, and he half expects her to ask about his conversation with Opal, but she remains quiet. Just because she chooses not to speak doesn't mean there isn't anything worth saying. It's often the silent ones who have the keenest intuition.

With her gaze downcast, it's hard to tell what she's thinking, so Felix motions to the space in front of him, hoping to catch a glimpse of what's brewing behind those jaded eyes. It isn't that easy, though. Arden keeps her gaze lowered, then says, "After you."

Felix palms the key, his hand tightening over the metal. As much as it pains him, he obliges her. Perhaps he'd been wrong. Perhaps there really *isn't* anything worth saying.

RYDAN HELSTROM

TRY AS HE might, Rydan can't help but watch Arden as she follows Felix to the portal that leads to their designated wing. Surely Vira's noticed but, much to his surprise, she's too busy talking out loud and pointing at the many marvels of Midvale.

"Would you look at these bookcases and these vines—the extent of this place!" She rushes ahead of him, nearly falling in line beside the others. "I mean, I thought Orihia was something, but this place? Just *wow*."

He angles his head, urging her to come back over. "How about we let the others go first?"

"How chivalrous of you," Vira teases.

Arden must have heard him because she quickly glances over her shoulder, forces a smile, then disappears into a shimmering curtain of violet and indigo.

"Why are you acting like this isn't one of the coolest places you've ever seen?" Vira's skipping back over to him when she suddenly brings herself to a stop, as if realizing the answer to her own question. "Because you've already seen it before. With Arden," she says quietly.

Let the damage control commence. "Come on now, that isn't entirely accurate. We only saw the entrance." He points to where they're currently standing. "So *this*, right here, right now, is all new to me." He leans over and presses a soft kiss to her cheek. "And I'm experiencing it with *you*."

Indignation flashes across her eyes but, thankfully, it doesn't linger. She extends a hand to him, which he gladly takes. "Ever entered a portal before?"

"If it's anything like transporting . . ."

"Oh, no. This is *much* smoother."

"Thank the lords for that," he murmurs.

He squeezes her hand as they walk into the portal together. With a single blink, he's crossed the threshold into the northeastern wing. And, based on the bronze plaque that's hanging on the wall, they're right where they need to be, in chamber five.

Rydan breaks his grip from Vira's to pat his chest and stomach. Still in one piece. He turns to look behind him, but the portal's gone. "I figured I'd feel—"

"Sick? Woozy? Disoriented?" Vira finishes. "I told you— *way* easier than transporting."

"Perhaps Haskell should take note."

She laughs, then walks over to the door that displays the matching emblem on their key. "This must be it." She runs her index finger over the symbol—the point of an arrow facing west, then scoffs. "How fitting."

"What is?"

"This is the ancient rune for fire."

Rydan raises a brow. *Seems Lane might know more than she's willing to let on.*

Vira inserts the key into the lock before rotating it a quarter-turn to the left. Just as Lane had alluded to, the door creaks open and the key disintegrates. Its remains float through the air, encircling each of their wrists in a flurry of ash.

Rydan can't help but stare in awe as the ancient symbol is etched ever so faintly into his skin. "So this must be what Lane meant when she said *we* become the key."

"Probably for the best, seeing as you tend to lose the things most important to you."

Even though she says it in jest, her remark cuts deep. He knows she's referring to the crescent fire—as well as his accusation that *her* brother was the one to take it—but as much as he wants to strike back, he bites his tongue.

Change the subject. Fast.

It isn't all that difficult, seeing as he *does* have a burning question. "We got up here, but how exactly are we supposed to get back down?"

"*Voco ostium,*" Vira says, not bothering to look at him or further clarify the gibberish she's just said. "I swear, sometimes it's like you purposely tune people out."

"Voco *what?*"

She sighs. "You summon it. The portal. And you do that by saying," she lowers her voice, "*voco ostium*—except way clearer and a bit louder."

"Was this something Lane mentioned?"

She nods while giving a hasty click of her tongue.

"My mind must have been elsewhere."

She gives him a knowing look. "Must have been."

He hangs back as she steps into their room, recoiling at the thought of following her. "I'm going to see what else is up here."

She sighs, waving a hand in the air. "I'll be here."

Before she can change her mind or invite herself to join him, Rydan's bounding down the hall, wondering if chamber five has a bar or something similar where he can get a stiff drink. Vira most certainly wouldn't approve. Arden wouldn't either.

Hasn't stopped him before.

The slate stone beneath his feet is smooth, soundless, and nearly transparent, the walls a shade of deep plum with faerie lights floating both above and below him. With the number of doors lining either side of the hall, this particular chamber has no end in sight—that is, until he reaches a giant glass window that *must* be enchanted, given the fact that Midvale resides in a cavern, because the image on display is that of a snowy mountaintop, much like the range that borders Sardoria.

He sits on the ledge overlooking the faux scenery, feeling taken aback when he feels a gust of wind that most certainly *isn't* imagined. *They really go all out here.* He takes another look at his wrist, tracing the shape of the rune, before bringing both hands out in front of him. They ignite almost instantly, golden flames dancing atop his fingers.

"Looks like you've got just what you need to keep yourself warm."

Even though there's no mistaking to whom that brusque voice belongs, it still startles him. The flames extinguish just in time for Rydan to push himself off the ledge—before he can cause any real damage—and greet Haskell. "I thought you'd be in your room?"

"Eh," Haskell says with a shrug. "Would it be weird to say that I miss my previous company?"

Rydan's not sure if he means Arden, or him and Vira, so he just says, "Not weird at all. Avery can be a handful."

"That he can be." Haskell heaves a deep sigh as he looks out the window. "Reminds me a lot of Lirath."

Rydan follows his gaze. "It does. Speaking of, I don't think we ever properly thanked you."

There's a mischievous glint in his eyes, one that makes him look ten years younger. "I got all the thanks I need." His expression suddenly shifts into a somber one. "You know, I couldn't quite believe it when I learned that Arden was alive. You and Vira played a much larger role in that than you realize."

"Really? How so?"

"I knew the minute I handed you my pocket watch. In Chialka. The recognition on your face was undeniable."

"That was precisely the moment I realized who you were. That you were Arden's brother. That Arden *had* a brother," Rydan says thoughtfully.

"I've noticed the looks the two of you have been exchanging. Back in Orihia. Just outside Midvale. I pick up on that kind of stuff. Arden can be a bit of a closed book, but if there's anything you need to talk about . . ."

"Thanks, Haskell."

"Don't mention it." He doesn't press further. "Well, I'm off to continue my quest for water, seeing as Avery could use *a lot* of it."

"I take it he still isn't feeling well?"

He shakes his head. "I can't tell if it's the libations or the travel or something else entirely. Perhaps it's a combination of things." He runs a hand along his beard. "Then again, he's been much more interested in brewing tonics of the herbal variety—some more potent than others. Says his magick hasn't felt the same since the ritual you two performed in Orihia for the fallen illusié." He shrugs. "In any case, water should help."

Rydan attempts to hide his concern with a laugh. Why would Avery feel ill so long after the ritual? Especially when he himself has never felt better? "Well, good luck with that. And if you need any help, you know where to find me." He angles his head toward the hallway. "In chamber five."

"We're right above you. Chamber six," he says ruefully. "Although our window shows a lava spring bordering on eruption instead of serene, white-capped mountains. I much prefer your scenery. Reminds me a lot of home." He clasps his hands together. "Well, I'm off to do my rounds. Figured I might as well visit each chamber so that I can transport to wherever I might be needed. These portals give me a headache."

Rydan does his best not to gape at him or lecture him about how much *better* the portals are than his transporting.

To each their own.

"See you around," he calls out before disappearing in a flash of emerald light.

Rydan turns back toward the window, his gaze landing on the blustery winter landscape. He wouldn't dare say it, but of all the places he's ventured to, Haskell's cave in Lirath was the one place he felt *free*—like he didn't have to constantly watch his back.

Something tells him that Midvale will be the exact opposite.

CERYLIA JARETH

CERYLIA'S REQUEST TO room with Opal came as a bit of a shock to both her *and* the rest of the group, but she has her reasons . . . as a queen should. Given the recent string of events that have transpired, keeping Opal as close as possible is, without a doubt, a priority.

Lane had been gracious enough to bestow upon them a chamber that houses two very large, very *separate* living quarters. As soon as they'd arrived, Cerylia had veered to the left, opening the double doors to the first room. Decent, what with its array of velvet armchairs, rectangular wooden-carved coffee table, small stone hearth, and Victorian-style king-size bed. One look at the clawfoot tub almost has her sold, but something tells her to hold out.

"I'll take this one," Opal says, no doubt having eyed the clawfoot tub. "Nightly baths and fires have become a sort of ritual for me."

Realizing she's standing in the center of the doorway, Cerylia drifts to the side before giving Opal as warm a smile as she can muster. "I'll be just across the hall."

Opal gives her a small nod, then enters the room before shutting the giant double doors with hardly any restraint. Cerylia brushes off the frank response, turns on her heel, and heads across the sitting room to the next set of double doors. She rests her palms against the handles, praying that she's chosen well. With a small push, the doors open to reveal . . . *a sanctuary.*

As far as she can tell, there are multiple rooms *within* this room—and not only that, but she has a small arboretum that doubles as a balcony, and a much larger hearth than Opal's, the quartz-infused stone chimney climbing all the way up the length of the room, leading to a dome-shaped cathedral-style ceiling. Her bed, with its many arches and spires, is also Victorian-style, and extends almost the entire length of the back wall.

There are multiple wooden-paneled armoires with delicate carvings engraved on the sides; a well-lit vanity with illusié-infused faerie lighting; and a plush ivory rug that engulfs her in pure bliss from the very moment she sets foot on it.

Halfway across the room, the door to her left leads to an elegant washroom, also donning a clawfoot tub underneath a particularly large skylight; another vanity with every oil, soap, tonic, and apothecary item she could possibly think of; a wrought-iron door that leads to yet *another* balcony; and, to top it all off, a walk-in closet with only the finest silks and satins in an array of robes, gowns, and cloaks.

Speaking of which . . . she removes one of the velvet hangers and unhooks her cloak before hanging it on the nearest rack. She rolls her neck from side to side, smiling as she continues to explore her new room—but not before sliding into some finely woven gossamer slippers.

Leaving the garderobe behind, she trails the tips of her fingers along a bronze-plated mirror before settling on door number two. A gentle push reveals her very own arcane library. The mere sight of it is enough to make her knees buckle. The room is circular and quite wide, its walls lined with shelf after shelf of ancient texts—books she'd been convinced she'd never get the chance to study or read, much less hold—books she was certain were destroyed by those who were, well, *less inclined* to regard illusié in the manner they so deserve.

Floor to ceiling shelves, climbing at least seven stories high, surround her, along with the tallest ladder she's ever seen. The ladder, however, isn't for climbing, as she can clearly see from its shimmering form. Much like the walkways in Orihia, it takes her where she wants to go, so long as she indicates the shelf number. A bit different than the floating bookshelves in the lobby downstairs, but she likes its old-school feel—with just a flair of modern magick.

A square marble desk, twice the length of her, sits in the middle of the library, until she realizes it's actually four smaller desks that have been shoved together. It piques her curiosity as to who'd occupied this room before her and what sort of business had been conducted here—something she'll likely never know, seeing as nothing's been left behind . . . not even an open book.

Excited at the prospect of finally discovering how to regain her extracting abilities, Cerylia has to force herself to leave the beauty of the room and keep exploring. When she arrives at the last and final door, save for the arboretum, she can't help but notice that it's locked. Seeing as her only key had disappeared upon entry, she's at a loss for what's behind door number three. She presses her ear against it, not sure what she's expecting to hear, but there's only silence.

"Odd," she murmurs to herself as she takes a step back and sets her hands on her hips. She's eyeing the door, studying its every nook and cranny, when something familiar catches her eye. Embedded in the bottom left corner, running parallel to the door frame, is the hilt of a dagger sans the blade. *It can't be.* Her stomach drops as her fingers graze the Trendalath emblem carved into the leather binding. She squeezes her eyes shut, hoping that when she opens them again, the very same dagger that Aldreda Tymond had used to murder her husband will somehow disappear.

But it remains, in all its taunting glory.

Beyond such a heart-wrenching discovery, a larger realization looms. If the dagger is here, then at one point or another, Queen Aldreda Tymond was a resident of Midvale. When or for how long remains to be seen, but that would also mean . . . Aldreda was illusié. And that this was her room.

"I have no choice but to uncover what's behind this door," Cerylia murmurs as she runs her hands across the surface, hoping to find an entry point; but, much to her chagrin, she comes up short. She takes a step back to survey the door in greater detail when a voice startles her.

"My, my, perhaps I should have done a full walk-through."

Cerylia whirls around to find Opal at the entryway.

The girl waggles her eyebrows. "My mistake, I didn't mean to startle you. I've just finished settling in. I hope you don't mind . . ."

"Actually, I'm just now getting settled myself," Cerylia says as she casually backs away from the mystery door, hoping Opal won't ask questions.

"Well then, pardon the interruption," Opal says, but not before her eyes flick to the door.

Damn it.

"I'll leave you to it," she says, disappearing into the foyer shortly after.

Cerylia blows out a long breath. *As if she weren't already on edge . . .* She drops into one of the leather armchairs and kicks her slippered feet up on the coffee table, momentarily admiring the delicate design. Handcrafted, no doubt—and from The Isle of Lonia, if she had to guess. Surely a gift Dane would have surprised her with, had they gotten the chance.

Instead, she's occupying the very room of the woman who'd murdered her husband in cold blood, knowing that what lies behind that locked door could very well answer the questions that have plagued her for a decade.

DARIUS TYMOND

WITH HIS STAFF gone missing, Darius is warier than ever as he roams about the castle, suspicious of everything and everyone. He passes by the courtyard, his gaze settling on each of his Cruex assassins. Hidden in the shadows of an alcove, he watches out a narrowly cut window in the stone. One disturbing thought after another floats across his mind.

How many of them are like Lane?

Did they know of her intent?

Did Braxton somehow get to her? Or vice versa?

He fists his hands at his sides, feeling the edges of the amethyst ring as it digs into his skin. He'd made such headway with Braxton, such progress—all wasted.

With both Lane and Braxton missing, as well as Hugh, Darius will eventually need to announce something along the lines of their disappearance. Elias's non-return had been one thing—*that* he could brush past without anyone catching wind of potential foul play. But three Cruex? As the most skilled assassins in Aeridon, it will undoubtedly raise suspicion. But, seeing as Braxton and Lane have betrayed their sworn oaths—and thereby everyone in and around Trendalath—perhaps he can lump Hugh in with the lot and turn their fellow Cruex against them . . .

In all the years of his reign, he's never experienced such disloyalty—unless, of course, you add his late wife and the Savant's Caster into the situation. No, this had all begun with the only female assassin he'd deigned to allow into the Cruex ranks.

Arden Eliri.

Rydan had followed in her footsteps.

Then Lane.

And now, his very own blood, his son—Braxton.

Traitors. Every last one of them.

The time will come where he won't need any of them anymore. A lonely journey, no doubt . . . but, then again, hasn't it been that way already?

With a fleeting look at the assassins, Darius presses off the stone wall and flings his robes behind him. Lying to the Cruex should work in his favor; the Savant, however, are an entirely different story.

They've already started to question his authority, his strength, what with Clive's untimely break from the dungeons. He'd asked each of them to fortify the castle after his recent unexpected encounter with the Caster, with the intention of keeping him out for as long as possible. Darius knew that locking him up was a long shot to begin with. And because he can't kill the bastard . . .

The staff. Damn that staff. It's the one thing, besides this ring, he'd never misplace. And as much as Clive loathes his very existence, he wouldn't dare steal it. No, that's been an unspoken agreement between the two of them. His life for what that staff gives Darius access to.

Which means . . . it was either one of the Cruex, one of the Savant, or Cyrus. Although his advisor *has* been mostly by his side for weeks—unless, of course, he's off somewhere performing some delegated task. Not to mention, Cyrus knows what's at stake. He knows where he'll end up if he so much as flinches at the idea of betraying his king.

Quite the risk to take . . . but not entirely impossible.

His head pounding, Darius finally arrives at his chambers, yielding to solitude for the evening. If he's going to put on a show for the Cruex *and* the Savant, he must be at his best—and that requires sleep and a light conscience, only one of which he has control over.

It certainly isn't the latter.

BRAXTON HORNSBY

TIME IS LOST on him here—wherever *here* is. Days, weeks, *months* could have gone by, and he wouldn't even know the difference. The last shred of sanity he's able to cling to is that of seeing Opal and Felix . . . and Arden. That green and gold shimmering orb amongst a backdrop of muted gray. Although he'd called out to them, *reached* for them, they hadn't heard his desperate cries.

But that had somehow been different . . . different than when he'd seen Rydan. While the former had seemed like merely a projection—some fantastical illusion—Rydan had appeared . . . *real*. Lifelike. Not a fabrication at all, but a figure sewn and stitched into this world.

Braxton's sitting cross-legged on the ground, the metal crest mocking him from its place against the base of a "tree", if one could even call it that. Everything here is dead, gray, dreary, *lifeless*—and yet, Rydan had been here, very much alive. Or so it'd appeared.

What is he supposed to make of that?

Braxton's staring intently at the crest, at the engraved flames, when it dawns on him that he hasn't had anything to eat or drink in, well, *however long* he's been here. He places his hands against his stomach, waiting for it to rumble with pangs of hunger, but there isn't a single sound. He deliberately moves his hands to his throat before clearing it, expecting it to be parched, but he isn't thirsty in the slightest.

"So that answers one question," he says aloud to nothing and no one. This place must be of illusié origin; if not, the alternative is that he's, well, *dead*—and that just can't be. He can still feel his heart pounding, blood pumping through his veins, the very *life force* with each breath he takes, no matter how shallow it all might feel in the moment.

Okay, so . . . not dead, then.

Before pushing himself to his feet, he sweeps the crest from the ground. His gaze settles on the very trail he's walked down what feels like a hundred times—*over and over and over again.* The scenery doesn't change; there's no "checkpoints" or "markers" to indicate how far he's gone; and there's no end in sight.

It's maddening.

If not for the faint glimmer of hope that seeing his friends had provided, he probably would have bashed his head in with the damn crest. *Morbid, but true.*

Blowing out a long, convoluted breath, he takes a step forward. Then another. He keeps his gaze pointed at the ground, knowing that, if he looks up, he'll only become more disheartened than he already is—if that's even possible. He must admit, this is a pretty low *low.*

There's no getting around that.

In an effort to distract himself, he begins to hum softly about ten minutes in, a tune his mother used to sing to him. It's been some time since he'd last heard it, but the melody has remained crisp in his mind, like a well-preserved flower. The tune is soft and gentle, flowing and graceful, just as his mother had been.

The gravity of the situation—his mother, her death; his father, his deceit; his being stuck here with little to no hope of escaping—begins to weigh on him, but Braxton manages to whistle it away, the sweet harmony ringing in his ears.

Lane knows he's here.

She knows.

Lane knows I'm here.

It's the only thought that propels him forward as the melody blends into his surroundings, ultimately fading to become the very essence of this place . . .

Which is absolutely *nothing*.

ARDEN ELIRI

I LEAVE THE door open as I make my way into my—*our*—chambers, with Felix mere steps ahead of me. The room we've been designated is quaint, and the first thing I notice is that there's only one bed. One washroom.

One *everything*.

"Oh, you're going to *love* this," I murmur sarcastically.

"Love what?"

I straighten at his voice. Its soft edginess. Its cautionary trust. Its fading hopefulness. I think that's what Felix and I have in common. We're walking contradictions, forever skirting the line between one extreme and the other, never quite meeting in the middle—or at least not long enough to make any real progress. And so, our relationship is like fire and ice—hardly ever fluid, like water—but lords, how we *need* to be like water. For both our sakes.

With this in mind, I walk further into the room and look at him. He's leaning a shoulder against the doorframe, arms overlapped across his chest, one leg crossed over the other. His russet hair is tousled, getting longer by the day, and his eyes appear darker than the midnight sky itself; except for the faint glimmer that only I know how to make brighter—on those rare occasions where we do happen to find ourselves "in the middle".

I'm really hoping that *now* is one of those times.

"Our room," I answer, waving a hand at our charming surroundings.

He leans into the door further before pushing off of it, then slowly takes his time as he meanders around the room, running his hand along the antique walls and their many brass fixtures. "A little cramped for my taste," he finally says, quietly.

I don't say anything knowing that, if I open my mouth to respond, I'll regret whatever comes out. Instead, I just stand there, stone-faced. And it's in that momentary pause that a new feeling washes over me—one of being *done* accommodating his needs. Done entertaining his juvenile demeanor. Done with the tension I never asked for—the *relationship* I never asked for.

Suddenly feeling reborn, I turn away from him, walking to the double doors at the edge of the room before gripping the handles. "I'm sure there are other accommodations available if you ask Lane." It's not meant to be a jab, and it thankfully doesn't come across that way. My suggestion is sincere. I don't want either of us to be uncomfortable *or* miserable, seeing as we'll probably be here for a while.

Juniper sidles up next to me as I begin to open the doors to what appears to be a balcony housing an extensive, enclosed herbal garden. The plants are awash in moonlight, and even though I'm fully aware that Midvale itself is in a cavern, the night sky above me feels as real as the times I've spent staring up at the stars in Orihia . . . more specifically, the night I spent with Felix.

I'm so entangled in my thoughts that I don't know when or how Felix came to be beside me, but here he is, seemingly caught in the same memory as I am. His fingers delicately graze mine, and I can feel the immense heat from his body as it builds and builds. Even so, as his hands wrap around my own and he turns his gaze toward me, I keep mine fixed on the faux sky above.

He doesn't utter a word . . . but he doesn't need to. Nor should he. It's just now dawning on me that silence has always been our "middle". The space between. The pause. The moment just before a breath and just after a smile. Words have never served us—*don't* serve us—like they do most people. Our connection goes beyond that, to a place that only we understand both the simplicity and complexity of.

Only when I feel his stare reaching into the very depths of my soul do I tear my gaze from the sky. My eyes search his, seeing and feeling, feeling and seeing. I grip his hand just a little bit tighter, knowing that I've reached him when he reciprocates the gesture—as if to say, *"I'm not going anywhere."*

Neither am I.

❧ ❧ ❧

I awaken to the soft thud of a heartbeat beneath my ear, and an entanglement of limbs amidst a heap of blankets. I smile, taking in the scent of sandalwood and myrrh as I draw lazy circles across Felix's chest. He stirs, but not enough to wake entirely. When I begin to slide out from underneath his arm, he pulls me back in and lifts me on top of him. We're both completely bare, save for the mound of blankets between us. I press a kiss to his neck, right below his Adam's apple, then gently trail my lips up to his jawline, then his ear.

"Good morning to you, too," he murmurs. Beneath my mouth, I can feel the grin that's spreading across his face.

"Mmm, is it really morning?" I bury my face into his shoulder, about to roll off of him, but his hands meet my hips almost instantly, keeping me in place.

"Not so fast." Delicately, he brings me upright so that I'm sitting directly on top of him, bare-chested, bare-faced, bare . . . *everything.* His eyes rove my body as his hands trail my skin—up my arms, along my collarbone, down my breasts. He lingers there for some time.

I snatch his hands in jest. "If I remember correctly, you *played* enough last night."

"And what of making up for lost time?"

I raise a brow. "From the looks of it, we'll have plenty of time." What I don't say is that I'm not sure how long we'll be staying at Midvale, but something tells me our time here will be lengthy—and perhaps I'm okay with that. Maybe even *more* than okay with it.

To be away from Trendalath and Sardoria and the Mallum and the "real" world. To have a break from it all.

"It's all logic with you, Eliri."

I know he's only joking, but the way he says my name—using my last name like that . . . it reminds me of Rydan. I don't recall Felix *ever* calling me by my last name. To say it doesn't sit well with me is an understatement.

Trying not to display my every thought prominently on my face, I force a smile and plant a quick kiss on his cheek. Fortunately, before either of us can say anything else, there's a knock on the door. And as much as I hate to admit it, there's a small part of me that wants it to be Rydan standing on the other side.

"I'll get it," I say, bouncing from his lap and over to the armoire.

"Are we really being summoned this early?"

I scoff. "It's not *that* early." I point to the window where the illusion of sunlight is spilling through. "At least, not according to Midvale's enchanted windows." I pull one of the silk robes from the armoire before wrapping it around myself, not bothering to look in the mirror as I head for the door.

The knocking continues, louder this time.

I open it, hoping that my tone is welcoming enough to hide my disappointment. "Oh, hello," I say to the lanky man standing before me. "May I . . ." I don't get the rest of my thought out as recognition washes over me. I've seen this man before. With Rydan. When we first stumbled upon this place, before we were suddenly ejected from the Veil.

"Casimir," the man says, eyes gleaming as he introduces himself. "I can't even begin to tell you what an honor it is to finally meet you in person, Lady Eliri. Well, I suppose I can, seeing as I *did* try the first time you were here—"

"Who is it?" Felix's gruff voice carries across the room.

I ignore his question and shake Casimir's hand, stepping into the hall as I shut the door halfway behind me. "Yes, I've been wondering when I would see you again. I'm terribly sorry about our last encounter." My voice is hushed, but Casimir doesn't take offense.

"Lady Devall informed me of your arrival. We are just thrilled. Absolutely delighted, if I do say so myself."

Before I can get another word in, Felix swings the door open, nearly knocking me off balance. He looks between me and Casimir. "Are we being summoned?"

Casimir blanches at his tone. "In a manner of speaking, yes." He looks a shirtless Felix up and down, disapproval written all over his face. "You must be Sir Barlow."

"You can call me Felix."

"Right." Casimir shifts his attention back to me. "I'm here to show you to our fortnightly convocation, seeing as you're newcomers." A blush crawls across his cheeks before he quickly adds, "Well, new to Midvale, not to illusié. But the Archmage insists that all newcomers attend, and it just so happens you've arrived at precisely the right time."

"Lucky us," Felix murmurs.

I elbow him in the side, not taking my eyes off Casimir. "We would be honored. If you'll allow me to freshen up—"

"I'll make my rounds and return at half past the hour to gather both you and Sir Barlow."

"Felix," he repeats, clearly annoyed.

Ignoring him yet again, I ask, "Formal attire, I presume?"

"You'll find freshly pressed cloaks in your armoire."

I give him a warm smile. "That'll do, then. Thank you, Casimir."

With a quick bow of his head, he takes off down the hall, vanishing from sight. I'm about to scold Felix for being such a grump when I turn to my left and realize that he's gone, too. I step back into our room and close the door, spotting him at the armoire.

"I hope you like purple," he says from over his shoulder. "Because the gray one is much too large for you."

I join him, taking the cloak before laying it on the bed. "I wouldn't exactly call this purple," I say as I run my hand along the fine linen, admiring the black velvet lining the hood and the oversized brass button engraved with the Caldari emblem. "It's more like a deep violet, nearly verdot-colored." I turn the cloak over, expecting to see *something* symbolizing the Haven itself, but there's no crest, no emblem, no anything.

"That's as purple as purple gets."

"Perhaps you need to get your eyes checked," I say, throwing the cloak around my shoulders and fastening the button. When I turn around, Felix is already dressed, looking even more dashing than usual.

Between the sheer black attire underneath his storm-gray cloak and his purposely unruly hair, he embodies all that is *danger incarnate*. What I would give to be back in that bed, running my hands through each tendril, wearing *only* these cloaks. His gaze sizzles with intensity, and I don't even care that he might be reading my thoughts *or* amplifying my feelings. We'd already ravaged each other last night—who's to say my imagination might hinder that? Certainly not with the current scene that's playing out in my head. If anything, it's just adding fuel to the fire. The lupine smirk on his face only signifies that he approves.

I make for the washroom, sensing him eagerly trailing behind me. Once I reach the threshold, he whirls me around, our cloaks dancing as one with the brisk movement. He begins to unfasten my button when I suddenly raise my hands to meet his. "Tonight," I say, my voice sultry and low.

He relaxes his grip before sliding his mouth along my jawline to my ear. "Wearing *only* the cloak?"

A fire ignites within me as I play with the thought once more. I don't bother to speak my answer, knowing very well that he already has a front row seat to what I'm imagining. His response is easily felt, as the length of him hardens against my thigh.

I slowly back away, equal parts pain and desire etched across his face. "I'm holding you to that." He points to his temple to indicate that he's *seen* everything I've seen, everything I've just imagined.

I give him a devious smile before waltzing the rest of the way into the washroom to make myself presentable. Within minutes, I've cleansed my face, ran a comb through my hair, and even managed to tint my lips using a dark berry rouge, as well as rub some color into my cheeks. As an assassin, I'd never really been taught to care about my appearance, but there's something about wearing a formal cloak that changes things.

I emerge from the garderobe at the precise moment Casimir knocks on the door. With every step I take, Felix devours me with his gaze. "Stunning," he purrs, as he takes my arm in his. "But then again, you always are."

I flash him a genuine smile, then open the door.

"Lady Eliri. Sir Barlow." Casimir beams. "Follow me."

FELIX BARLOW

CASIMIR'S HEAD BOBS in front of them as they make their way to the convocation, but what Felix suspects will be a dog-and-pony-show is the furthest thing from his mind. Ravaging Arden, on the other hand, is pretty high up there. Her cheeks seem to darken as she glances over her shoulder at him, her eyes weaving a tale that only he knows how to read. Desire blooms in his chest as he takes her in—the imperfectly pinned up hair, the deep crimson of her lips, the stars in her kohl-lined eyes. A smile pulls at the edge of her mouth before she turns to face forward again.

The feeling dissipates, however, as they pass by a portrait of a falcon mid-flight. Midvale Arcane Haven is everything Xerin warned him it would be—warm, inviting . . . and highly unpredictable. Knowing what he's here to do, the secrets he's here to uncover . . . it's beginning to weigh on him. To think, all this time he'd been worried about failing; never had he considered the consequences of success.

Until now.

Knowing what he knows now, can he really follow through with it? Moreover, is it worth what he'll have to sacrifice?

Thwarting plans may not be his forte, but steadfast conviction certainly is. Lest he forget, he has amplification on his side—and what's more powerful than human emotion?

The thought stays with him until they reach the entrance to the convocation. Casimir gestures to the velvet curtains. "This is where I leave you."

Arden nods her head in thanks. She's about to open the curtain when Felix places a hand on her shoulder. She pauses but doesn't turn around. He moves in closer so that his mouth is mere inches from her ear. "We don't have to stay."

The statement doesn't seem to register at first but, once it does, Arden whirls on him. "Did I hear you correctly? Because we've only just arrived."

Felix takes both of her hands in his. "I don't think we're going to find what we're looking for . . . not here."

She angles her head to the side, observing. Questioning. "And what is it, *exactly*, we're looking for?"

His mouth runs dry not only at her tone, but at the way she's looking at him. Like she can see right through him and this stupid ploy that doesn't seem to be working *at all*.

"Because *I* thought," she continues, not bothering to give him a chance to respond, "that we came here to meet more people like us. To build strength in our numbers. To stand a fighting chance against King Tymond. Against the Mallum."

It pains him to think about just how much she doesn't know.

It dawns on him then that, even if she agreed, even if they did leave, never to return to Aeridon again, he'll never get the ending he's been obsessing over since they crossed paths that day in the Thering Forest. Where two separate lives become one. Where two souls merge despite the inevitable chaos surrounding them . . .

He'll never get to call her home.

A pang hits him square in the chest, forcing him to loosen his grip. He tries not to unravel completely as she pulls away from him. As suspected, the urge to amplify is all too present, but he reins it in, just like so many times before.

Arden gives him a weary look, her eyes searching his for answers. "Are you coming or not?"

Felix lowers his head, unable to bear the confusion and uncertainty he's surely causing her, yet again. "Yes."

She doesn't take his hand nor wait for him to follow. He grimaces as she stalks ahead and turns the corner down the hall, leaving him behind with nothing to keep him company but his thoughts.

RYDAN HELSTROM

RYDAN JOINS VIRA in their box seats, of which there are many. "We're the first ones here," he whispers as they lower themselves into the plush chairs.

"Well, I wouldn't say that," Vira says as she leans over the rail, nodding at the massive convocation and the many boxes that *are* indeed filled. "Almost every seat appears to be taken, at least from here."

"I was talking about *our* box," Rydan says as he turns around behind him. "Do you think the rest of the group got the message?"

Vira sets her hand atop his. "I'm sure Casimir, or someone of similar rank, visited each of the chambers to announce it." As if on cue, Haskell and Avery glide through the black velvet curtains, chatting and laughing about lords know what. Haskell's eyes meet his, and Rydan gives him a quick nod, to which he reciprocates.

"Ah, well if it isn't our two lovebirds," Avery says, a mug of mead sloshing as he falls into the chair behind Vira.

She turns around and rolls her eyes at him. "Seems you've found the bar," she quips. "Which isn't at all surprising, I might add."

Rydan cracks a smile. "What, you couldn't be bothered to indulge the rest of us?"

Avery shrugs. "Maybe next round. I don't know what we're in for, so I wanted to come prepared." He takes another drink, gulping loudly. "Where's everyone else?"

"There they are," Haskell says, slapping his hands on his knees before rising to give his sister a hug. "And might I say, you look remarkable."

Blocked by Haskell's bulky figure, Rydan discreetly leans into Vira before turning his head for an unobstructed view of Arden. His gaze softens as her eyes float just above where he's sitting, as if she's suddenly been frozen in time, a portrait of absolute perfection. The top half of her hair is pulled back into a messy braid and is secured with a crystalline pin; her cheeks are tinted a deep burgundy, as are her lips; and her cloak is the perfect shade of purple, the contrast against her olive skin only bringing out the golden flecks in her emerald eyes.

Remarkable doesn't even begin to cover it.

Rydan clears his throat to greet her when, as he should have expected, Felix appears to her left. He shoots a lethal glance at Rydan before directing his attention back to Arden, offering her his hand as they take their seats in the back row.

Rydan grimaces as he turns back around in his chair. His sharp intake of breath immediately gets Vira's attention. "Everything okay?"

Without meeting her gaze, he nods before bringing his elbows atop the railing, as if suddenly enthralled by whatever's occurring in the seats below. "It seems Her Majesty is running late."

"Rydan," Vira scolds. "I'm sure she and Opal will walk through those curtains any moment now."

"I wouldn't be so sure about that." He shoots her a sidelong glance, then angles his head at one of the boxes clear across the other side of the room—where none other than Queen Cerylia Jareth and Opal Marston are seated.

"That's odd," Vira says, squinting. She whirls around and tugs the sleeve of Avery's cloak, nearly causing him to spill his mead everywhere.

"What the hell, Vira?"

"Look," she says, pointing. "As if our chambers weren't separate enough . . ."

Out of the corner of his eye, Rydan senses Arden stirring. She leans forward so that her chin is nearly resting on Vira's shoulder. "What's going on down there?"

"Looks like it's just us tonight," Rydan answers.

Arden flicks her gaze to his, emerald meeting gold in a startling clash. She looks like she *wants* to respond—and in more ways than one—but with Vira sitting right between them, she doesn't. Instead, her eyes drift from Rydan all the way across the convocation hall. The subtle shift in her expression tells him everything he needs to know.

"I'm sure they'll catch up with us afterward," Vira says lightly. "Now turn around and pay attention. It's about to start."

Rydan lingers for a moment, hoping to exchange silent communication with Arden like they had for so many years in the Cruex, but her gaze remains fixed straight ahead. If he's being honest, he doesn't blame her.

He resumes facing forward just as the lights begin to dim. Seemingly out of nowhere, a floating platform appears in the center of the hall. Rydan looks up and down as the projection is duplicated both above and below where they're seated, giving *everyone* a front row seat, no matter where they happen to be sitting. From the looks of it, there's an infinite number of boxes, climbing in all directions, that surround the circular hall. If he had to guess, he'd assume their box was in the middle, but it's hard to say when his surroundings are so skewed.

A crystal-clear voice, one he recognizes to be Casimir's, fills the empty space. "Ladies and gentlemen, esteemed illusié and faculty, please allow me to be the first to welcome you to yet another exhilarating assembly of the minds."

Applause erupts from all around.

Casimir lifts his hands in the air in thanks. Only when the applause wanes does he continue, "We have some newcomers in the northeastern wing, our very own Caldari, who have only just arrived yesterday. Please join me in welcoming each and every one of them."

Without warning, their box is showered in a ray of white light, illuminating them to the audience. Surprised, Rydan plasters a smile onto his face as those in the surrounding boxes applaud, some even going so far as to whistle and shout, and just when he feels as though he's about to break a sweat, the light finally dims.

"Oh, thank the lords," Rydan mutters under his breath.

"Who knew we were such icons?" Avery quips half-drunkenly from behind him.

Rydan, as well as the rest of the group, ignores him as Casimir goes on to say, "We're also welcoming a very special guest tonight, a mage we haven't seen since she last attended our lovely institution during her former years. And, dare I say, she's made quite a name for herself. I am honored to announce that Queen Cerylia Jareth, Aeridon's most esteemed Extractor, has returned to Midvale Arcane Haven."

A hush falls over the room as whispers begin to circulate. The pause is not only noticeable, it's near deafening.

"Clap for your queen," Felix growls from the back row, as he begins to do just that. Arden joins in, followed by Haskell, Avery, and Vira. Dumbstruck, Rydan brings both hands together, the feeling suddenly very foreign to him.

And that's all it takes to get the others clapping, too.

Avery lets out a boisterous howl that sounds somewhere between a hyena's cackle and a wolf's mating call.

"Right, that's enough for you, then," Haskell says, ripping the mug from his hands.

Rydan turns around. "I'll take it."

"Isn't much left."

Rydan shrugs and, just as Haskell is passing him the mug, Arden's gaze drifts down to his. Her expression hardens as she watches the exchange. He tilts his head, albeit slightly, before raising a brow at her, then the glass itself. She doesn't give any other indication as she lifts her chin and brings her focus back to the stage.

At least she'll know where to find him after this is over.

CERYLIA JARETH

CERYLIA CONTINUES TO wear a smile as Casimir finally finishes his speech. She hadn't been expecting to be singled out like that—certainly not after having just arrived the day prior. She'd barely settled into her chambers, let alone *decided* whether or not she was going to stay or for how long.

Leaving all matters of Sardoria to Delwynn had been a grueling choice—not because she doesn't trust him, but because of what she's worked so hard to cultivate and maintain. Regardless, her advisor is the best—and only—person for the job, and so, somewhat begrudgingly, she'd temporarily resigned her post as queen. She'd much rather risk *that* than the alternative: never regaining her extraction abilities. Without them, illusié doesn't stand a chance against the Mallum or any future threats the entity's existence may pose. And so, she's returned to Midvale, knowing that, at some point, she'll have to face the one person she'd disappointed years and years ago . . .

"Queen Jareth?"

She's startled from her thoughts as she turns toward the voice, wondering when the old man now seated beside her had arrived and how long he's been sitting there. "My apologies. Do I know you?"

"Templar Odell," the man says, extending his hand in greeting. "You probably don't remember me, but—"

"Oh, yes! Yes, of course I remember you, Templar," she enthuses. "I haven't seen you since . . . well, since I left Midvale as a student." She hates the way her voice drops, the underlying weakness there.

The Templar gives her a reassuring smile. "I've always been rooting for you, you know. You've made quite the name for yourself as Queen of Sardoria. Midvale had no choice but to take notice."

"Thank you," Cerylia whispers, feeling overwhelmed with gratitude. "It's been a long road."

"That it has." The Templar falls silent for a moment. "Tell me, are the rumors true? About the Mallum breaching Sardoria castle?"

"I'm afraid so." Cerylia pauses, not quite sure how to accurately vocalize her thoughts. "One of our Caldari lost their abilities that night. I, fortunately, wasn't in the line of fire."

"Line of fire?" He raises a brow in confusion. "Why would you be worried about that? Your ability as an Extractor is a part of the Sacred Trinity."

Cerylia turns in her seat so that her entire body is facing him. "The Sacred *what*?"

Templar Odell blanches. "Oh, dear. I suppose our findings over the years never made it to your doorstep."

"What are you talking about?" she demands, panic blooming in her chest.

"The Sacred Trinity includes three distinct illusié abilities that the Mallum, or any entity of darkness, for that matter, is unable to absorb or touch in any way. Extracting, Rescinding, and Channeling. The Mallum could still technically kill you, yes, but, as long as you're alive, your abilities are safe."

Cerylia regards the man with wide eyes. "Well, that certainly would have been information worth having," she mumbles.

"We sent a messenger falcon with a scroll," Templar Odell says, scratching his head. "Come to think of it, we never did see the bird again . . ."

Cerylia doesn't hear the rest. Instinct tells her Xerin had something to do with intercepting that scroll, and for no other reason than to keep her in the dark. She grasps for a deeper understanding as she chews on her lower lip, but she's interrupted before she can make heads or tails of the situation.

"Your Greatness?"

A different voice tears her from her thoughts. "Yes?"

"The Archmage will see you now," Casimir says before turning his attention to the man seated next to her. "Apologies for the interruption, Templar."

"Not to worry," the old man says with a wave. "It's time for me to retire for the evening anyway. I bid you both adieu."

"Goodnight, Templar," she says, gathering her robes as she rises from her seat. She faces Casimir with what she hopes is a look of calm. "I'm ready."

He nods before saying, "This way," then disappears through the curtains.

Her heart pounding in her chest, Cerylia follows suit, not wanting to lag too far behind, but also preferring to keep her distance. Casimir utters an invocation, to which a portal appears shortly after. He gestures for her to go first. She musters a polite smile, only taking a deep breath once she's passed where he's standing.

Within seconds, she's no longer in the middle of the great gathering hall but standing in front of an ominous-looking door with so many trinkets, fixtures, and knobs she can hardly pinpoint which one might be used to actually open the damn thing. At her side, Casimir joins her and draws something into the door with his forefinger—a symbol of sorts. The inscription glows a faint gold before seeping into the door and disappearing altogether. From the other side, she hears a click followed by another. And another. Casimir tilts his head back and forth, as if counting, impatiently tapping his foot against the deep-hued hickory flooring. Finally, the door slides back and to the left before vanishing into the sidewall—certainly an upgrade since the earlier days she'd spent here.

With a slight lift of her chin, she follows Casimir into the oval-shaped room, trying not to flash back to the many conversations (and reprimands) she'd experienced over the years. She'd always been a wonderful student—the professors had said so themselves—but her zest for learning was often taken a bit too far when it came to incorporating any "hands-on" experience. Her abilities, while admirable, are also lethal—as she'd been so thoroughly reminded, time and time again, in this very room.

The wooden pillars surrounding the room are also made of hickory, although stained a few shades lighter than the floors, and lead to a pointed ceiling, the only thing in the room *not* made of wood, but of indigo-colored glass. Between each of the pillars, against the wall, are bookcases with some of the oldest tomes known to their kind. The thick layer of dust and multitude of cobwebs indicate that many of the texts haven't been referenced in some time. As a young girl, she'd ached to get her hands on those books—to see what mysteries and magick lined those pages. That feeling hasn't changed.

Perhaps the Archmage would oblige her this time . . .

Casimir steps off to the side and, before Cerylia knows it, she's standing in front of a woman she hasn't seen in over two decades. Her confidence wavers as the Archmage looks up from the pile of parchment on her desk, quill in hand. Her ivory eyes rove Cerylia from head to toe as a small smile cracks her face like sun-dried leather.

"I see our cloaks *still* aren't to your liking?"

Thankfully, there's a playfulness to her tone, and Cerylia relaxes almost immediately. "They're quite lovely, Archmage Galdor, but I prefer to stay true to Sardoria."

The smile sticks to the old crone's face. "You may leave us now," she says to Casimir.

Cerylia angles her head, watching out of the corner of her eye as he takes his leave. She can't quite put her finger on why, but she'd much preferred his presence—especially now that the tension is mounting. Or perhaps it's all in her head . . .

"When I'd gotten wind of your arrival, I almost didn't believe it. Certainly unexpected. Maybe even a little presumptuous."

True, Cerylia hadn't left Midvale on the best of terms. She'd secretly hoped that all had been forgiven *and* forgotten—but given the now solemn expression on Cyfrin Galdor's face, it's clear she'd been hoping for the impossible.

"I can't even begin to express my appreciation for welcoming me back into the Haven. And please, let me be the first to apologize for how I left things."

Cyfrin drops her gaze, then gently sets the feather quill down on the desk. She rises from her seat, palms face down on the freshly inked parchment, and leans forward ever so slightly. Her elongated silver roots give way to a mane of stunning frost-white hair that weaves and flows down her shoulders and over her chest, all the way to their resting place, just above her hip bones. Twines of ivy, in the palest of pinks, are braided and woven into each delicate strand of her hair, pinned into place by metallic leaves. Crafted of the finest silk, her silver cloak is embellished with clusters of selenite and amethyst crystals. The hood, a deep shade of purple with silver thread embroidered throughout, creates a mesmerizing design that seems to come to life with each dalliance of the light.

Somehow, Archmage Cyfrin Galdor looks *exactly* the same as when Cerylia had attended Midvale—not a year younger, not a year older. But, while her physical appearance may not have changed, *something* about her has. Secrets line the old woman's eyes, hiding in their wrinkled corners, unwilling to reveal themselves to just anyone.

But Cerylia isn't *just anyone.*

"I may not have wanted you to leave, but your mind had already been made up—especially after you'd become so enamored with that Dane character."

The way she says it brings Cerylia right back to when she'd been near Arden's age, being scolded and reprimanded for unrequited love. "We ruled for a time, you know," she says, more quietly than she'd intended. "Together. In Trendalath."

"I'm well aware of Aeridon's history," Cyfrin says sharply, "although sometimes I wish I weren't."

Her remark stings, but Cerylia doesn't dare show it.

"Even *together*, you couldn't keep the Tymonds from sieging and taking what you'd so rightfully claimed."

Anger heats her from within. "Perhaps if we'd had the support of the very place that had raised us—*educated* us—we'd be reciting an entirely different timeline of events."

Her words hang in the air, heavy and unrelenting.

Cyfrin presses her mouth into a firm life. "Perhaps that's so."

When she doesn't say anything else, Cerylia musters the gall to ask, "Why have you asked me here?"

The Archmage angles her head with a bemused expression. "Why, to welcome you, of course."

The tension that's grown between them during the course of this interaction is nearing unbearable. Cerylia gives a slight bow of her head before saying, "I thank you for your hospitality and for taking the time to offer a personal welcome, but might I request I take my leave now? The journey here has been quite taxing."

A shadow flickers across Cyfrin's eyes. "Of course, Cerylia. We'll resume our conversation at a later time."

The lack of respect in choosing *not* to use her formal title is blatant and unnerving. Cerylia wouldn't dare stoop that low. So, with dignified grace, she bows her head once more. "Until then, Archmage Galdor. I look forward to it."

An outright lie, she doesn't bother to look the woman in the eye as she raises her head, turns on her heel, and makes for the door.

DARIUS TYMOND

DARIUS STEPS OUT of his chambers, not feeling the slightest bit refreshed after nine hours of sleep. It's as if Aldreda herself had returned from the dead, tossing and turning, bestowing her restlessness upon him. She'd always been a light sleeper, which is why she'd opted for her own chambers—well, that, amongst other reasons.

Clearing the wretched woman from his mind, he glances at the guard stationed by his door. "All gathered, I presume?"

"In the Great Hall, as you requested, Your Majesty."

"And all are accounted for?" A bit of a trick question, seeing as so many have fled, but Darius waits for a response, nonetheless.

As he should, the guard hesitates. "I believe so, Your Majesty."

Darius gives him a curt nod, taking his time as he heads to the very heart of the castle itself. The guards scurry to open the doors as he approaches, hardly making it in time for him to glide right through, unscathed. Usually when he enters a room, all eyes turn to him—a sign of respect—but every single member of the Cruex *and* the Savant keeps their gazes locked straight ahead. The blatant disregard is almost enough to rattle him, but it only motivates him further—and he's going to need it if he's to get through this meeting.

He doesn't bother to climb the steps of the dais, but instead turns to face them so that he's not towering above the group, but, rather, is *on* their level. If this is going to work, camaraderie is key. He stares at each of them with grave intent, going down the line to ensure they *feel* his presence—his wrath. No one dare cross him.

When he finally speaks, his tone is that of what nightmares are made of. "For some time, I've been questioning the allegiance and devotion of these ranks." He makes a sweeping gesture across the room, even going so far as to include the King's Guard. "I question whether or not you still take your solemn oath seriously . . . if you ever did to begin with."

At this, Ezra Denholm steps forward. "I most certainly do, Your Majesty."

"As do I," Percival echoes.

There's a collective murmuring amongst the group.

"When I initially requested that you work together, to combine forces and intel, I had certain expectations—and, as treacherous as they might be, those expectations included revealing your fellow cohorts for any and all deviant behavior." He pauses, letting the words fully sink in. "As you know, Clive is no longer among our ranks, and that is, in part, due to the scheming of Lane Devall and Hugh Darby."

Unease ripples through the room, notably amongst the newer Cruex recruits.

"And what of your son?"

The question catches Darius off guard. He looks to the inquirer, Benson Hale. *Ah, yes.* The Caster and the Conjurer—they'd certainly gotten off on the right foot.

"Has he, too, not gone missing?" Benson looks at the line of Cruex to his right. "I certainly don't see him present."

"My son was a mere *pawn* in their scheme." Darius knows it isn't the truth, but Braxton is *his* problem, and his alone, to deal with . . . when the time comes.

"And what of Cyrus?" Benson challenges.

"What *of* Cyrus?" A familiar voice echoes from the back.

The others turn their heads as Darius lifts his gaze, settling on the one man who had been there, in the tunnels, with him. The one man who, besides him, knows the truth. "As you can clearly see, Sir Hale, Cyrus is here and accounted for."

Cyrus doesn't bother to fall in line beside either the Cruex or the Savant. Instead, he takes his place directly in front of the king. "Unlike you lot, I've actually been *out there*—outside these walls—looking for the perpetrators."

"How did you—?" Benson starts.

"He's my advisor. As is customary, he was the first to know." Darius gives Cyrus as warm a smile as he can manage. "And it seems, by his actions, I was correct in honoring him with such a title."

The Savant's Multiplier, Julian Enfield, steps forward, his ebony eyes full of concern. "Your Majesty, are you to say that we are now not only after the Caldari, but also Sir Ridley, Lady Devall, *and* Sir Darby?"

"And Sir Kent." Hugh may have found out what Darius had done to his poor cousin, Elias, but, fortunately, that secret had died with him. Darius raises a brow at Julian. "It seems family has a tendency to stick together, no matter the consequences *or* the downfall."

"I worry that there aren't enough of us to fulfill your request. Where might they have traveled to if we can't seem to locate them, no matter our skill or resources? Who could possibly be offering them asylum?"

Darius nearly lunges at the Multiplier for such an absurd conjecture, but Cyrus intervenes just in time. "I have reason to believe that if we continue to search the Roviel Woods, we will find them. Perhaps our strength is not in numbers, but in ability. With the exception of one *Clive Ridley*, the remaining targets are, more or less, untrained, inexperienced, and quite naïve."

"But they are to be captured and brought back alive?"

Darius looks to Landon Graeme, the Savant's Curser. "Only Sir Ridley, Lady Eliri, and my son. The rest you can do with what you will. Those three require a fate much worse than death—but, by all means, Curser, do your worst."

A sinister smile snakes its way across Landon's face.

"Now, if there are no further questions," Darius says, already heading for the double doors, "this meeting is adjourned."

BRAXTON HORNSBY

BRAXTON KEEPS RETURNING to the same spot as when he'd first arrived here, which isn't hard to do, seeing as this place is a never-ending loop—an infinity trail. He lifts his gaze, letting it float higher and higher into the gray abyss. No sunshine. No clouds.

No "weather" to report.

Every once in a while, he'll think he's heard something and turn his focus skyward—but so far, it's only been in his mind. A figment of his imagination.

How he wishes this whole place was merely that.

He's replayed those last moments with Lane more times than he can count, desperate to notice *something* that might point to a way out. That flicker of hope is beginning to dull, in danger of being snuffed out entirely.

Thoughts like . . .

What if this is it for the rest of my life?

What if I never make it out of here?

What if I'm forgotten?

What if . . . there's nothing to live for anymore?

To *see* the same thing, day in and day out. To *do* the same thing, day in and day out. To not need rest, or food, or water. To have no entertainment. No social interaction.

No purpose.

He wouldn't wish this on anyone—not even someone as despicable as his father.

Memories. They're all he has to cling to. To try to remember what things used to be like. What laughter sounds like. What food tastes like. What rest feels like.

What it is to *feel* other than completely . . . numb.

He cannot forget what he knows. What he'd discovered. That Darius had murdered both Hugh and Elias in cold blood; and that his father has killed countless others, given the stockpile of bodies sitting underneath Trendalath castle.

That Cyrus knows.

That Lane saw it, too.

That he and Arden are cousins. That she's still alive.

That he hopefully still has a home to go back to . . . *if* the Caldari will have him.

Each repetition keeps the flame lit, keeps it burning just a little bit longer and a little bit brighter. But, as with all things, repetition grows old. Is *he* growing older here? It's difficult to say. The crest is hardly a reflective surface and, even if it were, it's not like there's enough light to see—forever residing on the fall of dusk and the cusp of dawn.

He lowers his gaze from the void above, swallowing his disappointment. If only he knew *why* he could see Arden and Felix. And Rydan. And how.

Lane knows I'm here.

Lane knows I'm here.

Lane knows I'm here . . .

The mantra carries him along the trail, beginning once again with no end in sight.

ARDEN ELIRI

I STIFLE A yawn as we return to our room, hoping that Felix hadn't caught it, but the way he whirls me around and pins me to the wall indicates otherwise.

"Now, Arden . . . we shouldn't make promises we can't keep. Wouldn't you agree?" His tone is playful, yet feral. Desire burns deep within his eyes. "What you said earlier, what I saw in your mind . . . it's the only thing that got me through that dreadfully long convocation."

His gaze sears into mine, igniting me from the inside out. I fumble for words, no longer feeling an ounce of exhaustion. "Who says I'm not keeping my promise?"

His eyes darken, mouth rigging to the side. Just above my shoulders, he presses his hands, which are on either side of me, into the wall even harder, his cloak draped behind him like a silken mist. "I may be mistaken, but I could have sworn I saw you stifling a yawn just moments ago."

I don't respond but, instead, purposely flick my eyes to the growing bulge along the side of his leg. Slowly, I roll my attention back up and over every square inch of his body. I take my time before finally settling on the smooth curve of his mouth. I unmercifully let the tension build before whispering, "Perhaps you should wake me up then."

I can feel the heat in his stare, as if everything he'd held back earlier is now on the verge of erupting. *Good. I could use some . . .*

Before I can finish the thought, he's pressing himself against me and twining his hands in my hair, unhooking the crystalline pin that's holding half of it up. It clinks against the floor as his mouth meets mine—ravenous, *hungry.*

I meet his desire head on, parting my lips just enough for him to slip in, to taste me. Greedily, he explores the space— my teeth, the roof of my mouth, the inside of my lower lip—as if searching for something precious he's lost. I lean into his touch further, my tongue meeting his as we dance around each other, the arousal building to a crescendo.

I snake my hands down his trousers in what little space remains between us. Although I graze the button, I don't unfasten it right away. Instead, I go lower, until I'm feeling him, gripping him, in all his impressive length. My hand glides even lower, teasing him, circling the bulky head over his pants. He groans as he tenses, briefly separating his mouth from mine before relaxing into the sensation. His hips begin to move in small, rhythmic thrusts as he drops his mouth to mine once more. The kiss deepens as he grows hungrier, even more starved than before, and I know I've got him when he suddenly pauses, his heated breath filling my mouth as my hand moves back and forth—faster, harder.

"Arden," he groans, moving his hand across the waistline of my pants. His fingers graze my lower midriff, gentle but yearning. He expertly dips past any and all fabric that might hinder him from reaching his destination before finding my center. I shudder as the pad of his index finger, warm yet also cool to the touch, moves up and down, slowly working me. A soft moan escapes me, something I know has the capability to unravel him entirely—to know that *he* is the source of that pleasure, of the sounds I'm making . . . the very ones I'm unable to control.

He grazes his teeth along my lower lip before gently clamping down, then draws them along my jawline until he reaches the middle of my neck. The sheer pressure of his mouth against me is enough to make me throw my head back, his tongue flicking as he gently pulls and releases against the sensitive skin. We continue to stroke each other until his hand dips far enough to feel the reaction he's caused.

He pulls away from me then, his expression purely primal as he takes a step back, then another. He raises his hand and slowly traces his mouth with his index and middle fingers—the same fingers that had just been exploring the very depths of me. My wetness gleams on his lips. "Take everything off," he orders. "Except for the cloak."

His voice is low, his tone brusque, and as much as I despise being told what to do on any given day, this is different—especially when he's treating my very essence as something to *savor*. Coating himself without tasting me.

Not yet anyway.

I hold his gaze as I slide off my pants and unbutton my blouse, happy to be rid of them. Way too formal for my taste. As promised, the cloak stays on.

His eyes dilate, chest heaving when he sees that I'm bare underneath. "I stand corrected," he says, his grin growing wider. "It seems you *were* prepared to keep your promise."

I smirk, my eyes drifting to his trousers. "Your turn."

He obliges, quickly unfastening the button before removing them altogether, then briefly drops his cloak so that he can pull his tunic overhead. Hard, defined muscle ripples along his arms, his chest, his stomach, all the way down to his legs. I can't help but stare at the hardness of him, both upper *and* lower.

"Seems you came prepared as well," I note.

"What can I say? I aim to please."

I stalk toward him, my desire sharpening like a blade, until I'm standing directly in front of him. He watches me closely, a predator hunting its prey, observing every move I make. Without looking at him, I bend all the way down, close enough for him to feel my breath as I say, "You forgot something." I reach for the hood of his cloak, pausing, instead of returning upright. I look up at him through my lashes, very much aware of what this particular position does to him.

His expression is pleading, borderline desperate, but his words surprise me. "Not until I taste you first."

I angle my head, still looking up at him. "But I'm right here," I say, running my own two fingers over my lips, just as he'd done moments before.

His throat bobs and something shifts in him then— something cataclysmic. He lunges for me, pulling me up by my arms before pressing his body against mine. The cloak flutters from my grip, falling to the floor in a pool of gray as his hands grip my hips, my arms locking around his broad shoulders. He slides his hand down and around so that it's pulling my right leg up to curve around his back. He grunts at the insatiable way I move my mouth over his, exchanging the taste of myself that's still present on his lips.

Pushing and pulling against each other, I swiftly raise my other leg so that I'm straddling him. He catches it with ease, pulling me up higher before walking us over to the bed. I can feel him throbbing beneath me, my own need pulsing just above his shaft. He flings me onto the bed, towering over me, a male in his dominance. I'm laid bare for him to see, my breasts peaked at the sheer thought of what's to come next.

"How do you want me?" he growls.

There isn't even a moment's hesitation as I turn over and stick my backside into the air.

"Not even a warmup," he chuckles darkly. "Well, if that's the case, we won't be needing this." From behind me, his arms wrap around my sides before pulling the now-wrinkled cloak over my head and tossing it to the side.

Before I can so much as laugh, let alone smile, he's entering me, slamming me into oblivion, over and over again. I let out a voracious moan, which nearly sends him over the edge, panting with each delivered movement. I arch my back more, wanting every inch of him to fill the space between my legs, then eagerly lift my chin. He acts instantaneously, roughly wrapping one hand around my throat, just enough so that he can feel my throat bobbing, feel the sounds I'm making—*feel* what he's doing to me.

The physical restraint around my throat is enough for me to unleash myself, arching even more while he bucks harder. His grip tightens, his breath ragged as he drives deeper and deeper. The pressure builds in my neck, my chest, the apex between my thighs.

"Felix," I gasp, choking out his name.

A sign that we're both nearing climax, he removes his hand from my throat and, still thrusting, leans over me while dragging that same hand to my center. Slow, circular movements turn wild and untamed, so that I'm riding him uninhibited, inviting him into me fully.

"Arden," he pants, breathless—but his fingers don't stop and neither do my hips. We're undulating wildly against one another until I feel myself ripple against him in a massive wave of release, my body shuddering at the impact. My warmth fills the space he's already claimed, and I'm fully aware of what that does to him. I can hear him hiss my name again just before he tenses, then pours into me unrestrained.

His hands drop to his sides as we both collapse onto the bed, him faceup, me facedown. I turn my head so that my cheek is flush against the sheets, just in time to see the gleaming satisfaction in his eyes. He sets his palms, one over the other, against his heaving chest, then rolls his head to look at me, hair unruly, his body slick with sweat.

I smile at him. "Maybe the cloaks weren't such a good idea."

"Are you kidding me?" he says in mock disbelief. "They were a *great* idea."

"They certainly didn't last long."

He considers this before saying, "I must admit, while you look stunning in purple, I much prefer your *natural* color." He winks. "Perhaps we can work the cloaks in better next time—"

"Next time? Now who's the greedy one?" I tease.

He stills, a smirk creeping onto his face as he playfully reaches over and cups my backside, scooting me closer to him. I happily curl into the nook between his arm and shoulder, inhaling the intoxicating scent we've just created.

"You know, I'm only greedy when it comes to you," he whispers as he presses a kiss to the top of my head. "I can't help myself."

The words fill me with deep satisfaction. I lift my head, meeting his gaze. "I never said I wanted you to."

A shadow flickers in his eyes, a ghost of a smile touching his lips. "Then I suppose I won't."

"Good," I say, ducking my head back down. Even though I can't see him, I can feel him smiling.

"Goodnight, Arden," he whispers.

I wrap my legs around his and gently press into his chest, unable to stifle that damned yawn any longer.

"Goodnight, Felix."

⋘ ⋘ ⋘

I wait for Felix to fall asleep, which doesn't take long, before sneaking out of our room. If Rydan's constant stare tonight told me anything, it's that he needs to talk to me . . . *alone.*

I suppress my guilt as I summon the portal to take me back to the main hall. The journey here had felt long, coupled with that lengthy convocation? What I *really* want to do is crawl into bed and sleep, uninterrupted, but it seems there are much larger things at stake.

Namely Opal and her motives.

The portal materializes near the entrance, me along with it. There's a clanking of keys as the girl behind the desk opens and closes drawers at an alarming speed, hardly noticing my abrupt arrival.

"Excuse me?" I say.

She looks up with eyes the color of steel. "Yes?"

"Where might I find a place to get . . . libations?"

She smirks. "Southwestern wing. It's called Tap's."

"Thanks . . .," I say, drawing out the word, hoping she'll tell me her name.

"Cassandra."

"Thanks, Cassandra."

She doesn't bother to ask my name, just resumes placing the keys in their assigned drawers.

I walk to the far side of the hall before summoning another portal—this one to the southwestern wing. I expect there to be a multitude of levels, like in our wing, but I don't have to go searching far because I can see a rustic brass sign just ahead with box letters that spell out T-A-P-S, and a large bell by the entrance. The hall is lined with portrait after portrait of those I assume to be illusié—whether living or dead, I can't tell. Ivy grows up the walls, framing each portrait in its own mesmerizing way, and the floor beneath me is a mossy green. It closely resembles the actual ground of the forest, and when I reach down to touch it, I'm nearly convinced that it is.

I'm more than tempted to take off my boots and walk barefoot along the pathway, but now isn't the time. I have more pressing matters to attend to. I hurry along, trying to take in as much as I can of this greenhouse-esque landscape, until I finally reach the door to Tap's. It's made mostly of frosted glass, which makes it difficult to see inside. I grasp the elongated handle and push it open. The bell rings upon entering.

It's late, past midnight, so I'm not surprised to see the many empty tables and chairs. The bartender looks up from polishing a glass and sets it down before picking up another.

I wind through the maze of furniture until I'm just steps away from the counter. Right before my very eyes, the glass he'd set down fills with an amber-colored liquid. Without so much as a word, he gestures for me to take it, then angles his head at something behind me.

I slide the glass toward me and bow my head in thanks before turning around. Almost immediately, my gaze settles on a familiar face across the tavern. Rydan's downing what appears to be his fourth glass of mead as I approach the table.

"Cheers," I say, startling him. I remove the hood of my cloak (yes, *that* one), then set my glass down and take the seat across from him.

"I was hoping that it was you, but honestly, I wasn't counting on it."

"Why not?"

"Felix seems to keep pretty close tabs on you as of late."

My cheeks warm at the remark. "I suppose I could say the same about Vira."

He looks at me then, completely stone-faced. After a few seconds, he cracks a boyish grin, the golden flecks in his eyes gleaming. "Touché, Eliri. Touché."

Something a bit like guilt coils inside me as I meet his gaze. I steady my hands around the glass, tapping my fingers against it. "Remember when we'd sneak off after training? To that hidden alcove just below the kitchen?"

"You mean the cellar," Rydan says pointedly.

I sit back in my chair with a smile. "Is *that* what that was?"

"With that seemingly endless supply of ale, mead, and verdot? Of course it was. What else would it be?"

"I don't know. I guess I just assumed it was a part of the castle that had been long forgotten."

"With how stocked it was, I can see why you'd think that. Seems Tymond has enough to go around for all of Aeridon and then some."

I can't help but scowl at the mention of the king's name. "This is such a mess," I whisper. "I still can't believe I'm related—"

"Don't go there," Rydan says, shaking his head. "Not right now. Not when you're drinking."

"Yeah, well, it's not that easy to block out."

"Yes, it is." He gently takes my wrist and lifts my arm so that the glass is level with my mouth, then tips it toward me. "A few more of these and it'll be a distant memory."

"Is that why you do it?" I ask. "To forget?"

He releases a heavy sigh. "We've done a lot of fucked up shit, Arden. And we can sit here and blame Tymond all we want, but at the end of the day, all that blood . . . it's on our hands. It always will be."

I stare down at my glass. "He would have killed us."

"He's trying to do that now. What's the difference?"

His meaning dawns on me. "We were just kids—"

"Exactly. *Children.* Trained to do the unfathomable."

I shake my head, searching for the right words. "That may be true but . . . we chose different. Here. Now." I reach my hand across the table and set it on his, my fingers curling into his palm. His distraught gaze meets mine once more.

Seeming to blink back what I assume are tears, he breaks our grip and rakes his hand through his hair. "I suppose that isn't what you came here to talk about though, is it?"

The sharpness in his tone causes me to pull my arm away. "No," I say rather harshly. "I suppose not."

"We need to talk about Opal."

Unwarranted rejection whirs through me. "Are you sure now is a good time?" I narrow my eyes at the empty glasses. "Wouldn't want *you* to not be thinking straight."

"I'm thinking just fine," Rydan counters. "If anything, this *helps* me think."

"Like that time you showed up to Cruex training completely inebriated?"

He picks up his glass, then pauses. With a tilt of his head, he sets it down again. "Fair point."

I watch as he shoves the half full pint to the side. "I'm sure you noticed Opal wasn't in our box during the convocation."

"That I did."

"I'm concerned that she's manipulating Cerylia. I just don't know how."

"What if it's the other way around?"

I chew on my lower lip. "Could be."

"You want to warn her, don't you?"

"Of course I do. She's my aunt. The problem is, I don't know what I'd be warning her of."

"How about the fact that Opal's been using her abilities to mess with time, past events included?"

"But that's exactly what her abilities are for—that's why Cerylia offered her asylum in the first place."

"It would seem your aunt, then, has the intention of manipulating time."

I can feel my jaw harden at the accusation. "I thought we were talking about Opal."

Rydan shrugs. "We are. I'm just pointing out connections where I see them."

A pit forms in my stomach. "No. Cerylia is in this fight *with* us. She's against Tymond just as much as we are."

"What if Tymond isn't who we should be fighting?"

I search his eyes for his meaning. "The Mallum?"

He shakes his head.

"Then who?"

From the side, he slides his glass directly in front of him before downing its entire contents. It lands with a heavy thud against the wooden table. "Xerin Grey."

FELIX BARLOW

ALTHOUGH SLEEP HAD nearly found him, Felix had felt the lack of Arden's presence as soon as she'd gotten up from the bed. As tempted as he'd been to follow her, there's another more urgent matter that's weighing on him—namely, the reason he'd been sent to Midvale in the first place.

To find the room Xerin had asked of him will be no easy feat . . . especially in a building that is centuries old, like this one. Not only must he *find* this alleged mystery room, he must also do so under the cover of midnight, however fleeting, which really doesn't leave much time.

Even though Arden had left a quarter of an hour ago, Felix sneaks to the door to get a glimpse of the hallway. No sign of her, as he'd suspected. No sign of *anyone*, actually, which signifies that now is the perfect time to leave. He goes to the armoire and pulls out a fresh tunic and pair of trousers, unable to help his grin as he passes by the discarded cloak on the floor.

Focus.

Feeling woefully unprepared, Felix exits the room. At the very least, it would've been nice to have been given a map of the grounds but, then again, he doubts Xerin would want to risk entering Midvale—or the Veil at all, for that matter. Especially not with an Archmage as intimidating as Cyfrin Galdor.

Realizing that he has to start somewhere, Felix turns right and begins roaming the halls. He'd be foolish to think the room he's looking for would be among the residential chambers . . . no, what he's looking for would be private, secluded . . . *away* from roving eyes and curious minds.

Which leaves either the highest level or the lowest level of the haven—and, seeing as they're already deep, deep down in a cavern, he deduces he'll have the most luck searching the uppermost quarters. Now to get there . . .

He nearly trips over himself as he sees just the person who could provide him with such information.

"Late night stroll?" Lane says from down the hall.

Felix shrugs. "Couldn't sleep."

"Seems to be a common complaint among our ranks."

"I wonder why," Felix murmurs to himself.

"Is there anything I can help you with?"

He knows the accusatory tone is only in his head, but that doesn't stop his clipped response. "I'm not the one you should be asking."

Unbothered, she merely shrugs and turns to head in the opposite direction. "Have a good night," she calls from over her shoulder.

He doesn't return the nicety as he leans against the wall and waits for Lane to disappear through a portal. How high the haven goes is something he's acutely unaware of, but if there's one place he can go to get the information, it's the library. So that's where he'll begin.

He may not have a map, but common sense tells him that the library would likely be the focal point of the school, after the convocation hall, of course, which means it *should* be in the center of the massive institution, spanning multiple floors. Perhaps there *was* something Lane could have helped him with.

Just as he's about to conjure a portal, a flash of green light grabs his attention at the west end of the hall. Haskell appears amidst the fading light, nearly coughing up a lung.

Concerned, Felix rushes over to him. "You all right?"

Haskell's coughing doesn't cease as he waves a hand in the air. "I'm getting much too old for this," he says, cracking a smile, "but I suppose there's no need to tell you that."

"Perhaps if you stopped trying to set new records for yourself . . ."

"That's impossible with a place this size." His chest heaves again before taking a calming breath. "I'm convinced I could transport every single hour of every single day for the next month and still not cover the entirety of the grounds. Exhausting is what it is—"

But Felix is already onto the next. "By chance, have you come across a library while transporting?"

"I think the better question," Haskell says with a grin, extending his arm to the fellow Caldari, "is *which one?*"

RYDAN HELSTROM

RYDAN WAITS TO say anything further as he studies the expression on Arden's face.

"This is about what you saw in Opal's memory."

It's a clarifying statement more than anything else—even though it's quite clear that that's *exactly* what he's referring to. He gives her a solemn nod anyway.

Before either of them can continue the conversation, the bell at the front of the tavern jingles and Lane waltzes in. It's well past midnight, so it's a bit jarring to see anyone else frequenting the bar at this hour. Then again, he's only been here for a day and a half . . .

"Night owls?" Lane says as she hops over the counter and fills a long-stemmed wine glass with verdot. The bartender had long since retired for the evening. "Me too."

"Actually, I'm really happy you're here," Arden says, pulling an extra chair over to their table. "Join us, please."

Rydan shoots her a sidelong glance, one that says, *"You are?"* He folds his arms over his chest and leans back, trying not to be thoroughly irritated that he and Arden were just about to get somewhere with this whole Opal-Xerin fiasco.

"Midvale's convocations are always so *long* and so *boring*." She swirls the crimson liquid in her glass, then brings her hand to her mouth, as if she shouldn't have said anything. "Not that you all being here is boring or anything. Actually, that was probably the most exciting convocation we've had in months."

"So, you've been here a while."

Lane glances at Arden. "Yes. In and out. As you know, I was in Trendalath for a time. Being 'initiated' into the Cruex and what not."

Both Rydan and Arden stiffen, but Lane doesn't seem to notice. "For the past forty-eight hours, I've spoken with every Veil and Void expert in Midvale. I have no idea how to locate Braxton, how to get him *out*." She stares at her glass of verdot despondently. "I can't believe I let this happen."

"I'm sure however it happened wasn't your fault," Arden reassures her.

Lane looks at her with pained eyes. "What we saw—what he found out that day about you, and your mother, *his* mother . . ." Her lower lip trembles. "He knows you didn't kill her, Arden. I hope you know that."

Rydan can sense the shift in Arden's demeanor before it even happens. He reaches across the table and sets his hand near hers, barely grazing her fingers—his subtle way of letting her know he's here. The anguish that clouds her face is almost too much to bear.

"He knows . . . that we're related?"

Lane remains silent but nods her head.

Arden closes her eyes, on the verge of tears.

The silence is too burdensome, too heavy, so Rydan turns to Lane and says, "Whatever it is you happened to discover while you were in the Cruex, in Trendalath . . . can you tell us?" When she doesn't answer right away, Rydan presses, "Please. Whatever you know, *we* need to know. This group has had far too many secrets for far too long."

The voice in his head chides him. *You're one to talk.*

Arden opens her eyes then. "How did Braxton find out about our family? That we're related?"

"We followed Darius late one night." Lane's words are barely a brush of air. "We had no idea what we were getting ourselves into—but suddenly, we'd arrived at a reservoir in a giant cavern. Darius performed some sort of ritual." She furrows her brows, recalling the memory. "Within moments, we were pulled into a . . . a memory." Her gaze drifts to Arden. "A memory of Braxton, and his mother, and your mother—"

"And my brother," Arden finishes quietly, her eyes darting back and forth in resonance. "I was still in the womb."

"How did you—?"

Arden shakes her head. "I'd rather not get into that right now. Please, continue."

Lane toys with the stem of her glass, trying to regain her train of thought. "Braxton was hell-bent on finding you, but we knew we had to return to Trendalath so as to not raise any suspicion. Back there is where everything went wrong." She blows out a long breath. "It all happened so fast."

"What did?" Rydan asks.

"We saw Darius hauling a Cruex body *underground*."

Arden and Rydan exchange a glance. "Who?" they ask in unison.

"Hugh Darby." Lane chews on her bottom lip. "And Cyrus was with him."

Arden just stares at her.

So does Rydan. "What the—?"

"There's more," Lane interrupts.

Arden guffaws in pure disbelief. "How *much* more?"

"He's stockpiling bodies. Darius is. Underneath the castle. Hundreds. *Thousands*." Her voice shakes more and more with each word. "And when we confronted him—"

"Lords above, you *confronted* Darius Tymond?" Rydan says, a chill racing down his spine.

"We had to," Lane shoots back. "We were too far in. Knew too much. Apparently, he saw it that way, too. He summoned the Mallum right then and there, in that lords-damned tunnel—"

"Summoned?" Arden presses.

"That ring he wears—"

"Amethyst," Arden mutters, clearly remembering something.

"He tried to kill us," Lane goes on, "but Braxton grabbed me and shielded me as I searched for our only way out." She slips her hand into her cloak and pulls out a pocket watch, then lays it faceup on the table.

Rydan catches her meaning instantly. "To the Veil."

"And, unexpectantly, to the Void," Arden adds.

Lane's shoulders slump as she pushes her unfinished glass of verdot to the side. "I didn't know what else to do."

"You did what any of us would have done," Arden says her voice barely above a whisper. "The Mallum would have killed Braxton. Cerylia mentioned what happened in Sardoria, about the Mallum absorbing Braxton's deviating abilities. Furthermore, it would have taken *your* abilities, too."

"And what of your abilities?"

The question seems to catch Arden by surprise. "I . . . I wish I knew. I've come into contact with the Mallum more times than I can count, but . . ."

"But what?" Lane asks.

"Well, for starters, I've still been able to access Orihia. And second, I didn't get lost in the Void on our way here, to Midvale."

Now it's Lane's turn to stare. "Perplexing, indeed," she murmurs.

"You know what this means then?" Arden says, her eyes locked on Rydan. "It seems that we *do* have Darius to worry about after all."

CERYLIA JARETH

CERYLIA EXPECTS OPAL to be asleep after such a long evening, but when she returns to their chambers, the girl is wide awake, staring blankly at the fire in the hearth.

"You're still up," Cerylia comments as she closes the door behind her. "Mind if I join you?"

Opal doesn't break her gaze from the fire as she gestures to the chair across from her. "I'm surprised you're back already. I figured you two would have plenty to discuss."

Cerylia flings her robes over the back of the chair before falling into it. "How many times must I tell you, Opal?"

She finally turns her gaze. "I can't help that I know what I know. Sometimes my ability feels more like a curse than a blessing." Her expression is unnerving. "Sometimes I wish I didn't have it at all."

Cerylia studies her for a long moment. "I see. Well, you are incredibly gifted, Opal. Not many are blessed with such potent inversion abilities."

"I haven't changed anything, you know," she whispers. "About the past. As much as I've wanted to." There's an immediate shift in her expression, from solemn to sad.

"I know," Cerylia says. "It must take a lot of control—a lot of resistance on your part."

"That doesn't even begin to cover it." A heavy sigh.

"Are you able to foresee how changing things might work for the better?"

"Not exactly. There are too many timelines. Start altering too many decisions and the reality we both know would be far from the one we're currently experiencing."

"Perhaps that wouldn't be so bad," Cerylia counters.

"Perhaps." Her face softens. "You want to leave, don't you?"

Truthfully, she doesn't know what she wants. "It isn't that simple. As Queen, I have a responsibility to Sardoria, yes. But that responsibility is also tied up here, in Midvale."

"You fear you aren't strong enough."

Even though the words come as a shock, Cerylia nods slowly, wondering what exactly Opal's seen. "I suppose that's part of it, yes."

"It's a justifiable fear. In your current state, it *would* take your life."

An image of the Mallum flashes across Cerylia's mind. "If this is your attempt at getting me to stay, say no more."

Opal leans back in her chair, her stare settling once again on the fire. "I'm not attempting anything, Your Greatness. Just stating what I know to be true."

"If I might . . . perhaps you should consider taking a break from inverting? After all, we did just get you back to feeling like yourself." *And looking like yourself,* she's tempted to add.

Opal turns a cold gaze on the queen. "Does such a thing even exist?"

Cerylia doesn't know how to respond to that. Suddenly feeling exposed, she begins to rise from her chair, but Opal beats her to it. "Stay, Your Greatness. I was about to call it a night anyway. I'm sure you have plenty to think about."

"That I do." She narrows her eyes. "Sleep well, Opal."

"I always do." And with a flourish of her cloak, she disappears into her room.

DARIUS TYMOND

AS SLEEP CREEPS over his eyelids, so does another nightmare—this one of hellish proportions. As most of his nightmares do, it starts off pleasant . . . dare he say, *delightful*, until taking a turn for the worse.

It begins at the spring. The one-sided conversations, the begging and pleading, the eternal misery. Her voice, soft and innocent turned morose and dreadful, playing over and over again in his head.

How could you, how could you, how could you . . .

And then it all reels back. Rewinding. Skipping.

Back back back.

Until he's in that meadow again. Then at the edge of the sea. At the market. In the Roviel Woods. No one had gotten him to leave the castle grounds. Ever.

Always so convincing. So adventurous.

And he'd wanted to go with her.

He'd wanted to do everything with her.

Go everywhere with her.

They'd usually had a chaperone, who would later become his wife. *Sisters . . . you don't fall for sisters.* You especially don't fall for one and end up marrying the other. It'd been his biggest mistake, but also one he'd had no control over. Had the opportunity been there . . .

He would have chosen her.

"I would have chosen you." The words are heavy, filled with promises he'd never see through.

Emerald eyes search his. "But you didn't."

The basket falls from her hand, wildflowers spilling from the sides in a river of lilac and yellow—a river that quickly morphs into crimson. *Blood.*

He looks up only to find that her beauty has been replaced by a place he knows all too well. *No, no, no . . .*

Underground. Surrounded by stone. Dank. Musty.

Cobwebs hang from every inch of the mostly caved-in ceiling, making it feel even more claustrophobic. He rushes down the narrow corridor, his eyes adjusting to the darkness as he goes. He can't help but kick up dust along the way— dust made of bones, of ash . . . the very essence of death itself.

The long hallway dumps him into a burial vault in the shape of a hexagon. Another long stretch of walkway, surrounded by water, leads to a marble tomb. His feet begin to move forward, as if being pulled by some invisible force, as if this isn't the first time it's happened, but he resists. Plants his feet firmly at the edge.

You chose this.

Her voice haunts him. The one that used to bring him so much joy, so much peace . . . reduced to nothing more than shame and sheer misery.

"I never would have agreed to this had I known—"

"Now, now, Darius. Let's not say something we might regret."

A shiver snakes down his spine at the dreadful yet familiar voice.

"We had a deal. Or are you so blinded by your own guilt that you've forgotten?"

"How could I possibly forget?" He thrusts his hand into the air, expecting the amethyst to pulse with the movement, but there's nothing. His gaze travels up his arm . . . at the ring that isn't there.

"You look surprised," the voice hisses. "Like I'd ever let you skip the best part."

Darius feels his face pale, his focus shifting from his hand to the tomb. "I can't—"

"Take the suffering?" the voice mocks. "And yet that's what you chose for her. For the person you claimed to *love*."

"That isn't—"

"It's the price we pay for power. You, of all people, should know that better than anyone."

Bile rises in his throat, tears pricking his eyes, but he doesn't dare move. One step forward and he knows how this plays out. One step forward and he knows what he'll sacrifice. No matter what he says or what he does, there's no changing it. This dream is his own personal hell, curated especially for him by the remorse of his own actions—and those who'd witnessed just how heartless he'd proven himself to be.

"The longer you wait, the more she suffers," the voice croons. "She already knows your choice. She's already waiting. There's nothing that can save her from your selfish sacrifice."

Another voice chimes in, this one even more unnerving than the other—of the woman he'd slept next to the moment he'd been crowned king and she queen. Aldreda is soft spoken as she says, "We can do it together. Always together. From this moment on."

Blood boiling, Darius remains in place, knowing that, eventually, he *will* give in. Not because he wants to. Not because he chooses to. But because in order for the nightmare to stop, he must see it through. Must carry out his actions just as he had in the past. Must relive every deplorable, wretched, aching moment of it. Over and over and over again.

Only then will he wake up. Never refreshed, never energized . . . forever tormented by the ghosts of his past.

BRAXTON HORNSBY

THIS IS HIS own personal hell.

At this point, Braxton would rather be tortured for all of eternity than feel absolutely nothing. There's a certain distinctness to numbness, a tragedy all its own. Indifference, neutrality, apathy—he'd thought these akin to numbness, to the current state he's in right now. But it's so much worse.

It's the *absence* of feeling.

The stark realization that it isn't there. At all.

He may as well be a wraith, forever wandering, forever seeking that which he'll never find: a dead end for a lost soul.

This place is taking his humanity. Filling him with emptiness, draining him of hope, manipulating his thoughts and replacing them with what can only be pure, uninhibited psychosis . . . so that, eventually, he'll become just as gray, just as *muted*, as this place. Ceasing to exist. Blending into the backdrop. Never seen or heard from again.

"No," he murmurs, the word drying like ash on his tongue. At least he can still speak, can still utter a lords-damned sound. "I'm here. I'm here. I'm here."

It's not so much a mantra to remind him of his physical surroundings, but one to remind him that he's still a *person*. He still *exists*. He's still *Braxton*.

His gaze falls to the crest. *Why this?* How is it that, of all the times he's walked this absurd infinity loop, he's never come across anything else? How had the crest gotten here? Logic tells him it'd gotten lost, just as he had—but intuition tells him otherwise. Someone had placed it here. Intentionally. As if to hide it. To conceal it.

To keep it out of the hands of those it isn't meant for.

But it's in his hands now.

The crest could not have been formulated here. There's nothing with which to make it and, furthermore, no one to forge it. Which means it came from elsewhere.

He turns the metal over in his hands, tracing his thumbs along the indentations when . . . something flickers. Orange. His eyes shoot to one of the imprinted flames.

However brief it had been, it had *flickered*.

Pointing his gaze to the sky, he searches for a source of light—the sun, lightning, a mirage of his friends—but he's met with the same ashen gray as always.

He levels his stare at the crest. "Do that again," he whispers.

He eyes the center of it, relaxing his focus just enough so that all of the engraved flames are in his periphery.

"Please," he whispers.

But the crest doesn't respond.

It's enough to make him want to hurl it into the empty space. To be rid of it. He knows what he saw. Knows that something conscious had sparked bright enough for him to see it. Something conscious . . .

An unnerving thought rattles him.

He's the only thing alive in this place.

The only thing that can think, breathe, and, at one point *feel.*

Could it be? That the crest is also . . . *alive?*

Something a little like hope sputters in his chest. It's the first glimmer of anything he's felt during his time here. Gently, he sets the crest down on the ground before seating himself in front of it. If staring at this thing until it chooses to respond is what he needs to do, then so be it. Whether he's doing this or walking the loop or thinking himself into oblivion, he'll drive himself mad regardless. At least this way, there just might be a purpose . . .

And that alone is enough to get him to try.

ARDEN ELIRI

I COULD HARDLY sleep after the unexpected conversation with Lane and Rydan at Tap's. I'm trailing Felix, who's following Casimir, to our first ever lesson at Midvale. From what I've gathered, the courses are designed for every level of illusié—but as of late, the focus has been on restoration. It seems Braxton isn't the only one who's lost his abilities.

Braxton.

My stomach sinks at the thought of him, lost and floating in some nether realm, even though I know Lane's doing whatever she can to find him. She definitely has more experience and connections here than I do . . . still, I can't help but wonder if perhaps our familial connection might be more powerful than she realizes.

But then, that begs the question—what about me and my abilities? Here one minute, gone the next . . . and yet, I could still see Orihia; still made it *here*, to Midvale, without getting lost in the Void.

After passing a number of locked doors, Casimir finally stops at a large medieval-looking one that's emblazoned with the letter A. He signals for the both of us to enter. I'm halfway through the door when, out of the corner of my eye, I spot Rydan and Avery. No Vira.

They're headed straight for us.

I raise my hand in a small wave, briefly catching Rydan's eye. His mouth rigs to the side in a small smile. I smirk before bowing my head and disappearing through the door. I'm not sure what I was expecting to find, but certainly not a classroom. It looks more like an office, a study of sorts, and that's when I see her. The Archmage.

Cyfrin Galdor.

"Come in, come in," she says, sweeping her hands across the desk. "Welcome to my office. Please, have a seat."

Just as I'm about to interject that there's nowhere to sit, a desk with two chairs appears to my left. Unfazed, Felix ushers me into the seat closest to us before taking the other one. Shortly after, Rydan and Avery join at their own desk and set of chairs, just across the walkway. While we're getting settled, I briefly survey the area in front of me, noticing a discreet alcove behind the Archmage's desk. Something large, rectangular, and metallic is poking out of it, but between the distance and the shadows cast all around it, it's near impossible to tell what it is. I strain my eyes, hoping for a better look, when the Archmage steps into my line of sight, completely blocking my view.

I divert my attention as Avery clears his throat. "Will the others be joining us?"

"Perhaps later," the Archmage says. "For now, it's just the five of us." She settles her wintery gaze upon me before continuing. "Welcome, Arden. I cannot even begin to tell you how thrilled we are to have an Eliri amongst our ranks once more."

Her statement throws me off for two reasons. One being her use of "once more", which I'm choosing not to question aloud. And the second . . .

"My brother is also—"

"Ah, yes. Haskell. But he isn't in this room at present, now is he?"

"I suppose not."

She studies me for a long moment—uncomfortably long. Before I can get further clarification, she says, "I understand that you've had multiple interactions with the Mallum."

What an introduction. I can feel the entire room tense on my behalf. I suddenly understand why Avery's here—because he'd been with me that day on *The Corsair*.

"Yes," I respond, not wanting to incriminate myself further.

"Your ability to heal is no more, correct?"

"That is correct." I hate how meek my voice sounds—but this woman, her *presence* . . . she's a tier of intimidating I'd never imagined existed.

"Show me."

Perplexed, I stare at her. "Show you . . . what?"

"Your inability to heal."

I look to Felix, feeling completely lost.

"Do as she says," he grunts.

I rise from my seat, not sure how I'm supposed to show how I can *no longer* do something, but I approach the Archmage nonetheless. I join her on the slightly elevated dais, extending my arms out to her, palms facing up. She looks at me expectantly but doesn't offer further instruction.

I look down at my hands before closing my eyes, knowing that what I'm about to do won't work. I search and search for that inner white light, in all the hidden spaces that guard my innermost thoughts and feelings.

Relentlessly, I search.

With my eyes still closed, I suddenly feel two gentle hands pressing against my décolletage. A low hum begins to reverberate there before spreading throughout my entire chest, down the length of my arms, all the way to my fingertips. I open one eye, curious to see if there's anything surrounding my hands, but I'm dismayed to find that they appear normal.

I glance at the Archmage. She stands in front of me with her eyes closed, palms still pressed against my upper chest. I don't know if I should close my eyes again, if I'm potentially messing up whatever it is she's doing, but just as I'm about to, her eyes open. A chilling shade of ivory meets my own, the picture of death itself.

"I'm afraid it's true," she whispers, slowly backing away from me.

An audible sigh escapes Felix, but I don't dare break the Archmage's gaze. "About my healing abilities?" I clarify.

A solemn nod is my only answer.

My shoulders drop. "But how—?"

"That isn't to say something else hasn't taken its place."

It takes a second for me to fully register the words. "I don't understand. Illusié are born with their abilities. And I—

well, I was born a Healer." My gaze tracks across the room to Felix. To Avery. To Rydan. I don't mean for it to linger there, but it does. "Just like Rydan and Avery were born Ignitors. And Felix an Amplifier."

"But I've only recently discovered my igniting abilities," Rydan interjects.

"Precisely." The Archmage bows her head. "You and Rydan here . . . neither of you had the luxury of growing up with your parents, with the guidance you needed in order to develop your skills from an early age."

The puzzled expression on Rydan's face has me wondering the same thing: how Cyfrin knows anything about us when we've only just met her.

"It's rare among illusié, but some families are gifted with dual abilities where one skill is dominant in the child's formative years, the other slower to mature."

I suddenly realize why she'd said what she did earlier, about having an Eliri amongst their ranks *once more*. "You knew my parents? They . . . they studied here?"

Another nod. "A tale that doesn't end well, I'm afraid—or hasn't Queen Jareth told you?"

At the mention of my aunt's name, I can't help but feel completely in the dark. Yes, this has all been a recent discovery, what with Cerylia being my aunt and Braxton being my cousin . . . but I never realized just how little I actually knew about, well, *anything*.

"Well, then. I'll leave that discussion for the two of you. Haskell as well."

She's about to send me back to my seat when I interject, "So what *is* my ability, then? What were my parents'? One of them must have been a Healer—"

"It's not always guaranteed that both abilities will be transferred to the offspring. Or to more than one child, for that matter." Shadows darken her eyes. "There is, however, the possibility of them . . . *morphing.*"

Dread curls in my stomach. "So, you don't know what I am? Or the effect the Mallum may have had on me and my abilities?"

"I'm afraid not."

I'm only just beginning to process her response when Felix speaks, reminding me that we aren't the only two in the room. "So, why are we here?" he asks, his eyes darting between us. "What is the point of this 'lesson'?"

The Archmage blows out a long breath and, from that alone, I know the news isn't going to be something any of us want to hear. "After my last conversation with Queen Jareth, I've come to understand that you three"—she gestures to Felix, Avery, and Rydan—"have had the most significant encounters with Arden."

A blanket of confusion settles over the room.

"And by significant, you mean . . .?"

Cyfrin directs her gaze at Avery. "I mean that *you* were there when the Mallum attacked. On *The Corsair.*" She looks to Rydan next. "And you've known Arden longer than anyone here. You knew her *before* she knew about her abilities."

I glance at Rydan, immediately flashing back to our time together in the Cruex.

"And you," she says to Felix. "Well, it seems the two of you are—"

"I know what we are," he interjects. "And so does she."

Heat rushes to my cheeks.

A hint of a smile touches the Archmage's lips. "Very well. Don't shoot the messenger. I was only answering—"

"Well, I didn't ask, now did I?"

"Felix," I mutter, glaring at him.

"One of you did." Her tone is unforgiving.

"We understand why we're here," I say quickly in an attempt to calm the fire. "*All* of us. But how does that play into our lessons?"

"Until we can identify your abilities, Arden, we cannot have you participating in anything else."

"And how are we to do that?" Felix scoffs.

"By using your abilities *on* her."

Right then, it feels like a boulder has lodged itself in my chest as all I can think about is how I'd harmed Braxton. And Delwynn. *And* Felix . . .

Felix stands, his hands coming down heavy on the desk. "Come again?"

"The three of you will use your abilities on Arden."

"With the intention of harming her, you mean?" he shoots back.

The room is wide-eyed now, myself included. My throat tightens as I swallow the knot that's forming there.

"I know it may not be what you'd hoped to hear, but yes." Cyfrin presses her mouth into a firm line. "And we need all three of you, seeing as amplifying targets the emotions and igniting targets the physical. Each of your abilities will provide its own baseline for us to work with."

Avery and Rydan exchange a sidelong glance. "Why would you need two ignitors, then?"

Cyfrin leaves her post, walking down the low-raised steps until she's standing directly in front of Rydan. She places her hands on the table and leans in, but still speaks loud enough for us all to hear. "Because if my instincts are correct, you, Sir Helstrom, are no ordinary Ignitor."

FELIX BARLOW

THE ARCHMAGE CERTAINLY isn't making his time here any easier. He'd already suspected that coming to Midvale would open a lot of doors for Arden, but just how many doors was something he never could have guessed. Turns out Cyfrin Galdor may be a worthy opponent after all.

He's watching Arden as she absorbs the news about her abilities. First, surprise. Then delight. Worry and concern follow. Confusion. And then what he's been waiting for . . .

Acceptance.

Not an easy thing to do when your past has been mostly fabricated, with absent parents and little to no knowledge of Eliri family history—something Felix happens to be all too familiar with.

He shifts his gaze back to the Archmage, instinctively picking up on what she's feeling. Apprehension. Doubt. Almost like she's grasping at something . . . Perhaps he should amplify to get her to stop talking. Lords know the woman's said more than enough.

But Arden is wholly focused, soaking in each and every word as if they're the final rays of sunshine before winter's cruel onslaught. He may not be able to read her mind, but he can see her piecing it all together, the answers she hadn't even realized she'd been searching for until now.

He'd promised not to use his abilities on Arden and, in that excruciating moment Cyfrin announces she'll be forcing his hand, it takes everything in him not to lunge at her and claw those ivory eyes straight from her skull. Not only will he be required to use his abilities on Arden, but his intention will be to do the unthinkable . . . to harm her.

As if his every action isn't doing that already.

His mouth goes dry as Cyfrin finally dismisses them from the room. He's tempted to pull Arden aside, but not with the Archmage watching them like a hawk. Another time, then.

Dread coils in his stomach as Cyfrin's icy glare follows him to the door. She doesn't blink as he crosses the threshold. He jumps as the door slams shut behind him, an omen if he's ever heard one. It's clear the Archmage doesn't want him here—but to what end?

RYDAN HELSTROM

HE KNOWS BETTER than to ask questions. The Archmage is nothing if not cryptic.

"No *ordinary* Ignitor?" he says as the four of them walk out of the office. "I didn't know there were different kinds."

"That's because there aren't," Avery retorts, somehow managing to keep pace with him. "I've been an Ignitor my whole life. Not once did my parents ever mention anything other than being able to summon and control fire."

While Rydan hears him, he's acutely aware of how Arden and Felix were two steps behind them, but are now slowly fading into the background. He stops suddenly and whirls around. "What do *you* think?"

It's clear the question is directed at Felix, but that doesn't keep him from continuing onward. Rydan holds out his arm, instantly blocking the Amplifier's path. Felix's eyes snap to his.

"Anything you'd like to comment?"

The corner of his mouth turns up in a snarl. "I'm not an Ignitor. So no." He pushes Rydan's arm down before stalking off.

Arden takes his place, shaking her head. "What has gotten into you? We're all on the same team, remember?"

Rydan blows out a long breath. "I know."

Avery pats him on the back before saying, "Save that anger, mate. I'm sure the Archmage will put it to good use." He winks at Arden before taking off in the same direction as Felix.

When it's just the two of them, Arden gives him a dubious look. "What do you think he meant by that?"

"Doesn't matter," Rydan says as he slings an arm over her shoulder. "But if the Archmage thinks we're going to try to hurt you just so we can find out your abilities . . ."

Arden matches his stride, leaning into him for support. "Well, I suppose it was kind of her to excuse us for the day to, how had she put it? *Let it sink in?*"

"You think that's why Felix left in a huff?"

She shrugs her shoulders, the movement barely perceptible underneath the weight of his arm. "I know he doesn't want to hurt me. And neither do you."

"Hey now," he teases. "I think you owe me a few favors from our Cruex days."

"I probably deserve them, too."

He stops walking, placing his hands on her shoulders before turning her to face him. "Listen to me, Arden. Whatever you've done in the past wasn't intentional." His throat closes as he remembers the brutal end the Soames family had met—

at *his* hands. "You don't deserve hurt. You don't deserve pain." He shudders. "I'm starting to realize that no one does."

"If only Tymond could hear you now." She cracks a smile, but it doesn't meet her eyes. "It's just . . . I know what lingers there, beneath the surface." She raises her hands for emphasis. "Like you said at Tap's, there's so much blood on these, even if they look clean. Even if I've washed and scrubbed and nearly rubbed off my own skin in the process. Just because we can't see it anymore doesn't mean it isn't there. Like it or not, our skin carries our memories, especially the ones the mind tries to block out. It absorbs each and every death, traps each and every soul in the very veins of its killer."

Without realizing it, Rydan's moved closer to her, his mouth just inches from her forehead. "Remember, whatever you've done, I've done, too." He raises a hand to lift her chin until that stunning shade of green meets his. "And *worse.*"

She squeezes her eyes shut before wrapping him in a firm embrace. "I'm happy you're here."

He tightens his arms in response. "Likewise."

She eventually lets go, arms falling at her sides as she starts walking again. He can tell there's something more she isn't saying, but knows she'll come to it in her own time. They round a corner, her hand brushing his every so often, and he could swear the heat radiating from her fingertips feels much like his own just before igniting.

Side by side they walk, in complete silence, in no particular direction, until they reach a fork in the hall.

"Fitting," she mumbles, more to herself than to him.

"What is?"

A hint of guilt flashes across her eyes. "Path one. Path two. If I take path one and refuse to partake in these lessons for fear of seriously harming my friends, I could end up harming them even more in the future with an unknown ability." She looks to the right. "If I take path two and *do* partake in these lessons, we could all wind up hurt or dead. Or something worse." She shivers.

A swell rises in his chest, but he forces it down. "You know whatever path you choose, I'll be walking down it, too. Right beside you."

"I know," she says, eyes flashing with trepidation. "That's what I'm afraid of." She lowers her head. "I can't choose. I don't *want* to choose."

"Then I'll choose for you." Heaviness pulls at his throat. "I'll bear the weight of it, no matter the outcome."

Tears line her eyes. "But I already know what you'll choose."

"I know you do. Because it's what you would choose, too." He reaches his hand out to her.

She stares at it, lip trembling before twining her fingers with his. "Okay."

"Okay." He squeezes her hand tight, veering right.

Toward path two.

She follows.

CERYLIA JARETH

CERYLIA BARGES INTO the Archmage's quarters without so much as a knock. "Have you completely lost your mind?"

Cyfrin barely looks up as she sits at her desk, flipping through an ancient tome. "Is that any way to greet your Archmage?"

"Whose idea was it to treat Arden as nothing more than an experiment? And at the Caldaris' hands, no less!"

Cyfrin pushes her reading glasses up her nose, unfazed by both the outburst and the accusation. "Mine."

Cerylia marches over to the desk but before she can get another word out, the Archmage asks, "Who told you?"

"Not that it's any of your concern, but Felix."

"Hmm," she murmurs. "Not surprising."

"I won't allow it." Cerylia crosses her arms over her chest. "We came here for help—"

"And that's exactly what I'm doing. Helping."

The indifference in her tone is infuriating. In an effort to compose herself, Cerylia straightens and lifts her chin before saying, "Pitting them against one another is *not* helping. And if that's your idea of honing their skills, you are sorely mistaken."

Cyfrin arches a brow from behind her glasses. "Did I not do the same with you?"

The question strikes a nerve—a big one at that. "That was . . ."

"No different," Cyfrin finishes for her. "We did not know of your abilities and so we did what had to be done."

White hot rage churns in the pit of the queen's stomach. "It's exactly *because* of that that I will not allow my niece to go through it." She swallows the acrid memories burning the back of her throat. "Discovering my extracting abilities meant *taking lives*. Of my fellow peers. Of *your* students."

"And a worthy endeavor that was."

Cerylia nearly chokes on her own bile. "Worthy? *Worthy?* I killed innocent mages, no older than myself at the time—and for what? So that you could claim some glorious title from The Council? So that everyone would know *you* were the one to discover, train, and hone the skills of a lords-damned Extractor?"

Cyfrin stills. "You saved more than you killed. You know that."

Cerylia bares her teeth, the words coming out in a near growl. "And then I locked that power away so deep, not even *you* would be able to harness it again."

Cyfrin doesn't so much as flinch under the queen's lethal gaze. "And yet you've returned. Here. Desperate to harness that exact power you claim to have willingly tucked away." She angles her head, sheer will blazing in her eyes. "You came back because you need *my* help."

The audacity of this woman. Cerylia can hardly contain her fury as she says, "I came back because I knew what was at stake if I didn't."

"So you won't leave."

It isn't so much a question as it is a statement. "No. I won't leave."

"Don't forget, Cerylia. I know this game well. Idle threats will do you no good here."

She hadn't even threatened to take the Caldari away, to get them the hell out of here, but she hadn't needed to. Whether she admits it or not, Cyfrin knows all her moves—because *she* invented the damn playbook.

Slowly, the Archmage removes her glasses, setting the folded frames on the desk beside the substantial tome. "You will stay. So will the others. We will take whatever means necessary to discover Arden's abilities. Yes, there is risk involved, just as there was risk involved with you. I will not require you to supervise; however, I will ask for your support and for that support to be demonstrated to the group." Her ivory eyes narrow before she adds, "Willingly."

In a battle for control, the queen meets the Archmage's stare head-on. "It would appear I have some support to muster, then," she scowls. "I'll see myself out."

For the second time that week, Cerylia leaves the Archmage's chambers feeling utterly defeated.

DARIUS TYMOND

SAME NIGHTMARE, DIFFERENT day.

Darius sits in front of the gold-plated mirror in his chambers, desperately trying to cover the evidence of his night terrors. The skin beneath his eyes is sunken in, wrinkled— even more so than usual—and there's a tensed muscle in his jaw that won't relax no matter how many times he tells himself to release it. His hairline's receding, the once lustrous silver giving way to a dull gray, his forehead now etched with what appears to be permanent indented lines.

Withering away.

He splashes some cool water on his face, patting his cheeks before slipping on the amethyst ring. Perhaps he should have struck another bargain, one of eternal youth— but it's too late for that now. His guest will be arriving any minute now, hopefully with news that his imbecile court has been unable to provide.

Knowing that this is the best it's going to get, he swipes his robes from the door of the armoire and flings them over his shoulders. The jewel-encrusted crown sits idly by. He considers wearing it, but ultimately decides to leave it behind. What a silly artifact it is, especially with the power that lies just beneath his fingertips. He is the king, regardless of what he wears.

Just past dawn, the courtyard holds a haze of gloom. He'd requested that his guards remain at their posts, as he so often does whenever he has this particular visitor. He's walking along the stone-lined path, rounding thick rhododendrons and other colorful foliage, when he happens upon a small circular area, surrounded by boxwoods twice the size of him, to find none other than Xerin Grey awaiting his arrival.

"You're late," Xerin says, his tone clipped.

Darius doesn't so much as bristle at the remark. "Do you have the information I've asked for?"

Xerin arches a brow, the crimson in his eyes deepening in the budding light. "That depends."

"You're just as dependable as Cyrus."

"I'll take that as a compliment."

"It wasn't." His mouth tightens in annoyance. "So? Do you have it or not?"

"It was quite the list of tasks you gave me."

"I don't have time for games," Darius snarls.

Xerin tilts his head, amusement dancing in his eyes. "But isn't that exactly what this is, Your Majesty? A game?"

A chill lodges in the king's chest. He holds Xerin's gaze, knowing that if he shows any sign of weakness, it'll be the nail in his coffin.

"Have you located Clive?"

Xerin scoffs, turning away from him as he runs his hands along the waxy leaves of a blooming shrub. "No more than you have."

"And my staff?"

"Still missing, I presume."

Darius fists his hands at his sides. "What about Braxton?"

"I thought you tried to kill him?"

"I did. And I almost succeeded."

"Killing your own heir," Xerin taunts. "I really thought I'd heard it all."

Temper flaring, Darius takes a sharp inhale. "I take it there's no update there either."

Xerin flashes a wicked grin. "Please, don't stop your interrogation on my behalf. You might just get lucky with your next question—"

Before he can fully think through his actions, Darius darts across the small enclosure, hand gripping the base of Xerin's throat. The amethyst ring gleams in the rising sunlight. "Do not test me, Grey."

Completely unfazed, Xerin chuckles, the sound raspy as he breaks Darius's hold. "Your last request had something to do with Clive, did it not?"

Darius steps back, composing himself. "Don't ask questions you already know the answers to."

Xerin smirks. "I'm afraid a reversal is simply not possible. You will carry out exactly what you've agreed to. As will he if you falter."

"So, nothing noteworthy *or* new," Darius murmurs. "Why am I not surprised, coming from you?"

"Now, now," Xerin chides, "that's quite the assumption you're making. I didn't say I had nothing."

Darius crosses his arms over his chest. "Well? Spit it out, then."

"If I told you that I'd located the crescent fire," Xerin suggests, shadows darkening his eyes, "would *that* be something of interest?"

Darius can't help but mirror the grin that's snaking its way across Xerin's face. "Why yes," he says coolly, "I suppose it would."

BRAXTON HORNSBY

THE CREST IS guiding him.

It's actually *guiding him.*

Sometime over the duration of his staring contest with the inanimate object, it'd flickered again. He'd jumped to his feet, coaxing it to stay lit as if it had a functioning mind. Consciousness. Far-fetched, yes, but has it been working? Yes. And it seems he's also cracked the code on deciphering what the glimmers mean. A brightening hue means he's on the right track; the duller the color, the greater the need to retrace his steps or move in a different direction altogether.

Which is odd. Because the trail he's been walking *should* be that same infinity loop. But, somehow, it isn't. And while his surroundings haven't changed much, there's enough of a difference to know that he's no longer on the path he was before. There are rocks, shrubs—all gray, but never has he been so excited to *see something.* The path before him turns to cobblestone as the crest grows even brighter. He follows the auburn beacon along the winding path, anxious to know where it might lead.

If it dumps him back out onto that infinity loop . . .

He grits his teeth. *There will be hell to pay.*

He makes a right turn, only to watch the light dim before quickly retracing his steps, making a left instead.

"Where are you taking me?" he murmurs.

The crest seems to shine brighter in response.

"Here's hoping we're almost there."

If this is it—his way out . . . his chest expands at the thought. To see Lane again. And Arden. And the rest of the Caldari.

To have physical contact. Conversation. Emotion.

To feel hungry, tired, happy, sad . . . to simply *feel.*

He hadn't known how much he'd taken it for granted. Even the bad. The misdirected anger toward Arden. The betrayal of his father (yet again). Grieving his mother's death. The desire to confront Lane and tell her how he truly feels, regardless of her reaction . . . he'll take the bad over nothingness any day of the week.

"Are we almost there?" he whispers.

The crest doesn't grow brighter nor does it dim. Braxton looks up at the faint red hue of the cobblestone ahead—the only other color in this place besides the glowing orange of the light. He picks up the pace until he's in an all-out sprint. Wherever the crest is guiding him, it's taking him away from the muted gray of the Void. At that, Braxton lets out a loud whoop, continuing onward to the mystery that awaits.

ARDEN ELIRI

I FIND MYSELF in a ring that feels much like my Cruex sparring days, minus the fact that Felix and Avery are here. That, and the incredible height of the tower we happen to be in. Cyfrin had informed us that she'd be supervising at the top of said tower with a number of Healers on standby. I tried not to let that last part rattle me, but I understand the need for precautionary measures.

We have no idea what we're dealing with.

The thought that's been circling my mind for the past week.

I'm currently facing Avery, arms cast down at my sides, palms facing out, with my eyes closed. It's the least threatening position I can think of. But apparently, it isn't what the Archmage has in mind.

Cyfrin's voice floats down to us. "Open your eyes, Arden. You need to be able to see your attacker."

My attacker. My stomach turns as my eyes shoot open. I catch a glimpse of Rydan and Felix, who are both standing more than a few steps back from the ring. *Smart.* They look as jarred and unprepared as I feel.

I dismiss the thoughts, bringing my attention back to Avery.

"Sir Bancroft," Cyfrin's voice booms overhead. "If you'll do the honors."

Apology is written all over his face as he follows the Archmage's instruction and lifts his hands from his sides. His eyes close briefly, chest rising before sinking back down. A few breaths later and sparks are igniting from his fingertips, erupting into full-fledged flames. His gaze settles on me once again. He looks me up and down, side to side, clearly conflicted. "I don't know where to strike."

I wince, looking up the length of the tower, waiting for Cyfrin to answer—but we're met with silence.

"I don't know where to strike," he says again, louder this time. I can hear the frustration lining his voice—how much he *doesn't* want to do this.

"Avery, it's okay," I say. "I've handled worse, believe me." I briefly meet Rydan's gaze, hoping it'll help ease the tension. "I can't tell you where to strike. Neither can the Archmage. Or anyone here. Because if I know, I'll be able to deflect it." *Thank you, Cruex training.*

"*Go first*, they said, *get it over with,*" he grumbles. "I'm sorry in advance."

I nod as reassuringly as I can, then ready myself for the blow. I'm tempted to close my eyes again but recall Cyfrin's warning. *No more stalling, Arden. You've been sliced by weapons and punched square in the jaw by brutes twice your size. What's a little fire—*

It's then I start to feel heat building within my body, something I can't explain since Avery's still standing on the other side of the ring, arms in the exact same position as before. The sensation builds in my lower abdomen first, then travels up from the pit of my stomach into my chest, lighting me up like a hearth on a crisp winter's night. My throat burns as I open my mouth to speak, my larynx feeling as though it's caught fire.

"Stop," I hear a familiar voice order.

Avery's flames are immediately snuffed out, as are my own internal stirrings. I look past him to see Felix ducking and marching into the ring. "What are you—?"

"Physical targeting should be last," he shouts into the void of the tower above. "We need to set an emotional baseline first."

Avery doesn't bother to wait for the Archmage's confirmation as he retreats from the ring. Neither does Felix. He stands opposite me, his lean, muscular figure only further emphasized in the blinding overhead light. He marks his position with his feet, readying himself, then runs both hands through his russet hair. The expression on his face tells me everything I'd rather not know.

This won't be pleasant. And I'm sorry for that.

I brace myself, having absolutely no idea what emotion he'll choose to amplify. If there's one thing I know about Felix (and I know *a lot*), it's that he's incredibly skilled at picking up on the emotions I'd rather not show—the ones I'd saved for myself, and myself alone.

For some reason or another, I make the novice mistake of glancing at Rydan, and *that's* when I wish it were still Avery out here instead of Felix. *No no no.*

I can feel Felix reaching in, focusing my attention, pulling at threads of memories I don't want him—or anyone—to know about. I close my eyes, trying to remove Rydan's face from my mind, trying to think of *anything* else, but I can't. His features are imprinted on the backs of my eyelids.

Felix's connection syncs with mine, the tether locking into place, Rydan unknowingly coming along for the ride. *You made me look at him. You chose this.*

I did no such thing.

Then choose something else. Let go and—

Make me.

There's an unexpected glimmer of relief that allows me to open my eyes. I blink. Felix remains across the room from me, eyes still closed, and as much as I don't want to go back under, it's no surprise when I'm pulled in again. In a battle of wills, Felix is undoubtedly the master, no matter how determined I might be.

And then it's like we're journeying, on a traveling caravan, through my memories—and Rydan is at the forefront of them all. Heated Cruex sparring sessions, unforgettable late nights drinking in the cellar, graciously walking me back to my chambers each and every day after training. Our last mission together—my guilt and shame as I'd knocked him unconscious and left him there for dead—or as good as dead, once Tymond got ahold of him.

The thread he's pulled is one of camaraderie, of two assassins who knew nothing other than what they'd been trained to do. To kill, without question. To feel no remorse afterward. It's the path I want to keep Felix down, as hard as it is to relive. Because if he veers ever so slightly . . .

Which is exactly what he does. Like an idiot, I've opened the door and he's walked straight through it.

I'd only ever known Rydan. He'd been my closest companion, the only male in that whole festering group of assassins who'd given a shit about me. Who'd sparred with me and trained me without wanting to severely injure me. Who didn't look at my gender as a weakness or something to be mocked. He's always treated me as his equal, a true partner in every sense of the word—

Don't. Please.

I push back against Felix, pressing against the walls of my mind as if they could somehow form an even more robust barrier against him. My mind is strong, but not as strong as Felix's. And so there's no use. Not now.

Not while we're on the topic of Rydan.

My heart tightens in my chest as I try to hold the memories at bay, but they crash between us like a tide to the shore. Every time he'd walked me back to my chambers and hadn't stayed. Every time he'd helped me to my feet, guiding me by my lower back to the infirmary. Every time he'd swept my hair up and out of my face when my arms had felt like bricks after slinging my chakrams during target practice. Every time we'd snuck into the cellar and he'd clinked his glass against mine, eyes blazing with pure delight and mischief. Every time he'd reached for me and pulled me into a hug, burying his face into my shoulder. And that one time we'd . . .

"Enough!" I scream, not realizing I've done so until I hear the echo. Felix's eyes shoot open as I march toward him, fury lacing each step. "That's *private,*" I say through clenched teeth as I grab him by the neck of his tunic, twisting the sheer fabric in my hands. "Or have you forgotten what *boundaries* are? If this is some sort of game to you—"

Felix doesn't so much as flinch. "I'm only amplifying what's already there."

His response only angers me more. My eyes flick behind him, to Rydan, who's leaning against the perimeter of the ring, eyes wide. I bring my attention back to Felix, snarling. "And how exactly would digging into my personal history with a good friend of mine help us uncover my abilities?"

Shadows glint in his eyes. "Because *everything* is personal, Arden. As you'll soon come to learn."

His callous tone throws me for a second, but I don't dare unclench my fists from his shirt. Not until Cyfrin's voice interjects. He backs away from me, tugging at the bottom of his tunic to straighten it. He holds my gaze, a hint of sadness in those deep chestnut eyes, before calling out, "Avery. You're up."

I scoff, shaking my head as I push past him and out of the ring. "No. We're done for today." I don't bother waiting for Cyfrin's approval as I exit the ring and slam the doors behind me.

⊰ ⊰ ⊰

I toss my hand up in a brief wave as I stride across the lobby to Lane.

"Pardon me for saying this, but you look like hell," she says, pouring a glass of water from the pitcher behind the desk. "What happened?"

"Something I'd rather not talk about right now." I hadn't bothered to check my reflection after leaving the ring and the twisted person in it but, based on Lane's reaction, it's probably far worse than expected. Not that I care at the moment. I take the glass of water from her, finishing it in three gulps. "I'm here because I need a new room."

"Oh," she says brightly, fishing inside the drawer for another set of keys. "Well, I can move you and Felix to—"

"My own room," I clarify. "Felix won't be coming with me."

Her face falls. "I thought—"

"Yeah. I did, too." I sigh. "Listen, the training the Archmage has us involved in, it's . . . heavy." I try to keep my voice from breaking. "And, seeing as I'm the focus of said training, I'm going to need my own room. At least until this part of it is over."

"That won't be necessary."

My blood chills at Felix's voice.

"I'll stay with Haskell and Avery."

I spin around, facing him. "I don't want you staying with my brother."

"It's already been arranged."

Fuming, I turn back to Lane. "A new key, then, so he can't just barge in whenever he feels like it."

Lane's eyes dart between us, the tension building with each second she chooses not to respond. "I can do that," she finally says, moving things around behind the desk.

I hold out my hand, keeping my attention fixed on Felix until I feel the weight of brass in my palm. I close my fingers around it, then turn my head and flash her a genuine smile. "Thank you."

"Arden—" Felix starts.

But I'm already headed for the portal that'll take me to my chambers—alone.

FELIX BARLOW

"YOUR ARM, PLEASE."

Lane's voice shouldn't startle him but, for some reason or another, it does. "What?"

She points to his arm, then gestures for him to approach the desk. He obliges her, realizing he probably should have spoken with Arden in private.

"Didn't you give her a new key?"

She nods, pulling on his arm so that it's straight in front of her. "This is the only downside to *becoming* the key itself."

"And what's that?"

"The removal." She pulls a sheer, glossy sheet from one of the drawers, then wraps it around his arm. "This might sting," she warns.

Felix is observing the material when a key that's nearly an exact replica of the one she'd originally given him begins to take shape from underneath his skin. Small currents buzz along the outside of his arm, moving further and further inward until his entire arm is fraught with the sensation.

He's about to tell her that he quite literally can't feel a thing because his arm's gone numb when the buzzing subsides and a new sensation takes over. And there's only one word for it: pain.

"I promise I'll go as fast as I can," she says, deftly moving the material so that it's no longer wrapped.

Felix grits his teeth as shards of metal begin to surface from underneath his skin, piecing themselves together to form what he recognizes to be his original room key. "Can't you just conjure a new key? Or forge one?"

"We could, but precious metals are getting harder and harder to come by. Not to mention, we don't use this process often. Once you have a room and a key at Midvale, it's yours for life."

"Clearly there are some exceptions," he grunts.

"Almost done," she assures him, slowly lifting the sheet— and subsequent metal key—from his arm. Setting it against the desk, she pushes on the key with her thumbs so that it plops onto the wooden surface as if it's just come out of a baking mold. "All finished," she says before inspecting it and returning it to its drawer. "Now, given what you've just been through, are you sure you don't want your own room?"

Felix considers his options. "What wing?"

"Your new room would be in the same wing as your old one."

Arden may not want him close by, but he'll be damned if he doesn't complete what he's been tasked with. Having an individual room would also keep the questions at bay regarding his late night wanderings.

"I will warn you, though," Lane says, already rummaging through one of the desk drawers, "that if we have an unexpected guest arrive, there is a chance they could be assigned to your room."

Felix resists the urge to sigh. "How often does that happen?"

She shrugs. "Hardly ever. Although you and the Caldari showing up here was certainly unexpected." She pauses before quickly adding, "Welcome, but unexpected."

Even if a stranger did get assigned to his new room, at least he wouldn't have to explain his comings and goings—or risk getting distracted from the task at hand. "That should be fine," he concedes. "A new room it is."

She sorts through a few more keys before handing one to him. "Like I said, your new room will be in the northeastern wing, same as the original. It's actually nearby your old one, just down the hall and to the left." She references the yellow orb, its contents splaying out into a map.

Jackpot.

"Is there a map of the school I can borrow?"

Lane shifts her gaze from the glowing map, eyeing him curiously. "Not currently, no."

While sitting under her stare is uncomfortable, explaining himself would only further point to his guilt and heighten her curiosity. And that's the *last* thing he wants to do.

Felix brushes off her response as if it's nothing, then takes the key from her with a gracious bow of his head. "I appreciate your help, Lane."

"Don't mention it," she says, biting her lower lip as if she wants to say more. She tucks the yellow orb back into its drawer, quietly adding, "Just so you know, the Archmage is the only person at Midvale who can distribute a map of the grounds. It's the way it's always been."

Felix doesn't need her to elaborate any further. Cyfrin likely keeps the maps under lock and key for one reason and one reason alone: secrets. He's certain Midvale has plenty.

Don't they all?

RYDAN HELSTROM

RYDAN'S ON THE way back to his room when he's nearly sideswiped by an enraged Arden.

"Whoa," he says, raising his arms in the air, hoping she won't display the same aggression toward him as she had toward Felix. His attention is immediately drawn to the key in her hand. "What do you have there?"

"What does it look like?" Her tone drips with derision.

"But you already have a room . . ." He trails off as he puts the pieces together—or tries to, at least. "What happened in there?"

"Boundaries were crossed." She doesn't elaborate further.

"But I thought you and Felix shared everything."

"Like you share everything with Vira?"

Ouch. "Fair point."

Even though she isn't looking at him, her eyes narrow. "Do you see how that might be a misguided assumption?"

"I do now." They stop at her door as she attempts to jam the key into the lock with shaking hands. "Here," he says, gently guiding her. He can feel her watchful gaze as they open the door together, the key disappearing. The inked rune on the inside of her wrist disappears and is replaced with a new one, while he gets an *additional* symbol etched onto his skin.

"Oh . . . forgot about that," he says sheepishly.

"Better you than him," Arden says as she pushes through the door.

Even though she hadn't invited him in, he follows her inside. He closes the door behind him, watching as she removes the cork from a half-empty bottle of verdot.

"Light a fire, will you?"

He knows that tone all too well. After especially hard training sessions with the Cruex, ones where she'd slayed her targets but had received little to no praise from the king, she'd retreated to her chambers to curl up and sulk in self-pity. Rydan had always been the one to sneak libations from the cellar—and, on some nights, he'd even been able to get her down there without much of a fight.

He kneels by the hearth, flames sparking in his hands. It takes mere seconds to light the kindling. She plops a *very* full glass on the table behind him, the crimson liquid nearly sloshing over the edge. "So, it's going to be that kind of a night, huh?"

She falls into one of the armchairs, nudging him in the shoulder with her foot. "Only one glass for you. Wouldn't want Vira to get worried."

Something a bit like guilt coils in his stomach. He's hardly seen Vira over the past week. Their schedules have been so different, what with her working with other Summoners and him starting to work with . . . well, the Archmage. And Felix, Avery, and Arden.

"I doubt she'll notice. She's probably gearing up for her next lesson."

Arden arches a brow. "Trouble in paradise?"

Rydan shoots her a sidelong glance, watching as she drinks nearly half her glass. "Better slow down. Save some for the fishes."

She snorts. "Verdot-drinking *fishes*. Now wouldn't that be something?"

He smiles, happy that he was able to tamp down her rage, even if only for a moment. He's about to get up and sit in the seat across from her when, suddenly, she's no longer in the armchair, but sitting right next to him, on the floor.

"The boundary Felix tried to cross today? Was you."

The remark catches him off guard, but not enough for him to miss her meaning. "I see." He brings the glass to his mouth. "How far did he get?"

"Pretty fucking far."

Rydan nearly snorts out the wine he'd just drank. "Want me to kick his ass?"

"Would you?" She shifts her gaze from the fire, flames flickering in her piercing green eyes, dark hair falling down one side of her shoulder. Her lashes seem to grow thicker as her eyes drop and then lift again.

The words leave his mouth before he can reel them back in, before he can evaluate their consequence. "You know the lengths I would go for you. The lengths I *have* gone for you."

Something simmers beneath her gaze. Something familiar he hasn't experienced in a long while.

"What I mean is, I know you can hold your own. I've seen it with my own two eyes." He studies her, the way her expression ebbs and flows with his words. "But when there are things you want to protect, things that *belong* to you . . . no one should force that from you. Or force their way into the middle."

The nearly indiscernible tilt of her head coupled with the way her eyes close indicate that that's exactly what Felix had done. That look she'd given him earlier today, right before he'd amplified . . . Felix had pushed his way into their sacred place. It wasn't one they talked about much, or spoke of ever, really, but just because something is hidden doesn't mean it isn't there. And his feelings for Arden?

Well, they've always been there.

And always would be.

Because he'd been her first. Her first kiss. Her first *more than* kiss. Her first intimate experience. And she'd been his. Once they'd blurred that line between assassin camaraderie and lethal attraction, there'd been no going back. As much as he'd tried. As much as he'd wanted to hate her when she'd left him during the Soames mission. As much as he was *still* trying—and failing—with Vira.

Seeming to pick up on his thoughts, she moves a hand to his, grasping it tight. "We've been through hell and back, haven't we?"

"More than a few times, I'd say."

She smiles, but it quickly falters. "There's so much to unpack here. With the Mallum. With Opal. With Xerin."

"And now you're dealing with a nosy boyf—"

"Don't," she says. "You know I'm not one for labels."

"That I do know, all too well." He pulls his hand away and reaches for the fire, pretending to move around some of the logs so that they'll burn longer. Arden sighs, resting both hands in her lap.

"Well, I suppose there isn't much we can do while we're stuck here," he says.

"You're right about that," she whispers. "So it looks like the quicker we can discover my abilities, the faster we can get out of here. Which means I'll have to put up with you. And Avery." Her tone hardens. "And Felix."

He doesn't mention that even when they *do* discover what magick's been lurking beneath the surface that Cyfrin will likely want to develop it. Hone it. And that will take time— more time in Midvale.

"Perhaps you should talk to Cerylia."

"There's no way she'll let us leave. Not after what she's given up to come here."

"How is it that the Veil is the only place we're safe right now?"

"That's probably why the Council created it in the first place. And why nearly all illusié have left Aeridon and decided to hide out for decades upon decades." Her empty wine glass clinks as she leans over to set it on the table. "Until the Mallum's gone, why would they risk being anywhere other than the Veil?"

"It just seems kind of . . . cowardly, that's all."

There's an edge to her voice as she says, "Like when you ran away after discovering you were one of them?"

"Don't you mean one of *us*?" he corrects.

Her lips tilt in a faint smile.

"Yeah. Just like that," he admits.

A long silence stretches between them as they stare into the fire. Her voice is barely a brush of air as she says, "We can't let our time here be for nothing."

She's right. "What do you suggest?"

"If I'm not mistaken, this place is crawling with forbidden texts—texts that we were convinced didn't survive Tymond's purge."

"And?"

"If I can get my hands on enough research, maybe I can piece together these 'morphed' abilities. And perhaps you can find out more about the Soames and about the crescent fire. For all we know, there could be book after book written on the Mallum." Her eyes glint with something he hasn't seen in a long time: hope. "We're quite literally sitting on a trove of information."

Or a bunch of myths and legends with no actual bearing on reality. Even though he thinks it, he doesn't have the heart to say it out loud. It's only when she pushes herself to her feet that he realizes she means *now*. "Oh, so we're going then?"

"What, like you have something better to do?"

He glances at the fire and the glass of verdot in his hand. "Is that a serious question?"

She sticks her lower lip out in a pout before pulling him to his feet. "Come on, you can bring that with you. I'm sure there's a roaring fire in the library. It'll be like you never left."

"Somehow I highly doubt that," he says, swaying as he stands upright.

"Don't even try to deny that you've missed this." She grabs what's left of the bottle and scurries toward the door. "And put that out, would you?"

Rydan watches her for a moment, then spreads out the embers with his bare hands, covering the hottest of them with ash. He's barely finished doing what she's asked when she bounces back into the room and nearly drags him out the door.

⁕ ⁕ ⁕

The library is unnervingly quiet. He isn't sure what he expected, but this . . . it's as if no one's cared to enter this specific establishment in decades. Arden hadn't even so much as questioned the colossal bar across the door as she'd used her chakrams to hook one end and push it up and over.

"I see your strength hasn't waned in the slightest," Rydan remarks, following her through the enormous oakwood door. "Perhaps we should have checked with someone first—"

"Since when have you ever cared about getting permission?" she teases, waltzing into the library like she owns the place.

"I don't," he shoots back, cheeks warming. "It's just—"

"Seems your time with Vira has made you a little bit soft." She turns over a shoulder, her eyes more of a jade hue in the dim lighting. "You don't even carry a weapon anymore."

He stops walking, realizing that he can't argue with that. She makes a solid point. "We're a rare breed, you and I."

"That we are," she agrees, head tilting skyward as she observes the room. Mounds of books on endless shelves float around them, beckoning them to take their pick.

"Knowing that this library isn't the only one in Midvale is beyond my comprehension," Rydan comments, following her to the center of the room. "We'd need seven lifetimes to read all of these."

"Maybe for you," she quips before smiling and skipping off to the nearest shelf.

"Not everyone had their own private chambers growing up, you know."

She slides her head out from behind one of the wooden fixtures. "Not everyone was singled out and ridiculed every day for being the only female either."

She has him there. "Okay, okay, you win." He grabs one of the chairs before sitting in it with the back facing him. "It's not like Tymond's library was that impressive, anyway."

Arden rolls her eyes. "Just another perk of being a male Cruex, I suppose."

Rydan stills, studying her expression. "You weren't given a key?"

She nearly guffaws at the assumption. "Nope. Sure wasn't."

"But you passed nearly every assessment—"

"Not *nearly*. I passed every single one of them."

Rydan presses his palms into the back of the chair, gripping it tightly. "That doesn't answer my question . . . how?"

"I suppose some secrets aren't meant to be shared."

The way she says it instantly has him back in the Cruex chambers and all the times Ezra's books had gone missing. Percival's, too. It's not a difficult memory to dredge up, seeing as they'd gone on and on about it for what'd felt like days on end. "It was you!"

As if she can read his thoughts, she says, "I guess we'll never know."

He lets out a hearty laugh. "If you could have seen Ezra's tirades . . ."

A wicked smile creeps across her face. "Oh, I did."

Rydan laughs again. "My respect for you just grew tenfold."

"As if it weren't already there."

Rydan pops up from the chair, suddenly feeling the urge to join her at the bookshelf.

"Oh, so *now* you're going to help, are you?"

"Whatever you need, Madame Assassin."

She snorts, pulling a few books from the shelves and piling them on top of his arms. "These should get us started."

He follows her to one of the desks, his thoughts trapping him as he notices the way she moves across the room with that indelible swagger. He tries to swallow the lump that's forming in his throat as a memory surfaces, at one of Tymond's feasts, where she'd donned a mauve backless evening gown. He hadn't been able to take his eyes off of her the entire night. The way the satin had lain over the lower arch of her back, cupping her backside . . . he'd known of her sheer physical strength from their training sessions alone, but *seeing* it, displayed so prominently in that gown . . . it'd nearly taken his breath away. He could tell every other Cruex had had similar thoughts. But she'd only ended up with one of them that night . . .

Heat rushes to his cheeks and, as much as he doesn't want to, he forces himself to look up, away—anywhere that isn't *her*.

The dome of the library it is.

"You got quiet all of a sudden."

Her voice, coupled with the thump of books on the desk, instantly draws him back in. "Happens more than you might think," he murmurs.

She narrows her eyes as if she actually *can* read his mind and that possibility, although unlikely, nearly sends him into a spiral.

"Dare I even ask?"

"I'd rather if you didn't."

She's sitting across from him, one hand opening a book, the other on the adjacent stack. "And why is that?"

She doesn't look at him as she asks the question, nor does she actually seem interested in his response. He watches her hand as it traces each line of text, brows furrowed, gaze intently focused on each paragraph.

There's a tightness in his chest at the mere thought of how much more she'd had to go through versus the rest of her counterparts, including him. The exclusion. The judgment and mockery. The need to constantly prove herself. If you ask him, she's more of a fighter than all of them combined. A true assassin.

A warrior.

Her gaze tracks upward from the book. "There you go again, Helstrom. Giving me the silent treatment."

He smiles at the use of his last name, but it quickly fades as he recalls what he was just thinking about. "I'm sorry," he says.

Confusion knits her brows. "For what?"

"For that night."

Understanding settles onto her face and, for a moment, he's almost convinced himself that her new ability is indeed telepathy.

"There's nothing to apologize for." Her tone is firm yet soft at the same time.

"What I really mean is that . . . I'm sorry it only happened once."

Disbelief graces her features but it's so subtle, he's wondered if he'd imagined it. She lowers her gaze then, lashes thick in the flickering candlelight. "Me too."

It's barely a brush of air, but he hears it. The admission neither of them have ever had the courage to make. He breathes a sigh of relief. "I always thought you regretted it."

Her eyes flick to his. "Never. Not even once."

His heart thumps against his chest. "It would have complicated so many things . . ."

Her eyes are on his mouth now. "It would have."

His hands tighten around the arms of the chair. "I—I just thought you should know."

She doesn't take her eyes off of him as she slowly closes the book in front of her, then returns it to the stack. "Well, then. Consider me informed."

Her voice is breathy, almost raspy, and he can't help but hear the way she'd moaned into his ear when he'd pulled the satin up over her hips . . . the way it'd eventually pooled onto the floor, his trousers along with it. He grips the chair even harder as the fabric of his pants tightens around his thighs.

"Everything okay over there?" There's a playfulness to her tone, but her face is also flushed, which tells him he's not the only one feeling the rising tension between them.

"Never better." He smirks. "Any other questions?"

A coy smile tugs at the corner of her lips. "I suppose my only other question is . . . what are you going to do about it?"

The pulsing between his legs only intensifies as more of the memory comes flooding in from that night in her chambers. They'd started against the armoire, then the bedpost, the balcony . . . the moonlight pouring down on them as they'd slammed themselves into the cool stone railing. He'd shivered at the way she'd run her hands through his hair, pulling and tugging as if she couldn't get enough—as if it would never *be* enough—and him pulling and tugging right back, with more fervor, more *need*. There'd been the soft graze of her teeth as she'd bitten his lower lip, taking it between her own—tender, but hungry. And, his personal favorite, the sounds she'd made as he'd pumped into her, staring directly into that blazing emerald fire as she'd completely unraveled in his embrace. Not a single thread of pleasure had remained unexplored.

Until now.

Until every day since.

He can feel the heat building, hands tingling at the power that resides within them. He's seconds away from launching himself across the table when he notices something that dulls the fire almost instantly.

"Arden," he whispers, his gaze falling to her sides.

She glances down at her hands, at the faint sparks igniting at her fingertips. She looks back up, the fierce hunger that had just lit her eyes fading entirely. Fear takes its place.

"Rydan," she whispers back.

FELIX BARLOW

UNDER THE COVER of night, Felix slips from his new quarters into the hall. As much as he'd wanted to settle into his new space, the reality of the situation is bleak: Arden wants nothing to do with him; he's mere days away from failing Xerin; and, to make matters worse, he's under the antagonizing eye of the Archmage . . . which makes breaking into her office all the more risky. If Lane's reaction is any indication, asking for a map of Midvale is a death sentence.

Fortunately, he doesn't need a map to find said office, seeing as he's already been there once before. Under less than desirable circumstances, yes, but at least he knows the location. Conjuring a portal to the southeastern wing takes only seconds until he finds himself standing in a familiar hallway.

It's dark, eerie, even, save for the dim lanterns lighting the obscure path before him. If it wasn't already clear that this hallway isn't to be traversed after-hours, well, it is now. Just ahead he can see a structurally sound wooden door, emblazoned with a giant A. The Archmage's office.

He tries to quiet his heavy footfall, but the hollow chamber seems to not only echo but reverberate even the faintest of sounds. He can't help but notice the inscriptions on the other doors, of which there aren't many, that he passes by. To his right, M. To his left, V. A few steps down and to his right again, C. A few other doors remain without an inscription. Could the room he's looking for be behind one of these doors? It seems too obvious and yet . . . perhaps not.

Hidden in plain sight.

The likelihood that any of the doors would be unlocked isn't exactly high, but that doesn't keep him from trying the handle to the Archmage's office. To avoid leaving fingerprints, he wraps the edge of his cloak around his hand before twisting the knob.

Locked.

How he's supposed to get in when "they become the key" is beyond him, and probably something he should have considered before risking this little venture. Defeated, he turns back the way he came, carefully checking the other knobs along the way. Locked. Locked. *Locked.*

The library hadn't yielded any results—at least, nothing lucrative that he could use—which means he's running out of options. And time. Granted, he'd only visited one library thus far in Midvale. So perhaps his options haven't entirely run out.

He drags himself to the edge of the hallway, preparing to conjure a portal back to the northeastern wing when the unthinkable happens.

One of the doors creaks open.

A single glance over his shoulder tells him it's the door inscribed with the V. Even though it isn't the Archmage's office, he's really in no position to pass up the opportunity to at least inspect it. But as he approaches, he quickly realizes the door didn't creak open—it was pulled open.

By none other than fellow Caldaris Opal and Estelle.

Opal stops in her tracks, causing Estelle to nearly run into her from behind. "Fancy meeting you here—and at such a late hour," the Inverter says.

Felix raises a brow, his attention flicking between the two of them. "The same could be said for you." He takes a step closer, realizing why Opal's dragged Estelle into her midnight escapade. "You know, the point of cloaking is to actually *be* cloaked whilst gallivanting about."

Opal raises a hand to her chest in mock offense. "Fair point. However, have you considered that, perhaps, I saw you coming?"

"I'm sure you did. You seem to know a lot these days that you aren't willing to share with the rest of us."

The derision dripping from his tone is enough to make Estelle push her way in front of Opal, eyes lined with concern. "Harsh, Barlow. What's gotten into you lately?"

The way she says it sends a pang straight to his chest, one he knows he's completely and utterly at fault for. Estelle has been his closest companion in the Caldari for years—but joining forces with Xerin has only strained their relationship. The cracks have been forming for months now. It seems they're finally showing.

"Nothing," he says bitterly. "Just out for a midnight stroll."

"Down the hallway that houses the Archmage's office? At this hour? Unlikely. Unless Cyfrin is taking midnight appointments we're unaware of."

Felix clenches his jaw, teeth on the verge of grinding.

"At least we're not skulking around, *alone*," Opal adds.

He's about to out her right then and there, but doing so would essentially be outing himself—as well as what they're actually doing here. While he may not know the exact details of Opal's assignment, the fact that they're technically on the same team, working with Xerin, is enough to make him keep his mouth shut.

"Or perhaps you're alone because you're alienating every single person trying to help you—"

"Enough," he barks, cutting Opal's tirade off. "Let's just return to our rooms and pretend like none of this happened."

"Where's the fun in that?"

Estelle glances at Felix, a somber expression clouding her face. "We could do that . . . but aren't you the least bit curious as to what's behind door number four?"

Yes. Very much so. But instead, he says, "Why would I be? Like I said, I'm just out for a stroll."

"Come on, Felix," Estelle says, lowering her voice as she inches closer. "It's okay. It was the only one we were able to get into without damaging the condition of the door."

"Or its hinges," Opal scoffs.

He remains looking disinterested for as long as possible, letting them persuade him a little longer. Finally, after much unnecessary groveling, he agrees to follow them inside. Thankfully, the tremendous effort it takes to hide his smile goes unnoticed. His first assumption upon entering the room is that it'd be larger—*much* larger—but he can easily walk the entire perimeter in less than fifty steps. Speaking of steps, he isn't at all prepared for the sudden drop in the floor: a spiral staircase that extends down, down, down . . . farther than the eye can see.

Felix grabs onto the narrow metal railing, leaning over the edge to get a better look as to just how far down it goes.

"Don't waste your time," Estelle says. "Thanks to Opal's ability, we know it leads to the Vaults without having to trek all the way down there."

"And what did you discover is *in* the Vaults?"

Opal arches a brow in silent communication. "Nothing noteworthy."

Which Felix takes to mean nothing she wants to discuss in front of Estelle.

The Cloaker shrugs her shoulders, unaware of the subtle conversation that's happening indirectly between the two Caldari. "I think that's enough exploring for one night, wouldn't you say?" She stifles a yawn. "I'm sure Cerylia—"

Opal cuts her off right there. "Yes, the queen is probably expecting my return any minute now. I shouldn't keep her waiting."

Felix doesn't miss the look of confusion on Estelle's face. Whatever they're hiding must be due to Queen Jareth's bidding, but Felix knows better than to pry. He'll get the information out of Opal one way or another, but now isn't the time. "Indeed, it is rather late. I'd be glad to escort you back to your quarters."

Opal blanches at the offer, but Estelle graciously takes him up on it, linking her arm in his. "Lead the way."

CERYLIA JARETH

EXAMINING THE LOCKED door in her chambers seems to be doing more harm than good.

Head pounding, Cerylia pulls away from the keyhole, grabbing the half-full glass of verdot that's sitting next to her. Surely it isn't helping, but it's the only thing that seems to take the edge off as of late. She hasn't spoken with the Archmage since their last interaction. Everything worth saying has already been said. Cyfrin had won—at least, for the time being.

"What are you attempting there?"

Cerylia nearly spills the crimson-colored wine all over the carpet as she whirls around to find Opal leaning against the doorway to her bedroom. "I don't know how many times I've asked you to announce your presence, but it seems that, once again, it's fallen on deaf ears."

Opal's mouth presses into a firm line. "We're sharing the same chambers. I don't know where else you'd expect me to be."

"Training? Exploring? Inverting?" Cerylia mumbles. "Take your pick. Your options are endless, unlike mine."

Opal straightens at her callous tone. "But you're the queen."

"Not here I'm not," Cerylia retorts as she sticks a metal pin into the keyhole, jabbing it every which way.

"What's that supposed to mean?"

"Seems Cyfrin is the only royalty for miles." She's so focused on opening the damn door that she doesn't even notice when Opal plops down right next to her and takes a drink from *her* wine glass. "Right, then. Help yourself."

If Opal catches her sarcasm, she doesn't show it. Nor does it stop her from tilting the heavily fingerprinted glass to her lips. "I don't think that's going to work."

"And what might you be, an expert lockpicker? Any other talents you'd like to confess?"

Opal smiles, and it's the first genuine thing Cerylia's seen from her since . . . well, since they'd arrived. "What is that even? A hairpin?"

"Sure is." Cerylia twists it one more time before releasing it. Sighing heavily, she palms the door, head resting against the back of her hand.

"Why don't you just ask Cyfrin for the key?"

Cerylia scoffs. "You really *do* have selective hearing."

Opal shrugs. "We were assigned this room. I don't think that's by accident."

"If that's so, why would they lock one of the doors?"

"Maybe that's a conversation for you and the Archmage."

Cerylia narrows her eyes. "You know something. You've been inverting, haven't you?"

"I will neither confirm nor deny that."

Cerylia studies her for a long moment. She doesn't appear to be aging. In fact, she appears to be fully back to her old self. Even the spark in her eyes is there. "As long as you're being careful."

"Always."

She pauses before asking her next question. "Is there anything I should know about? Anything I'd find worthwhile?"

Opal finishes the last of the wine, carelessly letting the glass roll from her hand and onto the seat. "Not in the slightest."

"Perhaps we can fix that."

Opal eyes the door, then sighs. "Fine. I don't know what's behind the door, but I know Cyfrin has the key. I *also* know that she specifically tasked Lane with assigning us this very room."

"And you couldn't just come out and say that?"

"I just did."

Cerylia nearly flings the hairpin at the girl's head. "I meant earlier."

"I tried." She smiles. "Seems I'm not the only one with selective hearing."

Cerylia stifles a laugh. "Perhaps I should send *you* to speak with the Archmage."

"The key's in the Vaults, but only Cyfrin has access to it."

"How do you know this?"

She shrugs again, so nonchalant. "I followed her."

"And she didn't see you?"

"I didn't say I went alone."

At that exact moment, Estelle appears right next to Opal, violet eyes shimmering. "Please don't be upset. It wasn't my idea."

Cloaked. Of course.

"On the contrary, I'm quite impressed." Cerylia looks between the two of them, feeling a pang of sorrow at the closeness of the Caldari. She, too, had once felt that way—had someone she could depend on, no matter what. Tears prick her eyes, but she turns back to the door, clearing her throat as she says, "I'm assuming after following her, you know how to access the Vaults?"

Opal's eyes glimmer. "Would you expect anything less?"

"Can you take me there now?"

The two Caldari exchange a glance. "We should warn you, however, that it won't exactly be a quick and easy trip."

"And why is that?"

"Best if we show you."

⚛ ⚛ ⚛

Cerylia leans over the metal railing, taking in the sheer number of steps spiraling beneath her. *Hundreds.* Even if she were to sprint down the steps, it'd take hours to reach the bottom. Perhaps that's on purpose. Whatever Archmage Galdor has hidden down there is meant to stay put, away from prying eyes. The key to the locked door in her room must be rather important, then.

All the more reason to continue her pursuit.

She steps away from the railing, pondering her options.

"We've considered every avenue possible," Opal starts, seeming to follow the queen's line of thought. "The fastest way to get down there would be by flight."

She sighs. "Which means we'd need the ability of a Shaper." The thought of asking Xerin to intervene doesn't sit well with her in the slightest. "Unless . . ."

"We use a Transporter," Estelle says, eyes wide with the realization. "Why didn't we think of that before?"

But Opal's gaze is fixed on the queen. "What's wrong with calling Xerin?"

Cerylia tries not to look taken aback, failing miserably as she fumbles for a response. "It's just that . . . Xerin isn't here. At the moment, anyway. But Haskell is. And this," she sweeps her arm across the landing, "is something that can't wait."

"Do you think he's ventured to the Vaults yet?" Estelle asks.

"I'm sure he's covered every inch of this place, so long as the doors are unlocked and he has access," Cerylia answers. "Would you mind fetching him?"

"On it," Estelle says before cloaking herself in the night.

The awkward silence that stretches between her and Opal has Cerylia wishing she'd sent the Inverter along with Estelle. Fortunately, they only have to make small talk for a few minutes. Any longer and Cerylia might reveal something she'll come to regret.

Clearly, Opal has other ideas.

"Whatever it is you suspect Xerin is up to, don't let it interfere with what you came here to do."

Cerylia narrows her eyes at the remark. "And what exactly have I come here to do?"

Opal keeps her expression neutral. "To regain your extracting abilities."

"While that may be true, the reasoning behind doing so goes much deeper than that," Cerylia corrects. "I came here to ensure I can keep my people safe. Not only those who reside in Sardoria, but the Caldari as well." She clicks her tongue against the roof of her mouth. "If Xerin poses a threat to either—"

"Why would he?"

Cerylia keeps her gaze fixed on the Inverter. "You tell me."

Opal scoffs. "I'm not the one with trust issues. Just because Dane—"

"Don't," she interrupts, jaw clenching. "We're done with this conversation."

"You might be, but I'm not—"

"It isn't up for debate."

Just as Opal opens her mouth to make what is surely another snide remark, Estelle returns with Haskell right beside her.

"Evening," the Transporter says, bowing his head as he follows Estelle into the room. "Or I suppose I should say *good morning*, given the hour."

"Did Estelle have a chance to fill you in?" Cerylia asks lightly in an attempt to brush off the conversation with Opal.

Her nephew nods. "You were right to assume that I've been to the Vaults. And good thing, too, because those stairs are a real pain."

"At least you only had to walk down them," Estelle quips. "Imagine if you'd had to climb back up." She shakes her head. "Brutal."

"But a great workout, nonetheless." Haskell looks to his aunt. "Are you ready?"

"As I'll ever be." She links her arm in Haskell's, realizing that she needs further instruction. "Seeing as it'll just be the two of us, what is it I should be looking for?"

'The first thing you'll come across is a crystalline grid," Estelle answers. "It's hard to miss, believe me. But on the far wall, you'll see a collection of cabinets. Go to the one in the upper left corner and turn the quartz dial thrice to the right, then twice to the left, until it lands back in the center. The key will be in that cabinet."

Cerylia takes a mental note of the instructions, but something snags her mid-thought. "When you followed the Archmage before, was she opening the cabinet to remove the key?"

"On the contrary," Opal says. "She was returning it."

Intriguing. "And you're sure it's the correct key?"

"Unless my inversions are wrong." She leaves it at that. "I'll meet you back in the room," she says coolly as she grabs Estelle's hand and guides her out the door.

Cerylia doesn't waste another moment as she turns to face her nephew. "Let's get this over with, shall we?"

Ever prepared, Haskell hands her a familiar-looking tonic. "Bottoms up."

❧ ❧ ❧

Back in her chambers, Cerylia's pleased to find that, while Opal had probably intended to wait up, she'd fallen asleep in one of the oversize lounge chairs by the hearth. Tiptoeing past her, Cerylia enters her room, closing the doors quietly behind her. She eyes the locked door before walking over to it, then inserts the key. *Deep breath.* She turns it, eager to see what awaits.

Without even having to push, the door creaks open, its hinges on their last leg. She peeks her head inside to find complete darkness, as should be expected. She leaves the door open a crack, scanning the room for a lantern. There's one by her bedside, though it isn't lit. She makes quick work of going back into the den, tiptoeing around Opal, and using the hearth fire to light the lantern before returning to the door.

Once inside, it's clear there aren't any windows in the mystery room, not even the faux scene-scape ones she's seen around Midvale. There's no internal light source either. It's as if this room was meant to stay hidden, forever in the shadows . . . but why?

The room itself isn't very large, maybe half the size of her washroom, and it has Cerylia questioning why the door was even locked in the first place. But that question is quickly answered as she approaches the only object in sight—a circular indentation in the wall that's reminiscent of stained glass. The image is difficult to make out since some of the pieces are missing; but upon closer inspection, she realizes that what she's looking at isn't made of glass at all. It's made of gems.

Soul gems.

"As I live and breathe," Cerylia says, gingerly plucking one from the wall. As an Extractor, she'd become rather familiar with the concept of soul gems, but to hold one in her hands? To know that such a thing actually exists and isn't just fable? It's astonishing. Enough to take her breath away. Soul magick isn't to be trifled with, which is exactly why this door had been locked, why the key had been hidden in the lowermost part of Midvale. It makes sense now.

It also makes sense why she'd been assigned this room.

She pockets the gem, studying the pattern on the wall when she notices something peculiar. Using the spot where she'd removed the gem as a reference point, it seems there should be six more just like it—but they've all been removed.

Who in Midvale is performing soul magick?

Who even has the capability to?

Opal had said that Cyfrin was *returning* the key . . .

It's both puzzling and concerning, to say the least, but Cerylia doesn't have time to dwell. She considers replacing the gem back where it belongs but if it were to fall into the wrong hands, she'd never be able to forgive herself.

Although, who's to say the other six haven't already?

DARIUS TYMOND

XERIN HAD TOLD him to meet at the jaded spring tonight, so that's exactly what Darius plans to do. Cyrus is nowhere to be found, so, instead of taking the carriage to the base of the Vaekith Mountains, Darius decides to ride horseback.

Spring showers rain down on him the entire way, the trail morphing into a sopping mess. Rivulets eddy and flow, branching off into tiny streams along the edges of the Roviel Woods. A dense haze forms around him and, for a brief moment, he fears Clive may have returned to exact yet another act of vengeance—but when he rides up into Volkharn and arrives at the gates in one piece with his sanity still intact, he realizes that that isn't the case.

He doesn't see Xerin at first, not until a falcon, his tried-and-true form, swoops down from an evergreen tree. A golden glow follows shortly after, revealing Xerin in his human form. "Well?" he says, his eyes the color of the desert sun. "What are you waiting for?"

Darius holds his ring in front of the enormous metal structure. Like so many times before, the amethyst's iridescent glow unlocks the entrance. The gates swing open. He motions for Xerin to go first.

Without a moment's hesitation, the Shaper storms through the gates, nearly jogging to the spring. Darius follows as best he can, but his robes are soaked, as are his boots. He hastily strips off the former, not wanting to miss whatever it is Xerin has in store. He'd been hoping to see his staff again, that Xerin might have found it, but from the looks of it, it's still missing.

The familiar sound of rushing water greets him, and he steps onto the floating stones to cross to the other side. He arrives at the vine-covered wall just moments after Xerin, who's looking at him expectantly.

"I don't know how going to the spring is going to help without my staff."

Xerin forcefully grabs the king's wrist. "Lift the barrier."

Darius grits his teeth, then yanks his wrist from Xerin's grip. He scowls as he splays his fingers against the wall—searching, searching, searching. It takes longer than expected and he can feel Xerin growing impatient with each passing minute. Finally, the ring pulsates as soon as it makes contact—but as it's lifted, he notices a stark difference from before.

There's no water.

At all.

The growing haze above blocks any moonlight that might be trying to shine through, but even if there were any, there's nothing to reflect it. No waterfalls. No streams. No water lapping at the bank's edge. Just a giant cavern punched into the mountainside. A warning statement.

Darius's breath catches in his throat. "What's happened here?"

"*This*," Xerin says, walking further into the dusty cavern, "is what is at risk if you don't get your imbecile court to fall in line. Cruex, Savant, King's Guard—*everyone*."

"But without the water, I can't—"

"Speak to your beloved?" Xerin shoots him a sidelong glance. Pure disdain lines his features. "If you'll recall, that wasn't a part of the deal. Just an extra. An added bonus."

Darius shakes his head, anger swelling in his chest. "That certainly isn't how I recall it."

"Oh?" Xerin crosses his arms. "Perhaps we should bring forth our third witness."

Darius nearly keels over at the mention of Clive potentially being *here*, in this sacred place. "You wouldn't dare."

"Oh, I would." Shadows flicker in Xerin's gaze. "But I didn't. Not this time, at least."

As much as his shoulders want to sag with relief, Darius remains tense, alert. *Guarded.*

"But back to this," he says, gesturing to the empty spring. "You were provided that staff out of generosity. Nothing more. After all, the terms of soul magick require only that: her soul for unadulterated power. That's what you agreed to. That's what you're getting."

"I'm beginning to wonder when," Darius muses, his tone brusque. "It's been years and I'm still without—"

"And whose fault is that? How rapidly or sluggishly you summon the Mallum to absorb *all* illusié abilities is entirely up to you. You outlawed magick a decade ago, no?"

A slow burn crawls across the king's cheeks. He only nods in response.

"Ten years is more than enough time."

"Why do you think I started sending the Cruex on those missions?" Darius growls. "Why my recent focus has been to rid Aeridon of those who possess the abilities the Mallum has already acquired? It's almost complete."

Xerin regards him with complete and utter apathy.

"If I had known it was the last time—"

"Surely you wouldn't have taken it for granted," Xerin interrupts, making another sweeping gesture toward the barren pit.

He grits his teeth. "So, I can no longer speak with her."

Xerin clasps him on the shoulder. "Look on the bright side, Your Majesty," he whispers, his breath close enough to make Darius shudder. "Perhaps this will be all the motivation you need to finally execute the rest of our plans."

BRAXTON HORNSBY

THE PATH IS growing more and more colorful with each step he takes, his surroundings populating with an abundance of detail. Never did he think he'd be so happy to see a tree, a flower, a *weed*—but here he is, grinning like a damn fool.

The more he ventures into the unknown, the more questions he has. If the Veil was created by illusié, does that mean the Void was also created by it as well? Or is it just a consequence of trying to enter the Veil without magickal abilities? Everything has its opposite. By that logic, if the Veil is illusié-made, the Void must be, too.

This assumption grows even stronger as everything around him continues to fill in. No longer a world of muted gray, of *nothingness*—there's color. Saturation. Shadow and light. Physical objects. Plants and trees. *Life*.

It's almost as if, somehow, someone had managed to create a world inside the Void. Which would require magick. Which also means . . . if there's a way in, there must also be a way out—and possibly someone else residing here.

He looks down at the crest, gripping it tight. This was the only "thing" he'd found when he'd first arrived—and the only thing he's found since. Someone had to have placed it here, seemingly to hide it. But why? Whoever had hidden it must be exceedingly skilled (not to mention brave) to journey into this lords-forsaken place.

It's then, in the middle of trying to figure it all out, that his stomach growls. It's been so long that he nearly jumps out of his own skin at the sound.

I'm hungry? I'm hungry!

But *this*, his senses returning, poses a new conundrum. What is there to eat? To drink? And will he need to—

Suddenly feeling exhausted, Braxton's knees buckle, sending him crashing to the ground. It's grassy, so at least there's something to cushion his fall. His hand loosens around the crest as the feeling of his entire body shutting down takes over. Hunger pains greet him mercilessly, followed by a stabbing headache, twitching eyelids, and a dry and salivating mouth. He wheezes on the ground, trying to catch his breath after walking for days on end without a single respite.

He takes it back. He'd rather feel the nothingness than all of this. It's too much. Far too much . . .

He's about to give in to whatever awaits him on the other side when a voice floats overhead. *A voice? There's someone else here?*

The realization is a shock to his system—a shock he clearly can't handle right now. Braxton reaches for the fight within him, but it's no use. His world fades to black.

ARDEN ELIRI

THE SPARKS HAD only lasted a moment before fizzling out completely. I hadn't been able to direct them or use them or ignite a second time, no matter how many times Rydan repeated the lessons he'd learned from Avery.

Between that and the tension in the library, I'd excused myself shortly after those futile attempts, craving the silence and solitude of my room. A few days had passed with no visitors, no knocks on the door, and no lessons. Quite frankly, I couldn't care less that I've been missing some of my lessons. I know the Archmage will come knocking at some point, or send Casimir or another one of her cadre, but the thought of facing both Felix and Rydan right now? That little reunion is one I'm hard-pressed to put off for as long as humanly possible.

At least the time alone hasn't been a total waste. Masked by the night, I'd crept back to the library to gather more texts and have been researching and reading in my room ever since—unbothered and undisturbed. The books on morphed abilities are few and far between, but what I *have* gleaned is that yes, it is indeed possible, and that, just as the Archmage had said, there's no guarantee said abilities would be a blend of the parents'.

So, nothing new.

I'm belly-down on the bed with my legs kicked up in the air, feet crossed at the ankles, quill scribbling along a folded piece of parchment. Juniper's curled up across from me at the edge of the bed, eyes drifting open every so often. I finish writing the last sentence before dropping the quill and rolling my wrist in my other hand. I figure I might as well keep a diary while I'm here, especially after the incident with Rydan in the library. There'd been other moments, too . . . moments where I can't describe how suddenly I'd felt different, like something within me had shifted. It'd happened when Felix and I had pulled Rydan out of Opal's inversion. And just recently in the library with Rydan. Now that I think of it, accidentally hurting (and somehow also healing) both Delwynn and Braxton had felt off, too.

But I can't be an Amplifier because I haven't been able to amplify anyone else's feelings. And I'm not an Ignitor because my efforts in the library had yielded nothing. Even though the texts mention there's no guarantee of illusié parents passing down their abilities to their offspring, it sure would help to know what my parents' abilities had been. It seems the Archmage has left that conversation to Cerylia, and for good reason—but perhaps my parents had been just like me. Perhaps they, too, had started with one ability that had morphed into another. Perhaps it's why the Savant had murdered my mother—and why my father had vanished without a trace.

Heaving a loud sigh, I shove the parchment, quill, and stack of books to the other side of the bed. I pull the blankets up over my legs, apologizing to Juniper as the bed shifts underneath us. I lay my head on the pillow and stare at the ceiling. I know I'll have to leave this room eventually. I know I'll have to face Felix. And Rydan.

But not tonight. Not right now.

I'm relieved when sleep finds me easier than expected. With Juniper snuggled into my side, I sink deeper into the blankets and pillows, surrendering to the dreamy abyss that awaits.

❧ ❧ ❧

I jolt awake to a feral pounding on the door. Tangled in a heap of blankets, I nearly fall to the floor as I try to climb out of the bed. "Hang on!" I yell, my morning voice raspy.

I shove the blankets off of me in a huff, snatching the silk robe that's hanging inside the armoire before flinging it over my shoulders. I hurl the door open to find the last person I want to see right now, especially after just waking up.

Felix.

"You know what they say about three strikes."

Mouth dry, I cross my arms over my semi-exposed chest. "Do I? And here I thought *you* were the expert."

It's meant to be an insult but if it affects him even remotely, he doesn't show it. "We can't keep making up excuses for you," he says, his hand firm against the doorframe. "I don't think the Archmage has believed the last three, let alone the first one."

Who asked you to?

"So, get dressed. I'll wait."

I narrow my eyes at him. "I don't need you to escort me to my lesson—or anywhere, for that matter."

His russet eyes blaze with annoyance, but there's something else lining them, too. Sadness? It's hard to tell.

"You have nothing to worry about because I'll be taking a step back." His voice softens, as does the hard line along his jaw. "You'll be working primarily with Avery and Rydan."

A confusing blend of emotions swells within me. Do I want to repeat what we'd been through the other day? No. But do I still want Felix present at the lessons? For some reason or another, yes. Yes, I do.

"But what about the emotional baseline?" I ask in what I hope is a covert way to plead my case.

Felix averts his gaze as he glances down the hall. "I suppose that'll just have to wait. Perhaps we can find another Amplifier—"

"No," I interrupt, shaking my head as flashes of being in the Daegrum Chambers fill my mind. "It's already hard enough trying to figure this out—what I am, what I can do. I don't need someone I've never met coming into the picture with the sole intention of hurting me." I shudder. "I've already been through that once before, against my will, mind you, and it's something I'd rather not repeat."

At the mention of the memory, what he's so clearly seen in my mind, his face falls. "I hadn't considered that."

"Yeah, well . . ." I don't even know how to finish my thought. What more can I really say that hasn't already been said?

He lowers his head into his shoulder, chin dipping before saying, "You know, you stormed out before I even had the chance to apologize."

My arms tighten across my chest. "Can you blame me?"

A soft laugh. "That's not how I meant it. I meant . . . that I'm sorry. For . . . infiltrating. For crossing a line." He rubs his hand across the back of his neck. "I didn't know how far I was pushing until it was too late."

A lump lodges in my throat. "But you didn't stop."

A muscle ticks in his jaw. "I know."

Admission. Not what I expected.

"Why didn't you?"

The question must make him uncomfortable because he shifts between his feet. "I guess I wanted to know."

"Know what?" I press.

Shadows darken his eyes as he says, "If what we have— *had,*" he corrects, "was different."

"And?" I whisper, feeling hurt at his correction of using the past tense.

"And I realized that I can't compete with that kind of history." His voice is strained. "Our connection might be strong, Arden. But, sometimes, time outranks every other component." His hand flexes against the doorframe. "Time is the one thing I can't change."

I allow the words to settle between us—the harsh reality he's just laid out. "So . . . what, then?"

The gentleness in his expression fades as he regains his composure. "So, I'm here to escort you to your lesson— because I told the Archmage I would."

"Wouldn't want to get on her bad side."

There's a subtle tug at the corner of his mouth and my stupid heart flutters at the sight of it. "Give me a few," I say, about to turn away.

"I'll be here."

The ache in my chest grows as I leave the door cracked, knowing better than to invite him into the very room I'd expressly exiled him from. I splash some water onto my face and pin my hair back, then pull on a leather jumpsuit that Casimir must have had delivered at some point. I toss my obsidian cloak—*not* the purple one, lords help me—around my shoulders and make for the door. Felix offers his arm to me just like he had the night of the convocation. As much as I want to take it, I refrain from doing so. The last thing I need is to confuse myself even more than I already am.

I step into the hallway, waiting for him to walk beside me. He doesn't say anything, only drops his arm and does just that. We walk the rest of the way in complete silence, but even so, it's the most comfortable silence I've endured. I suppose I have him to thank for that.

We arrive at the training room, his hand grazing mine as we both reach for the door. "If you need me," he says, "I'll be just outside this door."

I look at him, wishing I could just make up my damn mind—but I know who's on the other side of that door. And I know the three of us in a room together is just asking for trouble . . . and a whole lot of hostility.

"You'll be here," I say, pointing right where he's standing.

"You have my word."

Heart still aching, I give him a small smile, then push open the door.

FELIX BARLOW

IT WAS THE last conversation he'd wanted to have with Arden, but a necessary one. Watching her enter the training chambers, alone, only to then be greeted by Rydan is almost more than he can handle at the moment. He averts his eyes, hoping it'll soften the blow, but nothing can dull the sting of the cold, hard truth they'd just discussed.

He can't compete with Rydan. Not with their history.

And certainly not with what Xerin's tasked him with.

He can only hope that this first training lesson will yield some sort of direction . . . for *him*. Knowing what she's capable of without concrete proof might very well be the bane of his existence, especially when he has someone like Xerin breathing down his neck.

Tick tock.

He peers through the small rectangular window, tempted to reach for the door handle. Stand by, he could just stand by . . . But that isn't what he'd promised her. Not in there—but out here.

Although her gait across the room is confident, he can sense her weakness: the timid flick of her gaze as she observes the room; the bob of her throat as she stares into the void above; the forced smile as she tosses her head over her shoulder. He's deep in thought when someone suddenly appears rather wraith-like beside him.

"First day?" Lane asks, angling her head at the window.

Her presence nearly causes him to jump out of his skin, but he nods, clearing his throat as he says, "Might as well be for all of us."

She studies him, curiosity brimming. "Haven't you all trained together before? Practiced your abilities on one another?"

"In a sense, yes," he responds, keeping his eyes locked on Arden. "But this is different. It's more dangerous. Lethal, even."

Lane scoffs. "Sounds like you've put a lot of trust in our Archmage."

Quite the opposite, Felix thinks, but instead says, "I wouldn't say that. I just haven't had proper time with her. Can you blame me?"

Lane sighs, returning her gaze to the window. "Archmage Galdor is a busy woman, and rightfully so. Not only does she oversee the entire school, she's also an esteemed advocate of the Council."

Ah. So that explains why he'd seen her leaving the Council's door in the middle of the night.

A woman who has her hand in everything might just be the kind of person to ally with—and certainly may be of interest to Xerin. But just how far her influence goes remains to be seen. Luckily, Lane seems like just the person to ask; but he's already prodded her once about the map to Midvale, which didn't exactly go as planned. Patience will serve him well.

It's also a luxury he doesn't have.

"Perhaps I should request a meeting," he muses aloud.

Lane looks at him as if he's daft. "Did you miss the part where I mentioned that she's an incredibly busy woman?"

Felix grins. "No, I heard that part, loud and clear." He doesn't elaborate further, knowing that most people, being uncomfortable with bouts of silence, can't help but continue talking to the point of oversharing. He's hoping that, in this particular scenario, Lane is most people.

"Don't get me wrong, the Archmage cares greatly about the concerns and well-being of her students," she says, unknowingly falling right into his trap. "And you are no exception to that. But between her duties at Midvale, her assistance with the Council, and overseeing the sacred illusié sites of Aeridon . . . well, 'incredibly busy' doesn't even begin to cover it."

Already, he's learned two things about the Archmage that he hadn't known before: that not only is she an avid supporter of the Council, she also actively assists them; *and* that she's an overseer of Aeridon's sacred illusié sites. The very information he seeks is right under his nose.

". . . Is that something you'd like for me to do?"

Realizing she's been talking this whole time, he nods absently, although he's not sure what it is he's agreeing to.

"Right," she says, shoulders straightening. "I can't guarantee anything will come of it, but speaking with Templar Odell can't hurt."

The blank look on his face must be rather telling because she immediately clarifies who Templar Odell is. "Unofficially, he's the Archmage's second-in-command. Get in his ear and you'll be in hers, too."

"Thank you," Felix says, giving her hand a shake. "I appreciate it Truly."

Lane smiles, but it's quick to fade—as it should, considering all she's just revealed. "If you'll excuse me," she starts without finishing her train of thought.

Before he knows it, he's alone by the door again but with one drastic difference: he's now privy to knowledge reserved only for the Archmage's cadre. A fine day it is when his questions are answered in one fell swoop.

RYDAN HELSTROM

RYDAN WATCHES FROM the corner of the training room as Arden hangs up her cloak and steps onto the raised platform to meet with Avery. He hasn't seen her since the incident in the library—that incredibly tense, yet heated moment between them—and he'd started to wonder if perhaps he'd imagined the whole thing. But seeing her again, meeting the quick glance she's throwing his way, he knows he hadn't.

It'd been very, *very* real.

He angles his head as he studies her. She looks bright-eyed and fierce, as per usual, but there's something else in her expression he can't quite place. It's only a flicker, and then it's gone. Clad in black skin-tight leather, she's come prepared—as one should when dealing directly with fire. Her chestnut hair is messily pinned up, wavy tendrils cascading down the sides. The way she looks reminds him so much of their Cruex days, he almost forgets that they're nowhere near Trendalath.

"You may begin," the Archmage says from overhead.

Huh, no lecture for missing her lessons? Seems they must have caught Cyfrin in a good mood. Either that, or she's hard-pressed for time. More likely the latter.

Avery moves to one side of the ring; Arden, the other.

"Ready when you are," he says.

Arden readies her arms at her sides, shifting between her feet to brace herself. Once she's situated her position to her liking, she gives him a nod.

A skilled Ignitor, Avery's hands are already alight with flames. Rydan can't help but look between them, hoping that, during her time away, Arden's found something useful about her newfound abilities, whatever they may be. From the disconcerted look on her face, though, it seems that isn't the case. Unease builds within him as he watches Avery narrow his eyes and direct his focus on her—on his *target.* "Here goes," he shouts in warning before taking a step back and thrusting his arms forward.

Orange and red sparks shoot across the room at a terrifying speed. The temperature rises almost instantly as the flames lick the sides of the ring. Within seconds, Arden is surrounded by an overwhelming blaze. Rydan takes a step closer, tension mounting. She doesn't appear to be affected—that is, until she starts screaming. The sound is amplified as the fire whooshes in and out and all around. Pure, unadulterated terror.

It's undoubtedly the worst sound he's ever heard.

Out of pain or fear, he isn't sure, but he rushes into the ring, nearly tackling Avery along the way.

"Stop!" he shouts. "Stop! You're hurting her!"

Panicked, he darts over to Arden, feeling helpless that his own ability would only make matters worse, and manages to pull her away from the scorching flames. She'd been smart to wear leather because the majority of her body is barely singed, but her hands?

Oh, her hands are charred beyond recognition.

Rydan's stomach turns at the sight and smell of burnt flesh, and it turns again when Arden lets out another agonizing scream. Wincing, he gently sets her on the ground with one arm cradling her lower back, the other blocking the view of her hands. "You're okay, you're okay. Look at me. Arden, *look* at me."

Her cheeks are crimson, forehead and neck drenched with sweat, hair half undone from the pin that's desperately trying to hold it in place. "Who decided," she says through clenched teeth, "that *fire* was a beginner lesson?" Tears line her eyes with each word she forces out. "I've been sliced and punched and kicked, but fuck." She shivers, an obvious reaction to the overheating that's occurring in her body. "Igniting is *not* something I want to mess with."

The smell of scorched flesh grows stronger, and it's enough to make him want to hurl. "I know," he says, hoping that conversing will take both their minds off of it. "Maybe now you can understand why I ran off that day in Sardoria."

She lets out another yelp, her body on the verge of shutting down entirely.

"Where the hell is the damn Healer!" Rydan shouts into the void above.

Before he can attempt to comfort her again, there's someone at his side—someone who practically shoves him out of the way as he takes Rydan's place.

"What the hell happened?" Felix growls.

"What does it look like?" Rydan retorts, pushing himself to his feet.

Felix glances at Arden's hands, anger burning in his gaze. "Why didn't you give her *gloves*?"

"We didn't know," Avery answers, jogging up next to them, face flushed. "It happened so fast—"

"You couldn't have controlled the fire a bit more? As a test?" Felix snarls. "You know, before sending the lords-damned blaze of glory to destroy her?"

Rydan cringes at the words, as does Avery.

"You two can leave now. I'll take care of this."

The condescension in his tone only strengthens Rydan's resolve. "You know, I was doing just fine with her before you got here. I was distracting her—"

"Is that so?" Felix's eyes flash with lethal intent. "I wasn't aware that shaking-to-a-near-seizure was considered *doing just fine.*"

"Maybe not, but at least I took her mind off of the pain." *However briefly,* he thinks but doesn't add out loud.

"Not well enough, apparently."

"Like you can do any better?"

Felix arches a brow, as if to say *challenge accepted.* "I may not be a Healer, but at least I can amplify the feeling of relief until one gets here."

Rydan looks at Arden, who's nearly unconscious at this point, then back at Felix. "Good luck finding even an ounce of relief to work your magick on—because based on what I'm looking at . . . it doesn't exist."

"Good thing I'm the expert, then," Felix retorts. "Now shut up so I can focus."

Knowing that he's right, Rydan bites back his need to remark further.

"And make yourself useful, would you? It shouldn't be taking this long to locate a Healer. The Archmage said they'd be on standby." Felix glares up into the void above, as if *that* will do anything. "Where the fuck are they?"

As much as Rydan doesn't want to leave Arden's side, Felix is right, yet again. Arden's no longer screaming, which means that whatever Felix is doing must be working. Feeling conflicted to stay but also to go find help, Rydan makes for the door just as Casimir comes barreling in with three Healers in tow.

"Lords, did you bring the whole infirmary?" Felix comments.

"We need you to stop amplifying," one of the Healers says.

"Over my dead body," he shoots back.

"It *will be* over hers if you don't stop. We need to assess her pain level to determine the most viable path forward," another says.

"Or I could just tell you." He eyes each one of them warily. "Before I got here, she was screaming, shaking, and sweating. As for the physical damage, well . . ." He gestures to her hands.

"Be that as it may, your abilities will interfere with her healing. So again, we ask that you stop. The longer you refuse, the longer it'll take for her to make a full recovery."

"Listen to them," Rydan says, teeth bared. "Stop amplifying, Felix."

Felix gives him a withering glare, then kneels next to Arden and presses a kiss to her forehead. He leans into her ear and whispers something, but it's too quiet for anyone to hear. A tinge of jealousy flares in Rydan's chest.

Arden's blood-curdling screams shatter the silence the minute Felix pulls away. And all Rydan can do is sit by helplessly and wait.

CERYLIA JARETH

TO AVOID RAISING unnecessary suspicion, Cerylia knows she must return the key to the Vaults sooner rather than later. Cloaked by Estelle, and in the company of Opal, they do exactly that without running into a single soul— but it's on the way back that they see a rush of Healers heading for the infirmary with a body in tow.

"Who is that?" Opal whispers.

Estelle stops walking. "It looks like . . ."

"Arden." Cerylia feels her face pale. "Uncloak us this instant." But as soon as the words leave her mouth, she sees the Archmage emerge from the training room, hurrying after the Healers and Arden, heading straight for them. "On second thought . . ."

Estelle glances to her left at a closed door.

It's all Cerylia needs to formulate a plan. "Wait for them to pass. We'll enter this room, uncloak, and head to the infirmary."

"What about the Vaults?" Opal asks.

Cerylia looks at her in disbelief. "In case you hadn't noticed, my niece is being rushed to the infirmary by not one, but *three* Healers." She bites the inside of her cheek. "Something must have gone terribly wrong."

Opal shrugs. "Nothing they can't fix."

Both she and Estelle stare at the Inverter as if she has no soul, but Opal doesn't seem bothered by it in the slightest.

"Fine," she sighs, shoulders dropping. "The Vaults will have to wait."

"No shit," Estelle retorts.

As soon as the group passes them, along with the Archmage, they move as a single unit into the room. Estelle uncloaks them and before anyone can say another word, they're back out the door and headed to the infirmary. When they arrive, almost the entire group is there, waiting.

"My, word does travel fast . . ." Opal murmurs.

"Please, everyone, stand back and let us work," one of the Healers instructs.

Estelle rushes over to Felix, who's flanked by Avery, Rydan, and Haskell. Concern is etched all over their faces. Cerylia briefly wonders where Vira is before joining them, Opal following reluctantly behind her.

"What happened?" she demands.

Avery exchanges a guilty glance with Rydan before saying, "I was just following the Archmage's orders, Your Greatness."

Cerylia looks around the room, but Cyfrin isn't present.

"I didn't know . . . I thought . . ." His loss of words, coupled with the growing remorse on his face, is enough to tell Cerylia that it was indeed an accident.

"Did she even try to defend herself?"

"It's hard to say," Rydan answers. "The blaze was so powerful and swarmed her so fast—if it had been me, I wouldn't have had time to react."

Avery bows his head in disgrace.

Their conversation is interrupted as Estelle, who's finally managed to pry Felix away from the incident, joins them, with him at her side. There's a noticeable shift in the room then, followed by a long bout of silence as they all just stare at one other.

It's Felix who speaks first. He turns toward Opal, eyes simmering as he says, "Fix this. Now."

Wide-eyed, she angles her head at him. "Come again?"

The two of them have Cerylia's complete attention, as well as the rest of the group's.

"Do your job and invert. Reverse time. Before this happened."

Avery presses a hand to his chest, as if suddenly filled with relief. "I forgot. She . . . she can do that. Can't you?" he urges. "Will you?"

Opal ignores him, keeping her attention solely on Felix. She narrows her eyes. "You know I can't do that."

"Why not?" Felix challenges.

Opal's tone lowers an octave, her face a frightening portrait of defiance. "You forget your place."

The words hang in the air as Cerylia observes the unspoken exchange between them.

"Fix this," he growls, refusing to back down, but Opal stands her ground.

Cerylia flashes back to the conversation she'd had with the girl about *not* inverting. "The Healers are doing a fine job," she interjects. "Just give them time." Before Felix can protest further, Cerylia turns away at the same moment Vira bursts through the door. The sight of her instantly reminds the queen of Xerin and how she'd stumbled upon both him and Opal meeting in an undisclosed location just outside the castle grounds. *Had her suspicions about the two of them been correct? Is Felix somehow also involved?*

Before Vira can announce her presence to the rest of the group, Cerylia takes her by the arm and ushers her into the far corner of the room.

Rife with alarm, Vira's eyes flick from the queen to the chaotic scene that's playing out just over her shoulder. "Is she okay?"

"She will be," Cerylia says. "Just an accident."

"Rydan?" Heavy concern lines her eyes.

"He was there, but—"

"Avery, then," she finishes in understanding.

Cerylia just nods, giving her a few moments to process.

"Is there anything I can do? Any way I can help?"

"I'm so glad you asked," Cerylia whispers, tucking them both into the shadows even further. "When was the last time you spoke with your brother?"

DARIUS TYMOND

DARIUS CAN'T RECALL exactly when Xerin had left, but if he had to guess, it's been at least a few hours. A few hours of stewing over what Xerin *hadn't* revealed about the crescent fire. A few hours of sitting in front of this barren pit that had once been home to the clearest waters—and to his beloved. He sits at the cavernous edge, silently wishing it'd swallow him whole. Lords above, had he known who he'd been striking a deal with all those years ago . . .

What once held his reflection now holds only the abysmal reality of his future. A future he's failing to deliver, minute by minute. But perhaps it's for the best. Perhaps this is how it'd always been destined to unfold.

"Well, this looks different than I remember."

Darius whirls around at the familiar voice, scowling as his gaze lands on the infamous Caster. "You are not welcome here."

"And yet," Clive sneers, "here I am."

Darius climbs to his feet, not daring to take his eyes off the man. "Which begs the question . . . why?"

"Call me sentimental." He shrugs. "You should have known better than to lock me up with the commonfolk. Bars and chains have done very little to hinder the Savant."

"Yes, I'm well aware." He drags his gaze across the Caster's worn face before once again settling on those soulless eyes. "But that doesn't answer my question."

Clive takes a few steps forward, edging his way along the side of the cavernous pit. "I suppose it doesn't."

Darius fists his hands at his sides, the intensity of the amethyst ring thrumming through his veins. "Enough."

Clive stops walking. He lifts his head, arching a brow. "I wasn't expecting him to actually go through with it." He nods at the vast expanse before him. "He wastes no time, does he?"

It's then a thought jolts Darius. "How do I know that this isn't just another one of your illusions? That you haven't been here the whole time, *making* me see this?"

Clive tilts his head. "And what purpose would that serve?"

Darius finds himself at a loss for words. The more he tries to wrap his head around a reason, the further he gets from a logical answer. He presses his mouth into a firm line, signaling to Clive exactly what he'd hoped to hide.

"No, this isn't an illusion." He kicks the dirt with the toe of his boot. "This is as real as it gets." When Darius still doesn't respond, he continues, "I came here because I've discovered something you've been seeking. Something your

Savant nor the King's Guard nor your Cruex have been able to deliver."

Darius lifts his head in mock derision. "Are you not my Savant?"

A lupine smile graces the Caster's wrinkled face. "After my time spent in the dungeons, I consider myself a free agent. Wouldn't you?"

Again, there's no arguing his logic. "Then why come here? Now? Why escape just to track me down again?"

"Because at the end of the day, we both want the same thing. And I have information that can help us achieve that."

Darius shoots him a sidelong glance. "I'm listening."

"Good. You'd better get that ring ready," he says as he produces a pocket watch from the inside of his coat. "Because I know where the rest of them are hiding."

BRAXTON HORNSBY

WHEN BRAXTON COMES back to, his body immediately resumes shaking out of absolute hunger, thirst, exhaustion—and pain. Can't forget the pain. He can hardly get a grip on his surroundings as the sheer intensity of his body shutting down takes center stage.

Honestly, it's a miracle he even woke up.

Before he can fully register what's happening, a hazy figure comes into view and leans next to him, lifting his head so that it's slightly angled. The seizing is making it difficult to focus, let alone keep his eyes open, but shortly after, he feels the edge of a glass bottle tip against his lower lip.

"I need you to trust me," a deep voice says. "Drink."

Braxton manages to get his wits about him just in time to grip the bottle of tonic with both hands and pour its contents into his mouth. A bitter, earthy taste greets him, quickly accompanied by a sage-like smell. Normally he'd cringe at drinking any sort of tonic, but his body is so desperate for sustenance that he gobbles it right up, swallowing every last drop. It takes mere minutes for the shaking to stop, for his eyesight to grow clear, for the hysteria to fade away.

Whoever had helped him has turned away now and is currently bottling up another tonic at a nearby workstation. Braxton can tell it's an older man, given his height, build, and posture, but there's nothing familiar about him, at least not from this angle. He supposes there wouldn't be, seeing as he's never been here before . . .

The realization he's physically *seeing* another person and is no longer trapped in the Void is jarring. *But the crest, where is the* crest . . .?

"Easy there," the man says as Braxton hurries to push himself up onto his elbows. "That mugwort and skullcap may work fast, but not *that* fast."

Braxton blinks, turning his head to get a clear view of who's speaking to him—who's just saved his life.

"Tonic's a poor replacement for what the body actually needs. We need to get you some food. Water, too. This would be so much easier if we were back at—"

His senses fully restored, Braxton can hardly believe his eyes. "*Hanslow?*"

The man turns to face him, lowering the hood of his cloak to reveal the same white head of hair, although it's a bit more sparse than the last time he'd seen him. His eyes glimmer with that spry, cunning nature of his, alight with all the secrets he's carried for so many years. Secrets he'd only revealed to Braxton when the King's Savant had shown up at the inn in Athia and forced Braxton to flee, leaving the innkeeper behind. Braxton was certain he'd left Hanslow for dead. The man who had taken him in after being on the run from Trendalath for three years. The man who had taken a chance on him and given him shelter and food and a job for seven years. Seven *years* he'd worked at Hanslow's inn. The man had become the only family he'd known—family he'd had to leave, yet again, due to his identity and abilities.

"I was certain they'd killed you that day," Braxton whispers, raw emotion welling up inside of him. "I was certain I'd never see you again."

"Seems this old man has a few more tricks up his sleeve," he says with a wink, "and not just bar tricks."

Braxton manages to push himself to his feet before stumbling over to the man, wanting to feel the embrace of his old friend, to know that this encounter is *real.* Arms full of warmth wrap around him.

"I owe you my life," Braxton says between shuddered breaths. "They were coming for me, and you—"

"Only did what was right. What he'd promised."

The second voice startles Braxton enough to pull away from Hanslow, eyes searching the shadowy alcove for the source. "Who's there?" he says, suddenly feeling timid.

"You can come out, Stanton. The boy isn't going to bite."

Braxton shoots Hanslow a sidelong glance, but there's no time for a response as a slender man with jet black hair emerges from the shadows. His wide emerald eyes and pointed nose are more than enough to give away the relation.

"Braxton," Hanslow says, "it's about time you met your uncle, Stanton Eliri."

Braxton is utterly speechless as he stares at the man in front of him, at the ghost his daughter had presumed him to be.

Arden's father offers him a sincere smile. "The pleasure is all mine."

ARDEN ELIRI

WHEN I WAKE, my mind is fuzzy, but the smell of burnt flesh clears things right up. I groan as I lift my arms, wincing at the thick bandages that are wrapped around my hands. I bring my chin to my chest, noticing the silk tunic and trousers I certainly hadn't been wearing prior to "the incident". The leather jumpsuit sits idly on the chair next to my bed. It's then I realize I'm in the infirmary, although I don't recall how I'd gotten here.

The creak of a door catches my attention.

"You're awake." Rydan hurries over, dragging a chair behind him. "How are you feeling?" he asks as he sits down.

"I've been better." Even though I don't intend for them to, the words come out slurred. "My skin feels like it's on fire, though."

Rydan winces. "That's because it was."

I hold up my bandaged hands. "How long do you think?"

"To heal?" Rydan tilts his head. "The Healers said a few weeks, maybe more."

I groan. "It'd probably go a lot faster if my own abilities hadn't disappeared. Or morphed. Or whatever's happened to them."

"Probably true, but," he says, digging around in his pockets, "I brought this."

He holds up a jar of amber-colored powder that I recognize immediately. "Turmeric." I can't help but laugh.

"I know it probably won't help *at all*, but—"

"You remembered," I finish, feeling sentimental.

He nods, then gently sets the jar on the table next to my bed. "I'm so sorry this happened, Arden. I don't know what the Archmage was thinking."

"It's not your fault." I heave a deep sigh. "Something like this was bound to happen. I only wish I could heal faster—"

"I may have some good news there, although I'm not sure you'll take it that way." He drops his gaze. "One of the Healers said—if you were open to it, that is—that they could try having an Amplifier present during your healing sessions."

I sigh when I catch his meaning. "To amplify the healing?"

He nods but doesn't smile. "The thing is . . ."

"Felix is the only Amplifier here?" I guess.

"That would be correct."

I sigh again as I raise my hands in front of my face, rotating them back and forth. "I don't think I have a few weeks to spare. Not with everything that's at stake." I attempt to wiggle my fingers, but the movement sends a shooting pain up both of my arms. Miraculously, I manage to bite down a shriek.

"As much as I wish I could disagree with you, I can't."

I look at him, at the strange remorse blossoming in his gaze. "This wasn't your fault, Rydan. It wasn't Avery's fault either."

"I know," he says, raking a hand through his hair. "But knowing that it's *my* ability that's responsible for your pain, for *this* . . . well, that's hard."

"If you really think about it, all abilities are responsible for pain, in one form or another."

"Not yours."

I give him a weary look. "You weren't there when I nearly destroyed Braxton's hands and Delwynn's legs."

"From my understanding, they're both doing just fine. More than fine, actually." He furrows his brows. "Is it possible your abilities morphed from healing, to destruction to something like . . . resurrection?" He scratches his head.

I look at him, dumbfounded. "How do you mean?"

"I suppose that would only make sense for Delwynn. He's able to walk again, right?"

"Yeah," I say, biting down on my lower lip, "but who knows if that was really my doing. More like a freak coincidence, if you ask me."

"Perhaps it was at *that* point your abilities were in the process of morphing . . ."

I shrug my shoulders, suddenly feeling exhausted. I stifle a yawn, unsuccessfully.

"Right, you need to rest," Rydan says, catching on. "I'm just happy you're awake and not . . . angry."

"No time for that," I say, maneuvering to the edge of the bed.

"To rest? Or to be angry?"

I shoot him a sly smile. "Who said it had to be one or the other?"

Before he can respond, Felix enters the room flanked by two Healers. "We'll take it from here, Helstrom."

Rydan whips his head to the door, and I can tell by the way his jaw tightens he wants nothing more than to tell Felix off; but he restrains himself and gracefully rises from the chair. "I hope you feel better soon," he says to me. Then, with a slight nod and not a single look at the company that's just entered the room, he makes for the door.

I watch him the entire way out, only looking at Felix when he clears his throat. "I hope we aren't interrupting anything," he says as he walks toward me. I notice him eye the turmeric sitting on the table, a smirk crossing his face. "I think it's going to take something a bit stronger than that to reverse this level of damage."

I reach for the small glass jar, realizing that I can't grab it with these stupid bandages. "It's not for that. It was a gift."

"Odd gift," he counters. He reaches for it but stops when he settles on my cutthroat stare. He doesn't take his eyes off of me as he snaps his fingers to call the Healers over to the bedside. "Why don't we get started?"

I hold his gaze as the Healers take each of my arms and begin unwrapping the bandages. As tempted as I am to look at the damage, I don't so much as bat an eye.

"How are you feeling?"

The draft in the room is relentless the way it stings and pierces my skin, but I force myself not to flinch. "Never better," I say through clenched teeth.

The Healers begin uncorking various tinctures and oils, and I instantly recognize the scent of aloe as it wafts across the room.

"You know," Felix says slowly, "this'll work better the closer in proximity I am to you."

I arch a brow. "Meaning?"

"Well, I can sit here and place my hands on your shins to amplify from the base up."

"Or?"

His eyes flick to the minimal space behind me. "I can sit there, with my hands on your shoulders, to amplify from the neck down."

The position he's talking about is one I'm all too familiar with. It's how we sat underneath the tree in Orihia. How we sit after we've . . .

"Fine," I say, interrupting my own train of thought. "Sit behind me."

He leaves my sight and it's then my gaze falls to my hands. My stomach turns at the dark discoloration and raised splotches covering my skin. As if the smell weren't already bad enough, the sight is sure to put me over the edge.

"Don't focus on that. It'll only delay the time it takes for you to heal," I hear Felix say as his warm body settles in behind mine. "Look up and lean back."

I don't dare argue, not with the somersaults my stomach is currently doing. I keep my arms extended at my sides, leaning back so that my head is resting on his shoulder, eyes now trained on the ceiling.

"Better?"

I nod against him. "Somewhat."

I nearly jump at the frigid gel the Healers place on my skin, but Felix manages to amplify at just the right time. The moment his hands hit my shoulders, a wave of relief flows through me. I exhale loudly, louder than I ever have before, falling deeper into the nook between his neck and shoulder.

"That's it," he whispers into my ear. "Much better."

I know that in order to do this, he has to be taking some of my pain. I can tell by the hardening of his jaw against my forehead that he's probably taking on more than he should. I want to tell him to stop, that I can handle it, but I feel so relaxed, so at ease.

My pain is nonexistent.

Because of *him.*

"I had no idea your ability was this strong," I breathe, almost sounding drugged.

"It isn't." Felix grips my shoulders tighter, the façade of his unbothered demeanor fading fast. "I've never felt this before. This is—"

"We haven't either," the Healers interrupt. They're looking at us, slack jawed, and, at first, I can't understand why. Until I look down at my body . . . which is now covered in a luminescent lavender light.

"Whoa," I breathe.

"Whoa is right," Felix says.

"What is it?" I ask. "What's happening?"

The Healers shake their head in disbelief as they remove their hands from my arms. "We . . . don't know."

I feel Felix inch away from me until he's no longer sitting and is standing at my side. "Your hands," he whispers.

I turn my attention to my hands. The smell is gone. And a purple light has completely engulfed them.

"Your healing light was white?" Felix confirms.

I nod my head as streams of purple whirl around my fingers, palms, and wrists, taking with it every inch of charred, discolored skin—almost as if it were *absorbing* it.

"What is this?" I ask again. "What's happening?"

But no one knows the answer. And that's likely because whatever *this* is . . . is my morphed ability.

FELIX BARLOW

XERIN WAS RIGHT.

Felix finally has the proof he needs—and from a freak training accident, no less. It seems the lords truly are smiling down on him, for one reason or another.

He feigns awe as he observes the lavender light emanating from Arden knowing that, within minutes, it'll fade. It'll have done its job this time around, but the same can't be said for future scenarios—namely, the one Xerin's drilled into his head from the very beginning.

Just as he'd predicted, the lavender hue begins to fade, leaving fresh, healed skin in its wake. The Healers murmur amongst one another, scurrying closer to get a better look.

"This should have taken weeks," the eldest one says.

"Months, even," another chimes in.

"I take it this hasn't happened before," Arden says breathlessly.

"You're a living legend," the second Healer whispers. "We must inform the Archmage at once." He breaks for the door, but Felix beats him to it.

"Not so fast," he says, ushering the group to a corner of the room, away from the door. "Can we all agree that what we just saw was borderline miraculous?"

Hesitation hangs in the air as they all look at each other before nodding in agreement.

"And what do we know about what we just saw?"

"Next to nothing," the eldest Healer quips while scratching his balding head.

"And how does the Archmage feel about," Felix lowers his voice, "*miracles*?"

The youngest Healer shakes his head. "She's all facts and logic."

Felix nods, relieved that the Healers are following his train of thought. "So, if you were to leave this room, right now, as a witness to what you've just observed . . . what would you tell her?"

The question is meant to stump them, to show them the error of their ways—and, thankfully, it does.

"We must conduct thorough research—"

"—Browse the archives."

"—Write a detailed report."

"—Find additional case studies, if such files even exist."

"Now you're talking," Felix says. "For now, let's keep this just between us." He breaks his gaze momentarily, catching Arden's curious stare from across the room. Even if she's tried eavesdropping, he's far enough away and has kept his voice low enough so that the most she might catch is a word or two—fragments when, out of context, make absolutely no sense.

He turns his attention back to the Healers. "Are we agreed?"

"Yes," the eldest says, the other two echoing his response.

"Good." He angles his head toward the door. "Best get to it, then. It sounds like you have a full schedule ahead of you."

"That we do," the eldest says, making a beeline for the exit. The others follow, shutting the door quietly behind them, leaving only Arden and Felix in the room.

"What was that all about?"

He doesn't have it in him to lie to her, so he says, "Research." *A half-truth will do.*

"They seemed quite keen on informing the Archmage."

"Only after they've conducted their research," he clarifies, sauntering over to her. "How are you feeling, by the way?"

She glances at her hands, turning them over as if she can't believe what she's seeing. "Honestly, I've never felt better."

Felix grins. "Good. Then what we did actually worked."

"Right," Arden says, not moving from her spot on the chaise lounge. "Except, what exactly *did* we do?"

"Like I said, the Healers' research should provide more insight. I wouldn't get too hung up on the details—"

She frowns. "But this is all I've been focused on ever since I found out about it. Even before then, before I knew of the possibility that abilities can morph. The details are important, Felix. They *matter . . .*"

It's obvious he's struck a nerve, so he makes quick work of sitting on the edge of the seat before taking her hands in his. "You've healed. *That's* what matters."

She holds his gaze, eyes searching for answers. "But how?"

Felix sighs, trying to hide his exasperation. "Give it time, Arden. That's all we can do."

"The others will want to know," she says quietly. "And I don't have an answer for them." She looks at her hands again. "Well, I *do* have the answer, right here—I just don't know what it is yet."

"Let that be enough."

"I'm not sure I know how." Her expression softens. "But I'll try."

Satisfied with her answer, Felix gives her hands a light squeeze before gently pulling her to her feet. "What do you say we get you a meal?"

Arden laughs as she heads for the door. "As long as it isn't burnt, you can count me in."

❧ ❧ ❧

The dining hall is surprisingly empty for the time of day, save for a few professors, but Felix is grateful for the uninterrupted time with Arden. At least, it starts out that way. From across the hall, he catches the gaze of an older man robed in all white. From the style alone, he can tell that his rank differs from the Archmage's cadre, the professors, the Healers . . . in fact, he hasn't seen anyone else donning the ensemble, which can only mean one thing.

It's Templar Odell.

Hoping that Lane had followed through on her offer to request an audience, he excuses himself from the table, leaving Arden to feast on her second plate alone. She doesn't seem to mind, given that her newfound abilities have rendered her famished.

Felix approaches the table where the Templar is seated, briefly using his amplifying ability to assess the man's mood. There's an air of calm about him, an overwhelming sense of serenity and peace. It immediately puts Felix at ease, but he notices that as he draws closer, the feeling diminishes. Amplifying further, he gathers that the Templar is a private man, somewhat of an introvert, and prefers the company of very few. Being approached in the middle of a meal by an absolute stranger is probably the last thing he wants, but that isn't going to stop him.

"Templar Odell, I presume?" He offers a hand in greeting. "Felix Barlow. My friend, Lane, mentioned that, given the chance, I should speak with you."

The old man looks up from his plate, eyes glimmering at the mention of her name. "About the selphinium, correct?"

Confused, Felix retracts his arm. "Well, no. I'm not sure who would be asking about selphinium since we don't have to worry about dragons down here." He raises a brow. "Do we?"

"Forgive me," the Templar says with a hearty laugh. "I get a multitude of requests these days, many of the herbal variety, although it's difficult to fathom why. I'm no Herbalist." He pauses, as if just remembering the question he's been asked. "And you are correct in your assumption, Sir Barlow. We do not have to worry about dragons in Midvale." He angles his head in invitation at the bench across from him.

"I hope I'm not interrupting your meal. If this isn't a good time—"

The Templar waves a wrinkled hand flippantly in the air. "It's as good a time as any. What can I assist you with?"

Felix can't even recall how many times he'd rehearsed exactly what he'd planned to say, but something about the Templar's presence has him fumbling over his words. "I, uh, well, I've been in the library most nights and suppose I have some questions about the research I've come across, and I figured who better to ask than the Templar?" He hates the inflection in his voice, the way it makes him sound timid and unassured.

The old man raises a bushy eyebrow, no doubt picking up on the nervous edge in Felix's tone. "And what research would that be?"

"Regarding illusié-crafted items."

Mid-bite, the Templar sets his spoon down. "To my knowledge, there aren't many texts in the Midvale libraries on the subject. You must have scoured the shelves, spent endless hours in our multiple libraries . . ."

Shit. Perhaps he should have taken a different approach. Panic begins to set in, but Felix is determined not to let it show. "I suppose I should have prefaced my response by saying that I come from an ancestral line of Keepers."

A bold-faced lie, but it's his only shot. The Templar may have knowledge of *what* the Keepers are responsible for, but very little on *who* they are.

His answer seems to give the old man pause. Finally, he asks, "Why not ask your family, then?"

Felix feigns grief by intentionally making his voice crack. "Sadly, they've all passed over and left little information behind."

The Templar pushes his plate to the center of the table before dabbing the side of his mouth with a linen. "I'm afraid I'm not at liberty to discuss the information that you seek."

"I know there's a spring," Felix says quickly, not wanting to be dismissed. "A spring that holds the power to destroy illusié-crafted items."

Intrigued, the Templar leans forward and folds his hands over the table. "Go on."

"I also know that the spring isn't the only piece of the equation. There's more than one—spring, that is. There's also the crescent fire."

"It would appear that you know more than most." The Templar studies Felix with inquiring eyes. "What would make you think I possess any knowledge about the springs, the crescent fire, or anything else related to the destruction of illusié-crafted items?"

"Honestly, it was a shot in the dark," Felix admits, "but I deduced that the Council, the Keepers, and the Archmage must seek counsel somewhere. Logic tells me that, as Templar, that would be you."

The old man cracks a smile. "You're sharper than you look."

Felix shrugs. "I'll take that as a compliment."

"It was meant as nothing less." The Templar's eyes drop to his hands. When he finally lifts his gaze, there's war waging within. "What do you want to know?"

"Two things." Felix shifts in his seat, settling in for what he hopes is a fruitful conversation. "First, where is the second spring located?"

Templar Odell angles his head in jest. "I suppose it depends on which you consider the first and which the second."

"I'm aware of the spring in Volkharn." He doesn't bother justifying his knowledge of the location. "Do you know the location of the other?"

"I do. And it's a place very few dare to travel."

In his mind, Felix recalls an old map of Aeridon, knowing that the location he speaks of would be outside the mainland. Not Athia. Not Drakken Isle, although that would have been a close second. Which leaves . . .

"The Crostan Islands," Felix says, ignoring the shiver running down his spine. Even on the map, the island looks foreboding, what with its skull-shaped outline. For decades, it's been said it's where illusié go to die . . . so to also house the spring that destroys items of illusié origin? It's almost too obvious.

Templar Odell only nods, confirming his assumption.

"I fear my second question is on the morbid side."

"Young man, with the things I've seen, not much can rattle me."

Felix grimaces knowing what he's seconds away from inquiring about might just result in his very last conversation with the Templar—or anyone at Midvale, for that matter.

"Best get on with it," he urges, glancing past Felix's shoulder. "Your friend looks as though she won't last much longer."

Felix turns to find Arden face down on the table, her arms cradling her head. At least she'd moved the plate out of the way before falling asleep or resting her eyes, he doesn't know which. He brings his attention back to the Templar.

Here goes.

"My second question," he starts, blowing out a long breath, "has to do with soul magick."

The Templar's face falls. "We do not speak of such atrocities here."

"Atrocities?" Felix shakes his head. "You misunderstand. On a conceptual level, if one were to—"

"Oh, my understanding is perfectly clear," the Templar snaps. "We do not speak of soul magick because it only ever ends in atrocity."

Felix ignores the old man's warning and asks his question anyway. "Can the spring extinguish such magick? Can soul magick be undone?"

"Are you asking if something that shouldn't have been done in the first place can be undone?"

"Yes."

"With a soul attached?" The Templar sighs. "No. Neither the spring nor the crescent fire can extinguish soul magick."

Felix tries to hide his relief—because that's precisely the answer he'd hoped for. It's an answer Xerin will be quite pleased with.

"Thank you for your time, Templar," Felix says as he rises from the bench. "You've been immensely helpful."

Before he can walk away, the old man grabs his wrist. "I don't know what you've involved yourself with, either willingly or unwillingly, but my advice is to get out as fast as you can."

"And if I can't?"

The color drains from the old man's already pale face, making him look even more ghastly than before. "Then I hope for your sake, and all those involved, that you pray to the lords above for forgiveness lest you be damned eternally, forsaking all future lifetimes."

Felix breaks free from the old man's grip. "Duly noted, sir," he says as he turns to leave the table. "Duly noted."

RYDAN HELSTROM

NOT BOTHERING TO check if Vira's in their room, Rydan continues to wander down the many corridors until he reaches yet another window with changing scenescapes. He tucks himself into the corner of the windowsill, gazing at the rainy forest in front of him.

"Isn't quite like the real thing, is it?"

Rydan turns just in time to see Avery joining him. He sighs, leaning his head against the wall. "No, I suppose it isn't."

"I used to love the rain when I was younger. I'd be outside, at the docks, regardless of the thunder and lightning striking just across the bay." He drops his gaze to his hands. "And then when I learned who I was, what I could do . . . I liked the rain a little less."

Rydan glances at him, then at his own two hands. "I know what you mean."

"We could have used some rain in the ring today." The words are choked as he speaks them. "I never wanted to hurt her. I can't be responsible for yet another illusié's death."

Rydan gives a firm shake of his head. "You won't be. Arden is fine, just injured. And you weren't responsible for any of the others." An image of the burning bodies of the fallen illusié flashes across his mind.

"This was supposed to be their safe haven—Orihia, Midvale." He shakes his head. "We were going to find a way to get here together. But I failed them. I'm the only one who made it." He wrings his hands together. "I don't deserve to be here."

"Yes, you do. You didn't know when or where the Mallum would strike," Rydan counters. "No one does."

"It could have taken me, you know," Avery whispers. "Or, at the very least, taken my abilities."

"Why didn't it?"

He shrugs. "It didn't want me, I guess."

This gives Rydan pause. "What do you mean, it didn't *want* you? Are you saying the Mallum is a sentient entity?"

"I wouldn't put it past it."

"That trip on *The Corsair*, when you were with Arden—"

"Its focus seemed to be directed solely on her, yes."

Rydan leans back into the wall. How many times had Arden come up against the Mallum? At least three? Maybe more? Surely more than any of them—and yet, she still has *some* magickal ability, morphed or not. Why hadn't it taken her life? If its sole purpose is to rid Aeridon of magick, of illusié, why leave one behind? Why leave *her* behind?

A rather long stretch of silence must have passed between them because Avery's just staring at him, the growing concern ever present on his face. "Where'd you go?"

"Just thinking."

"About her."

It's clear who he means. He doesn't have to specify.

Rydan just nods.

"I've had the same thought, believe me."

Rydan feels his chest tighten as he says, "There's no way she could be . . . *connected* to that thing, could she?"

"The thought's crossed my mind, although I've never said it out loud." He shifts in his seat. "With everything I've seen, anything's possible."

"So perhaps, subconsciously, you *did* want to harm her?"

Avery represses a scowl. "Like I said. Anything's possible." He pushes off the window to his feet. "If you ask me, you're much better off with Vira."

Rydan's ears burn at the remark. "And why is that?"

Avery doesn't bother turning around as he starts to walk away. "Because at least *she* won't get you killed."

CERYLIA JARETH

CERYLIA USHERS VIRA into her chambers, making sure to lock the door behind them. There's no mistaking the urgency, given the way she swiftly moves past the fireplace to fetch a partially full tea kettle and sets it just above the open flame.

Vira watches the queen as she moves back and forth, eyes wide with trepidation. "Is my brother in some sort of danger?"

"To be honest, I don't know." Cerylia rummages through cabinets and drawers until she finds a tray of cups, saucers, and teaspoons. She slides the ornately carved tray from its position in the hutch and sets it on the table in front of them. She slowly backs into the chair across from Vira, the girl noticeably on edge.

"It's been some time since I've seen him or tried to contact him." Her eyes flit to the flames licking the underside of the kettle. "Xerin has never been one for restriction."

Cerylia arches a brow. "But you are his family, are you not? His *only* family?"

Vira presses her palms together before relaxing them in her lap. A nod is her only response.

"I'll ask again. Do you have a way to contact your brother?"

She shakes her head.

"Do you know where he might be?"

An audible sigh. Another shake of her head.

"And the last place you saw him?"

"In Orihia." She cringes, but at what, Cerylia doesn't know.

"You have been furthering your training as a Summoner, yes?"

Vira studies the queen for a moment, then drags her gaze to the fire. In a split second, her demeanor changes entirely. "Yes."

Cerylia straightens. "How far along?"

"I've always been able to summon dragons. Learning how to summon other creatures as well."

"And those who have shaped?"

Her lip curls in what appears to be distaste. "Yes."

The embers of the fire spark then, mirroring exactly how Cerylia is feeling. "So, if I'm understanding correctly, then you *do* have a way to contact him?"

Vira holds the queen's gaze. "Not inside the Veil, I don't."

"Well, then," Cerylia says, folding her arms across her chest, "it's a good thing we have a way to get *outside* of it."

DARIUS TYMOND

DARIUS WALKS ALONGSIDE Clive in no particular direction as they roam the Roviel Woods, hardly believing what he's hearing. "They've essentially *cloaked* themselves?"

"Yes. Inside what's known as the Veil."

"And you've been there?"

Clive veers to the right of the makeshift path, an indication that Darius should follow. "I have."

"How?"

"The same way your son got away from you. And Lane."

Darius tenses at the memory. Lane had fumbled for something just before she and Braxton had disappeared in the tunnels, right before his very eyes. "And you know how to do what they did? To get there?"

Clive stops in his tracks, revealing a watch no larger than his palm. "Courtesy of the Chatham family."

"You stole it." Darius can't help but feel impressed. "Not surprising in the least, given your track record."

Clive loosens his grip on the chain so that the pocket watch dangles in mid-air, but before Darius can reach out and grab it, Clive expertly loops his fingers along the metal links and snatches it back into his palm. "Not so fast," he warns. "If we're going to work together, I need some assurances."

Darius narrows his eyes, already disliking where this is going.

"My first condition is that you stop using the Savant against me."

When he doesn't continue, Darius realizes it's because he wants a verbal confirmation. "I suppose that can be arranged."

"You *suppose*?" Clive gives him a pointed look, hazel eyes flashing. "Now that just won't do."

Darius sighs before saying through gritted teeth, "I will no longer use the Savant against you or attempt to turn them against you in any way."

Clive rolls his hand, waiting.

"For now *or* the foreseeable future," Darius adds.

Clive grins. "I can accept that. Condition two—"

"Who says you get more than one?" Darius interrupts.

"The one who holds the power to access the Veil." He flashes the watch for emphasis. "And that would be? Oh, right. *Me.*"

"It's always a game with you," Darius mutters.

"And it's always so serious with you." Clive arches a brow. "Games are more fun—although, I suppose not when you're prone to losing."

Darius bares his teeth. "I'm *King* of Trendalath. I'd say that's far from losing."

"It would be," Clive considers, "if it weren't for the puppet master pulling your strings."

"He's pulling your strings, too."

"Maybe so." Clive shrugs. "But I'm not at his mercy."

Darius bristles at the insinuation but knows better than to harp on it. "When this is over, you'll be telling a very different story."

"One can only hope."

Darius doesn't know whether to take the response as confirmation or outright contradiction, but it wouldn't matter either way. Things have never been straightforward with Clive. And they likely never will be. Which makes allying with him even more troublesome. But before Darius can change his mind, Clive starts talking—actually, more like *revealing*—what he knows . . . and it's more than Darius had expected.

"They're at Midvale Arcane Haven. Queen Jareth, The Caldari, your niece—"

Darius cringes at the mention of his relation to Arden, but doesn't interrupt.

"Not only are they there, but so are all other illusié. No doubt trying to sharpen their abilities and strategize against the Mallum." He gives a pointed look at Darius's ring. "The Veil was created by the Keepers as a way to preserve any and all illusié archives. Midvale Arcane Haven was originally created to serve that purpose, but, over time, it naturally evolved into an institution. When you and Aldr"—he catches himself just in time—"the late queen, lords rest her soul, banished magick and exiled illusié, they flocked to the only place they knew they'd be safe, especially with the Mallum at large. A place tucked away inside the Veil, where only illusié have access—and only *certain* illusié, at that." He holds out the pocket watch once again. "This is our ticket in."

What he's just said snags on something in Darius's mind. "You mentioned only certain illusié can access the Veil?"

Clive nods. "I suppose it's the Keepers' way of maintaining their checks and balances, to create a place that only they could access—a place where they would have absolute control over who entered. Enchanted pocket watches became the point of entry."

"But that watch doesn't belong to you."

"That it doesn't, but it hasn't stopped me from using it."

"Seems their 'checks and balances' could use some finessing."

"I quite like it how it is. Makes my job much easier."

He has a point there. "So," Darius says, "you've been inside the Veil. You've been to Midvale. How does that help our cause? I am not illusié which means, regardless of the use of the pocket watch, I am unable to enter the Veil. Which means the Mallum is also unable to enter the Veil as I am the one who can summon it. How can we absorb the remaining illusié abilities when our very tool to do so cannot gain access to the very place they're all housed?"

Clive shakes a finger before turning once again to walk down the winding path. "I figured you'd ask such a question. You'll be pleased to learn that I have a plan—one that involves pulling them out instead of drawing us in."

Darius matches his pace, hanging on his every word.

"You see, I recently discovered that, like all functioning things in this world, the Veil has a power source. It is what charges it, what composes it, what keeps it from disintegrating into nothing more than fissures and arbitrary sparks."

Darius catches his meaning almost immediately. "This power source . . . it's *inside* the Veil?"

Clive smirks. "That it is."

"And you've seen it?"

His face falls. "Not yet. But I have my suspicions regarding its location."

Darius can feel his temper flare. "So what you're telling me is that this is all based on a hunch?"

"Of course not. I've been through the Archives, meticulously piecing together sketch after sketch, layer after layer, until I discovered what looks like a grid."

Darius eyes him dubiously. "A grid?"

"A *crystalline* grid."

Oh. Well, that changes things.

"And where do you suppose this crystalline grid is?"

Clive regards him with such an amused expression that Darius knows the answer must be more than obvious—and yet, he waits for his answer.

"Where only the most important things are hidden," Clive says as he lowers to his knees, dropping the watch until it thuds against the mossy ground. "Out of sight. Out of reach." A sinister smile spreads across his face. "Just like your tunnels."

"Of course," Darius says. "Underground."

Clive nods, then swipes the pocket watch from the ground before rising to his feet once more. "There's one other thing I should mention. Something I'll need from you if this is going to work."

"Name it," Darius says, not wanting to waste any more time.

"It'll require the skills of the Savant's Curser. Is that something you can manage?"

For the first time in a long time, Darius gives him a nod of genuine interest and delight. "He's all yours."

BRAXTON HORNSBY

HE'D PASSED OUT again, not because seeing both Hanslow and Stanton had bored him, but out of sheer exhaustion from however long he'd been wandering the Void. While tonics come highly recommended, they have their limits. They only work so well—and usually just for the short-term. Who knows what the long-term effects of his unexpected visit might be.

The clanging of dishes causes Braxton to jolt awake, the smell of freshly baked bread filling the entire cavern. Having finally gotten some rest, he can now focus on where they are—someplace entirely unfamiliar, but oddly comforting at the same time.

Hanslow scurries over to him with a tall glass of water and a plate of sliced bread and butter. They appear to be in a study—an ancient one, at that—what with its many pillars and walls and shelves. Artifacts litter every surface as do maps, rolls of parchment, and books. *So many books.* It's dark, save for the hearth that's serving as not only a source of light, but as a cooking fire, too.

Braxton dips the edge of the bread into the ramekin of butter, devouring each delectable bite. He presses his hand against his mouth, his throat immediately going dry even though his mouth is watering.

"You might feel a little strange," Hanslow says, as if reading his thoughts. "Effects of the tonic, I'm afraid. No way around it. After a few meals, you should be feeling like yourself again."

A hearty chuckle sounds near the hearth. "Ever the eternal optimist, aren't you, Hanslow?" Stanton turns in their direction but doesn't join them. "Eat as much as you'd like. We have more than enough to go around, thanks to Hanslow here."

Braxton brings his attention back to the old man, finishing the last of his bread and downing the glass of water. Hanslow goes to take both his glass and plate, no doubt for a refill, but Braxton grabs him by the wrist, stopping him. "Where am I?" he whispers. "What is this place?"

Hanslow gently shrugs off his grip before sitting back down in the giant armchair across from him. The way the flame's shadows dance across the side of his wrinkled face make what he's about to say seem more ominous than it probably is. He looks at Braxton for a solid minute without saying anything, then suddenly turns his head to address the only other person in the room. "Stanton, what would you call this place, exactly? A hideaway?"

Stanton keeps his eyes fixed on the fire, only bowing his head once he decides to respond. "At first, it was an escape—

or, that's what it was meant to be, at least. But now?" He shakes his head before raking a hand through his ebony hair. "Now it feels more like a prison."

"Ever the doom-and-gloom type, aren't you, Stanton?" Hanslow echoes.

He shrugs. "Someone has to be."

By Stanton's demeanor alone, Braxton can tell they're about to get into it and, after what he's been through in the Void, any more stress to his system may as well be a death wish. "So we're no longer in the Void?"

Hanslow winces, bobbing his head back and forth as if he doesn't know how to accurately answer the question.

"We're on the perimeter of it." Stanton's voice is harsh, unforgiving.

"Which means . . ." Braxton trails off, looking at his empty plate, the empty glass. "There's food here. And water." He quickly does the math in his head, realizing just how long it's been since he'd been in Athia with Hanslow, when the Savant had come knocking at the doors of the inn. "You've survived this long? How?"

Hanslow moves his arm, gesturing toward the glass as if he's about to do something to it, but Stanton's scowl stops him. "What have we talked about? Wasting your magick on trivial things?"

"It isn't a waste. The boy might be thirsty. Again." Hanslow winks, clearly wanting Braxton to confirm his assumption.

Stanton storms over to where they're sitting, shaking the very ground he walks upon, and grabs both dishes in his hands. "You can just *tell* him, you don't need to show him. As for refills, there's plenty of bread on the counter and water in the well." He doesn't give them a chance to respond as he turns away and heads back toward the hearth.

But Braxton doesn't care about that. He's staring at the old man with wide eyes. "Hanslow . . . you're illusié?"

He gives a slight nod of his chin, eyes twinkling. "That I am. I'm an Elemental—although here, it's more of the herbal variety."

Braxton gapes at him, slack jawed. "All this time . . ." It explains why market runs had been so few and far between, why sacks of grains, wheat, and rice hardly ever ran out. How there'd *always* been food available at the inn, regardless of the season or the trading embargo Trendalath had enacted. In fact, the only time he can recall Hanslow actively retrieving food was when they'd gone fishing. He'd always assumed it was for sport, but perhaps there'd been a larger reason at play.

"You can influence nature?"

"Plants and crops mostly. We got lucky with the well." He turns over his shoulder, nearly shouting, "Didn't we, Stanton?" But Stanton merely rolls his eyes and ignores him. Hanslow grins, completely unbothered.

"So," Braxton says, trying to wrap his head around the fragmented information, "we're on the perimeter of the Void, which means . . ."

"We're also on the perimeter of the Veil. The sweet spot, as I like to call it."

Clearly annoyed by his cohort's banter, Stanton lets out an audible groan in the background.

"Well, if my rendition is so painstakingly dreadful, then why don't *you* come over here and explain it?"

Stanton mutters something inaudible, to which Braxton can't help but snort. "You're so much like Arden, it's uncanny."

A sudden silence, unlike anything Braxton's ever experienced before, falls over the room. Hanslow sits back in his chair, a coy smile tugging at his lips, like he'd known all along that this was exactly where the conversation was headed.

Slowly, Stanton walks across the room, the sound of his breathing growing shallow. He stops just inches from where Braxton's sitting, then lifts his gaze. Piercing green irises meet his own. "You've met my daughter?"

Only then does Braxton realize how insensitive his comment had been. He knows for a fact that Arden has no idea what had happened to her parents—that she's assumed them dead all these years—and here he is, not even considering that Stanton may have believed the same.

Braxton doesn't dare break eye contact as he says, "Yes, I've met your daughter." It's hard not to mirror the tears brimming in Stanton's eyes. "She's witty and charming, impatient and stubborn, but also one of the bravest people I know."

Stanton reaches behind him for something to steady his nerves, but since there isn't anything, Hanslow jumps up to guide him into the seat he'd just been occupying.

"I was almost certain that she'd been maimed or slaughtered or worse by that prick—" He stops himself as he realizes who he's talking to.

Braxton urges him to continue. "Please, go on. I don't think there's anyone who despises my father more than me."

"When did you see her last? Is she safe?"

"She *should* be with the Caldari." He scratches his head, the past feeling like a blur. "I was actually on my way to find her when I ended up here—well, not *here*, but in the Void."

"It got to you." Hanslow's voice is quiet, but firm.

Braxton doesn't need to speak the Mallum's name. Stanton and Hanslow are well-aware of the malevolent entity that lurks in the shadows of Aeridon. He simply nods his head in response. In that same moment, he feels a pang of remembrance, how he'd ended up here in the first place. "The crest," he murmurs, eyes searching the area around him. "What happened to the crest?"

"You mean that one over there?" Stanton points to the left side of the hearth and, as Braxton leans forward, he can clearly see that it's propped up against the wall. "That's how you arrived here, you know. Surprised us, to say the least. It's been years since I've seen anyone—well, besides this old-timer right here."

Hanslow rolls his eyes in mock offense. "You'd best count your lucky stars. You were on the edge of death before I got here."

"I was doing just fine," Stanton snaps before quickly softening at the sharpness in his tone. "But yes, I suppose the timing *did* work in our favor."

"Oh, he's being modest. Stanton here had almost exhausted what very little power he had left," Hanslow clarifies, speaking directly to Braxton. "And on the most trivial of things, no less."

Stanton scoffs. "I wouldn't call *survival* trivial."

"It is when there are others who can help you at half the cost."

Braxton's gaze darts between them, feeling somewhat lost but understanding that Stanton had been in serious peril before Hanslow had arrived. "So perhaps the King's Savant showing up that day in Athia was exactly what was called for . . . it's exactly what was supposed to happen."

The old man's eyes glimmer with satisfaction. "It always is."

"Did you believe we'd ever see each other again?"

"I hoped." Hanslow smiles. "Although I wish it were under different conditions."

Braxton studies him for a moment. "How do you mean?"

Hanslow angles his head toward Stanton. "Care to take this one?"

A muscle flexes along his uncle's jaw, eyes shadowed as he says, "We're not in the Veil, nor in the Void, but somewhere in-between. In another layer. I call it the Medial." He sighs, keeping his eyes fixed on the table in front of him. "This place is merely a step up from the Void, but not by much. We still have access to our abilities, unlike the Void, which is where you end up if you've lost them, as you did."

"So how did I get *here*?"

"Through that," Stanton says, pointing at the crest. "Although I've never seen anything like it, at least not here. It's of illusié origin and so it's drawn to that which it came. There's no magick in the Void, but in the Medial, in this pocket of space and time we've carved for ourselves, there is, however minimal it might be. The crest was just trying to return to what it knows and you . . . well, you just so happened to be along for the ride."

"The Veil is where Lane was trying to take me, before we . . . before I . . . got lost." Braxton looks between the two men. "If we're on the perimeter, if we're 'in-between', as you say, can't we get out and *into* Aeridon? Or, at the very least, into the Veil?"

Stanton gives him a sad smile. It's the first genuine emotion Braxton's seen from him other than annoyance and anger. "If it were that easy, do you think we'd still be here?"

"I suppose not." He draws in a breath. "So, what, then? How do we get out of here?"

Stanton looks to Hanslow. "I'll defer to you on that one."

"We sealed our fate long before coming here," Hanslow says, wringing his hands. "We knew that . . . well, that this might be it for us. It's a choice we made. A heavy one, but we did so willingly."

"So . . . there's no way out? This is it? We're stuck in the Medial? *Forever?*" It's exactly what he'd feared in the Void come true.

"Well," Stanton says, "there wasn't a conceivable way out until . . ."

"Until what?" Braxton presses, on the verge of a mental breakdown.

"Until you showed up," Hanslow finishes. "And with an item of illusié origin, no less."

"So my—*our*—fate rests in an inanimate object?"

"More or less."

Braxton sighs, but it isn't out of concern. It's out of relief. And mild disbelief.

Hanslow smiles. "I know exactly what this calls for. Celebratory tea." He hops up from the chair, winding around the table toward the hearth. "I think I can scrounge up some dandelion root and lemongrass . . ." His voice fades into the background as he begins rummaging through drawers.

Stanton chortles, shaking his head. "Was he always like this?"

Braxton grins, finally feeling a semblance of hope. "More than you'd ever care to know."

ARDEN ELIRI

I KNOW I won't be able to dodge Cyfrin for long, but I'll be damned if I don't at least try. Felix had asked the Healers to keep the incident in the infirmary between us—at least for the time being so we can try to get a grip on what had happened.

I'm affixing two fresh bandages to my hands as a cover, as I have been for the past couple of weeks. Thankfully, Cyfrin had let us all off the hook for training after the incident with Avery . . . I probably have Cerylia to thank for that. I know she's furious about the injury—my *fully healed* injury, that is.

I finish wrapping the bandages before checking my appearance in the gold-plated mirror, then head for the library. I shut the chamber doors quietly behind me, feeling a pang of guilt for how I've treated Felix since our arrival. Well, except for that first day, after the convocation . . .

It's difficult to justify my anger toward him when he's also the one who helped heal the damage to my hands—or so I've assumed. And then there's Rydan, who I've noticed has kept his distance since the whole fire debacle, especially after being kicked out of the infirmary by Felix and the Healers. It's crossed my mind a couple of times to stop by his chambers, but knowing that Vira could answer the door instead of him? No thank you.

Perhaps that's why I've been trekking to the library at the stroke of midnight every night since, in the hopes that Rydan might just show up or already be there. But, so far, it's just been me, countless stacks of books, and the roaring fire in the hearth.

I'm approaching the library during my nightly stroll when I notice the lights in the hallway flicker. Knowing that everything is powered by magick, it gives me pause. There hasn't been a single disruption at Midvale since arriving here. And, because of that, I've grown to expect that everything runs smoothly, that that's just the way it is and always has been. At first, I want to dismiss it as just a figment of my imagination, but then it happens again. And again.

My pace has already slowed exponentially, but I've now come to a complete stop at a crossing in the hallway. I can see the library straight ahead, but something tells me to look down the other hallways. To look left, then right. The hallway to the left appears normal, but the one to my right is noticeably darker. What's even more disturbing is that I don't remember this crossing being here, this "option" to go a direction other than straight. True, the library has multiple entrances on multiple floors and, tonight, I'd decided to take the route less traveled—but an inner voice tells me that something isn't right. That this hallway isn't supposed to be here . . . that it doesn't even *exist*.

Against my better judgment, I veer to the right, running my linen-wrapped hands along the walls. I can't help but notice how dull everything appears to be—the paint, the lighting, the décor, especially the portraits on the walls . . . even the floor beneath my feet is lackluster.

As each step takes me farther down the strange corridor, the more my mind screams at me to turn back, to just go to the library like I have every other night. But there's something vaguely familiar about the appearance of this hall—not of the hall itself, but in the *way* it looks. The outline is almost fuzzy, the corners, edges, and lines less defined, as if I'm walking through a haze, which doesn't make any sense because I'm *inside*. It reminds me of . . .

Being with Estelle in the forest.

That night at the tavern before it'd caught fire.

My blood runs cold.

Just as the recognition is sinking in, I see a shadow at the end of the corridor dart across the hall and, without thinking, begin to race toward it. I know it can't be the Mallum because the Mallum can't infiltrate the Veil—but that doesn't mean it can't be someone else with intentions just as sinister as the Mallum. Someone working for Darius, perhaps? Like the Savant.

If it's that copper-headed asshole, I'm going to kill him.

I grit my teeth as I pick up the pace, arms pumping at my sides. I veer left at the end of the hall, in the same direction as the shadowed figure. I don't have my chakrams on me, seeing as we're supposed to be safe here, so I make sure to stop and look around for something I can use as a weapon.

Given that magick is used for just about everything in Midvale, there isn't much in the way of tools lying around, but it's when I go to remove one of the large picture frames from the wall and break it in half that I realize I'm in *big* trouble. The frame slips through my hands, as if it were a ghost—or perhaps *I'm* the ghost in this scenario?

It's a trap, an illusion.

Suddenly feeling like I've walked right into the devil's lair, I double back and sprint down the hall like my life depends on it. Because, in all reality, it probably does. I'm tempted to return to my chambers, grab my chakrams and full assassin garb and return to this very corridor, and in a split second, I decide that's exactly what it is I'm going to do.

I reach the access point to conjure the portal to take me back to my room. I fling the door open, unwrapping the useless bandages from my hands before rifling through my armoire for my gear. I slip on the all-leather training uniform, then secure my chakrams in their holsters. I grab a small dagger that Felix had left behind and stuff it into my right boot for good measure. I pull my hair into a topknot and burst through the door once again, repeating the steps to conjure the portal to the exact hallway I'd just returned from.

I take off in a mad dash, the faerie lights whizzing past my head, my eyes fixed on my destination. It feels so good to run again, to *hunt* again, and as much as I hate Darius Tymond for what he's turned me into, there's also a lingering appreciation there. For my brute strength. My unrelenting focus. My killer instincts. *Literally.*

It may make me the villain, but I'm never, ever the victim.

And, to me, that's worth something.

I'm steps away from the crossing, *steps away . . .*

I skid to a complete stop. The library is ahead of me, yes. The option to turn left? Is also there. But the ability to turn right? Is gone.

I lay my hand against the now-sealed wall and press my ear to it, but there's nothing. Absolutely nothing.

Well, I suppose that isn't entirely true.

Because there *is* something.

An experience.

My knowledge of that experience.

Twice over.

I back away from the wall, hands returning to their rightful place atop my chakrams. There's a Caster in Midvale, which likely means the Savant know about this place. Darius, too.

I glance at my hands, at the damage that *should* be there, but isn't. *I* did that. That purple light, whatever it was, came from me. And if I can heal *that* kind of damage? Who's to say I can't exact an even greater degree of it?

While I may not be able to access the illusion I'd just been in, I at least know what's coming. I can sense it, a deep resonance in the very core of my being. Aeridon may be familiar with the brute power of assassins, but what about an assassin with illusié abilities? With not only physical forces at play, but unseen ones as well?

Now *that's* something the world has yet to see, the likes of which they've never seen before.

Perhaps I'll be the one to show them.

FELIX BARLOW

HIS NEWLY ASSIGNED room isn't nearly as nice as the one he'd shared with Arden. Incredibly cramped with lower ceilings and less space overall—he's really living the dream. To make matters worse, the shelves are stocked with books he's already read thrice over. Not much in the way of entertainment.

Surely *something* will happen to pique his interest . . .

And it does. When the lights flicker.

Thankful for the distraction, Felix snaps the book shut before swinging his legs over the armrest. He tosses the text onto the seat, observing the overhead sconces as he walks toward the door. He opens it, peering into the hallway for a potential disturbance, but there isn't one. Confused, he slowly shuts the door, wondering if he'd just imagined it.

Until it happens again.

He studies the pattern more closely this time—the dimming, the buzzing, the prolonged nature . . . this isn't a regular power outage. It's something he's seen only a time or two before.

The work of a Caster.

But the Savant? Here? Impossible, if memory serves him. And not a mention of it from Xerin, no less. Unless he'd intentionally been kept out of the loop . . . but for what purpose?

Scenario after scenario races through his mind. If Clive *is* here in Midvale, then Arden is in danger. As frustrated as she may be with him at the moment, he refuses to let anything happen to her. Not here, not like this.

From the armoire, he grabs a black cloak and swings it over his shoulders before fastening the button that joins the fabric together. With boots strapped on and a knife in his pocket, he makes for the door. But when he opens it, he's met with an unfamiliar sight. The hallway he'd just laid eyes upon now ceases to exist. An uneasy feeling washes over him as he takes not one, but two steps backward, back into the safety of the room. A gaping black hole swallows the door, swallows *everything* that had been on the other side.

It isn't real, he tells himself. As much as he wants to believe it, the precision of the illusion tells his brain otherwise. The way blackness encroaches on the edges of the room, the shadows crawling along the ceiling, the wraith-like hands reaching, reaching, reaching . . . It's enough to make him stumble until he's backed himself into a corner.

The shadows around him begin to pulsate as if new life is being breathed into them, revitalizing whatever darkness lives within. He can't help but wonder if everyone in Midvale is experiencing this—if Clive's power could even be that far-reaching, that *strong*. His question is answered as a form begins to take shape within the black hole. It's human, thankfully. A man. Wiry copper hair is the first feature to emerge.

The Caster himself.

Felix straightens from the crouched position he'd taken earlier, realizing that as long as Clive is here, he can't be near the others, near Arden. Which means the illusion is localized. The rest of Midvale is safe . . . for now.

"How did you get in?"

A wry grin stretches across the man's face. "What's it to you, Amplifier?"

Felix hesitates in his response, wondering just how much Clive knows about him, his past, his *true* intentions being in Midvale . . .

Clive chuckles, raising his hands to show that he isn't a threat. "They'll be coming for you. Consider this a friendly warning."

"I didn't know such a thing existed," Felix says, studying him carefully. "Who's *they*?"

"Who you really work for, despite your grievances," Clive sneers. "You should be glad, I suppose. No longer having to keep up appearances and all."

Felix freezes in place, debating his next move. How could Clive possibly know about Xerin? The conversations they'd had behind closed doors? No . . . this feels like a trap, one he won't dare fall into.

"I work for no one," Felix says, discreetly reaching for the knife in his pocket. "And, if I were you, I'd watch where I decide to cast. Because one misstep"—he smirks, flinging the knife directly at Clive's heart—"could cost you everything."

The knife sails in the air, but doesn't hit true. Clive is too experienced, too good at what he does. Within seconds, the shadows on the walls and ceiling have retreated, the black hole closing in on itself, taking the Caster along with it. The blade clangs against the door before falling to the floor.

Felix dashes over to it, kicking it to the side before flinging the door open. He's pleased to find that the hallway has returned to its original state with no Caster in sight. He can only hope that Clive has fled the premises and won't be making additional stops on his way out . . .

Arden.

The only way he'll know for sure is if he drops in on her.

While it may only cause more discord between them, it's certainly a small price to pay to assure her safety.

RYDAN HELSTROM

ONLY NOW DOES Rydan realize just how off his and Vira's schedules are. Seated in front of an unlit hearth, he glances at the grandfather clock in the corner of their room, his foot tapping with each passing movement of the second hand. *Tick, tock, tick, tock.*

It's well past midnight and, while he knows Summoner training is specifically scheduled for such a time, he can't help but feel a pang of guilt for not knowing the exact time of her classes—or how long they usually last. He's been so wrapped up in helping Arden that he's neglected what he and Vira have—that is, if she isn't completely fed up with him by this point. Contrary to his fiery temperament, Vira is calm, patient, and understanding. He's never seen such compassion shine through anyone like that before.

Which makes what he's doing even more disparaging.

Then again, when he'd accused her very own brother of stealing the crest, she hadn't taken it well, as he'd expected. But Arden had. And she's been a much more willing participant in solving that whole mystery than the person he's been sharing a bed with . . .

Regardless of the tension between them, Rydan knows he needs to reconnect with Vira, at the very least to check in and see how everything's going. But, by the looks of it, he'll be sitting here all night, alone, unless he actually *does* something about it. With that in mind, he grabs a lit lantern from the mantle, knowing that the hallway lights are automatically set to dim in the hours before dawn. Yes, he could just ignite his hands to lead the way, but the focus it'd require is something he just doesn't have the energy for right now. He grabs a black cloak, pulling it over his shoulders, before heading for the door.

The hall is quiet, as it should be at this hour. He walks along it, passing the many rooms lined along the corridor, trying to jog his memory regarding where Vira's training takes place. It can't be in the training room he and the others have been using—not enough space to summon creatures of dragon-size proportions—which then causes him to wonder if her training is even occurring inside of Midvale at all. If you ask him, summoning is very much an outdoor ability.

He calls forth the portal that'll take him to the main entrance, knowing that, if anything, it's probably the best place to start. Perhaps if Lane or someone else is at the front desk, he can just ask. But when he steps out of the shimmering gateway, he's surprised to see that the lights on the main floor are even more dimmed than they were in the halls, and that there's no one manning the front desk.

There isn't a soul in sight.

It's off-putting.

Cautiously, Rydan maneuvers around the giant room, feeling tempted to call out to anyone who might be listening. He doesn't even realize he's lurking along the edge of the room when a soft melody, like that of windchimes caught in a gentle breeze, indicates there's another portal opening, one *he* didn't conjure. He presses himself against the wall, tiptoeing over to a massive pillar that will surely hide him from view. There's a flurry of movement and footsteps, and that's when he hears her.

"Your Greatness, I just want to reiterate that, while I've had training, there's no guarantee that I'll be able to do as you've asked."

It's easy to put the pieces together without looking around the pillar and potentially giving himself away. *Vira's with Cerylia.*

A separate voice says, "I know I've been wrangled into this last minute, but, if I may, perhaps you should wait until daylight. Who knows what she might summon at these hours . . ."

The gruffness of the voice tells him that it belongs to Haskell. It's an odd trio to be wandering the halls, especially at this hour. Based on what he's just heard, Rydan does a quick calculation in his head. It seems Cerylia wants Vira to summon something—or some*one*—and, given that Haskell's a Transporter, it must be something that needs to be done *off* the grounds. Or, seeing as Haskell has a pocket watch, perhaps they're daring an attempt at going back outside the Veil.

An uneasy feeling washes over Rydan as he leans further into the pillar, as if doing so will help him hear better.

Cerylia's voice finally breaks the silence. "On the contrary, daylight will attract too much attention. And, as we know from experience, Vira's brother prefers to fly under the cover of night."

Rydan nearly loses his footing. *Xerin. They want to summon Xerin.*

He's about to jump out from behind the pillar to warn them of all the reasons they shouldn't try to contact Xerin, but it seems that someone else has beaten him to it. A fourth voice bounces off the walls.

"Stop," Opal says. "Before you go any further, there's something you ought to know."

CERYLIA JARETH

FROM THE GRAVE expression Opal wears, Cerylia can only hope that whatever she's about to tell them will lead to a worthwhile outcome. If this is merely a stalling tactic, the Inverter *will* regret her actions. Cerylia will personally see to that. They've had more than enough back-and-forth during their time together, so whatever it is Opal has to say, she'd better get on with it. And it better be good.

"Go on, then," Cerylia prompts. "What is it?"

"You were about to leave."

"Was it that obvious?" Haskell chides, clearly trying to disperse the mounting tension amongst the group.

Cerylia ignores her nephew's futile attempt, asking Opal once more, "What do you need to tell us?"

Opal glances at Vira, studying the girl for a moment too long, then flicks her gaze to the queen. "You shouldn't summon Xerin. It isn't a good idea."

"How could you possibly know that?" Vira counters, eyes narrowed. "Last I heard, you traverse the past, not the future."

Opal's lip raises in a half-snarl, but her voice comes out cool, collected. "And it's because of that that I *know* it isn't a good idea."

Cerylia raises a hand between the two of them. It works because they both fall silent. "What did you see?"

"Xerin isn't to be trusted. He's been meeting with King Tymond in Trendalath."

"That could not be further from the truth," Vira argues. "Xerin despises the king—all authority, actually." She sends a brief apologetic glance toward Cerylia. "If he were meeting with him—"

"He is. I can prove it." She looks to Cerylia with pleading eyes. "I've shown you the past before. I can show you his recent movements. His signature is all over Trendalath."

Vira opens her mouth, no doubt about to defend her brother, when Opal shoots her a glare so menacing that Vira closes her mouth and averts her gaze altogether.

Cerylia decides to ask Opal point blank, "Is that the reason why you were sneaking around Sardoria with him? Meeting in the woods? Why you risked your life to access memories inside the Veil?"

"Yes," Opal answers, a little too quickly. "I had an inkling that his intentions weren't pure and everything I've seen thus far has only confirmed my suspicions." She extends a hand toward the queen. "I can show you, if you'd like."

Cerylia takes her hand and, sure enough, there they are, traversing the past—mere bystanders in Trendalath castle as Darius and Xerin speak in hushed voices at the far end of the corridor. From this distance, it's hard to hear exactly what they're saying, but just the sight of them together makes Cerylia's blood run cold. "Why would he betray his own kind, especially when he was the one to round everyone up in the first place?" she murmurs. Opal doesn't hear her, but it doesn't matter because she likely wouldn't know the answer either.

They wait until Xerin shapes back into his falcon form and disappears through a window before leaving the inversion to face reality once again.

"Well?" Vira presses, eager for answers.

"Opal is accurate in her findings. Xerin has been meeting with King Tymond."

Vira's face falls, growing paler by the second. "It . . . it doesn't make sense. Why would he . . .?"

"I was hoping you'd be able to shed some light on that."

Vira gapes at Opal incredulously. "Well, seeing as this is the first I'm hearing about my brother betraying the Caldari, no, I don't see how I *could* shed any light." Her shoulders drop as she heaves a loud sigh. "I'm just as in the dark as all of you."

An uncomfortable silence follows until Haskell says, "What do you suggest we do?" The question is aimed at Opal, but even she seems to be at a loss for words.

"There isn't much we can do," Cerylia admits. "But summoning Xerin clearly isn't in our best interest, nor is leaving Midvale grounds." *You're not leaving,* Cyfrin's voice rebukes as it pops into her head. Damn that woman and her sixth sense. Even though this has nothing to do with the

Archmage, the satisfaction she'd get from knowing that she'd been right—yet again—is too infuriating for Cerylia to even consider right now.

"So we're to just . . . continue on? As if nothing has happened?" Vira asks, on the verge of tears. "What if the king is exploiting him? Or blackmailing him? Or is somehow using the Mallum against him?"

Denial. The girl's in complete and utter denial.

As tempted as Cerylia is to try and console Vira, the reality of what this means settles into her veins like ice. Xerin is a Shaper, meaning that, at any minute, at any point in the day, he could arrive at Midvale appearing as someone else. As the Archmage. As Casimir. As Vira. As *Opal.*

"We need to fortify the perimeter, every inch of this place. No one comes in. No one goes out."

"Another lockdown." The way Opal says it immediately sends Cerylia reeling to the past, back to Sardoria when the Mallum had infiltrated the castle.

"Yes," she confers. "Another lockdown."

"I'm afraid it may be too late for that," a voice says from the back of the room. Arden steps into view, her full-length cloak whirring behind her. Rydan follows, emerging from behind a pillar as if he'd arrived with her, but the way she glances back at him and furrows her brows tells Cerylia that he hadn't.

"And what information do you have?" Cerylia asks, already feeling exasperated. "Please, do enlighten us."

But she isn't at all prepared for the bone chilling news her niece has to offer.

"It's the Savant," Arden whispers. "They know we're here."

DARIUS TYMOND

IT'S GLORIOUS. Absolutely glorious.

"A little to the left," the Curser says, instructing Clive from the speculor that's floating in the middle of the chamber, casting a mirror image on the waters below. "A few more steps."

Darius isn't even bothered that the Curser has taken the lead on this endeavor because the sight before him is unlike anything he's ever seen. To think he'd seen it all . . .

How wrong he'd been.

Clive stalks around the luminescent grid, its power nearly blinding. It's in the shape of a wheel but, much like a labyrinth, winds in on itself in a sort of spiral. Placed intentionally along each curve of the spiral are crystals of all varieties—clear quartz, citrine, calcite, obsidian, howlite—and at the very center of the grid is a giant sparkling amethyst. It truly puts his ring to shame.

"There. Stop right there."

Landon's command pulls Darius from his thoughts and back to the present. He brings his attention back to the image the speculor is casting. "Well? Can it be done?"

Landon runs his hand over the bald patch that runs straight through the middle of his head. He narrows his eyes, pressing his already thin lips together. After a few long moments, he finally says, "It can. The obsidian will be the most difficult, as its properties are to deflect the very ability I'll be casting upon it—"

"But not impossible?" Darius interrupts.

Landon arches a brow, clearly annoyed. "No. Not impossible."

That's all Darius needs to hear. "When?"

Landon grabs the speculor from the center of the room, the image of Clive and the crystalline grid disappearing in a whir of light and particulates. "You do realize what you're asking of me, correct?"

"Yes. I do," Darius retorts. "So, when?"

"I feel I must preface my answer by reminding you that I've never cursed that many objects at one time, especially not such *charged* objects." He falls silent, shaking his head, as if the calculations are too tedious. "We're talking about taking down the entire power source of an illusié-made creation: the Veil. Something that took dozens of illusié to conjure in the first place."

"And are you not the most experienced Curser in Aeridon?"

Landon sighs. "I am. But this . . . this'll be a challenge—even for me."

"I don't care what it is," Darius snaps. "You knew what you were signing up for the minute you stepped foot in Trendalath and swore your loyalty to the Savant."

"That may be true," Landon says, "but there were never any guarantees that I—that *any* of us—could destroy something like this on our own. We were under the impression that that was what the Mallum was for."

Darius narrows his eyes. "And it is."

"Then perhaps if you had wielded its power and its presence more efficiently, any remaining illusié wouldn't have had the opportunity to run off—"

"Enough!" Darius bellows, slamming his hands down on the table. "That is quite enough, *Curser*."

Landon's cheeks redden at the insult, at the refusal to use his given name. He doesn't say anything further.

"Consider this . . . Clive is currently in the Veil, casting an illusion around anyone he encounters so that he can slip in and back out entirely undetected—so that he could show us everything we've just witnessed." The fact that he himself is singing Clive's praises right now is enough to make his stomach turn, but Darius continues, "Do you know how many people that is? Hundreds, if not *thousands*. He didn't question his abilities, nor did he doubt them. He simply did what he knew he could do. And you're telling me that you can't curse some *immobile* objects because there 'might be too many'?" The disdain in his voice is palpable. "Pathetic."

"It's no wonder Clive was desperate to escape," Landon shoots back. "Serving a tyrant like you—"

"Watch your tongue, Curser, lest you want it removed for good." Darius opens his palm, then closes it again, the amethyst ring glinting in the dim light. "And don't forget that your abilities are as good as gone if you refuse to do your part."

"And if I can't?" he scowls. "What if, physically, it isn't possible?"

"Then you best find another way," Darius growls, "or bring me someone who can. Because one way or another, this grid *will* be destroyed, whether it's by the likes of you or not."

BRAXTON HORNSBY

"SO QUEEN TYMOND is dead?"

The question hangs in the air.

Hanslow and Stanton are staring at Braxton in awe, as if he's just grown three heads after recounting the stories of the Caldari, the Mallum, and the Cruex—which, to be fair, *is* starting to sound like an old wives' tale.

"Yes," he says, trying his best not to take offense, "my *mother* is dead."

"I'm terribly sorry to hear that," Hanslow says, patting him on the shoulder.

"As am I." Stanton gives a quick nod of his head but doesn't offer much more in the way of condolences.

Braxton knows just what to say. "Arden was there when it happened."

At this, Stanton raises his head, eyes narrowing.

"For a time, it was assumed that she was responsible for the murder. I believed it—hell, all of Aeridon did."

Stanton clears his throat, the first sign of uneasiness Braxton's seen from him. "What made you change your mind?"

Braxton shifts in his seat, wondering if telling them about the speculor and the jaded spring is a good idea—if it's something they'd even have knowledge of. "How does the saying go? *Magick works in the most mysterious of ways.* Let's just leave it at that."

"So not only did my daughter try to get away from that tyrant, but once she did, she was brought back against her will, tortured, and forced to use the very abilities that he'd cast out so long ago?"

Hanslow whistles at Stanton's rendition, eyes growing wide.

"Yes." Braxton's voice is meek. "To put it bluntly."

Stanton suddenly turns away from them and walks into another room.

"He needs time to process," Hanslow whispers.

"Understood." Braxton glances to the hearth, the crest calling his attention. "I suppose I should consider myself pretty lucky to have found that, huh?"

Hanslow pours himself another cup of tea, taking his time as he stirs some honey into the steaming liquid. "I'm not so sure luck has anything to do with it, son."

"You think it was . . . *deliberately* placed in the Void?"

"Yes." There isn't an inkling of hesitation in his voice. The old man wraps his hands around the mug and leans in before saying, "In fact, I think someone was trying to hide it."

"But why? And who?" Braxton can hardly keep the many questions scattering haphazardly across his mind at bay. "Who could have that much power? To *deliberately* visit the Void?"

"That's precisely the question I can't seem to answer." Shadows darken the old man's eyes. "Yes, the Mallum is a terrifying entity, but whoever *this* is . . ."

"They've been around for ages," Braxton finishes. "Since the dawn of illusié itself . . ." As soon as he says it, there's only one person that pops into his mind. The one member of the Caldari who's been around for lords know how long.

Xerin.

"You look as though you've seen a ghost." The old man's eyes are wide with concern.

"Hanslow, there's something we need to talk about," Braxton says, shuddering at the chilling realization. "We need to talk about what happened in Athia . . . *before* the Savant arrived at the inn."

The innkeeper holds up a finger before pouring them both a fresh cup of tea. "I'm all ears."

ARDEN ELIRI

IT'S CROSSED MY mind more than once to leave the library—and everyone in it—to inform the Archmage of what I'd witnessed in these very halls . . . but there's something in Cerylia's expression that stops me every time she goes to speak.

We, as a group, had decided *not* to talk about the Savant or Xerin—or anything for that matter—out in the open, especially not in the Midvale lobby. A single pair of curious ears at just the right moment in time can do more harm than good—something we've all learned the hard way. And so, I'd rounded up the group and escorted them to the library, pointing out the very hall (and its now convenient nonexistence) where I'd had the strange encounter.

Everyone's talking amongst themselves, no doubt trying to decipher my news as well as Opal's. Speaking of . . . the

Inverter is awfully quiet, given everything that's just occurred—almost like she'd expected an interruption of some sort to take the focus off of her and point it elsewhere.

"You're sure it was the Savant?" There's an edge to my brother's voice.

"I'm sure." I shudder at the memory of the Daegrum Chambers. "And if you don't believe me, I'm sure Opal here would be happy to confirm."

I must catch her by surprise because she quickly clears her throat, her eyes scanning the group somewhat nervously. "Of course. Although, *I* believe you. And I don't think that's necessary unless anyone here has their doubts."

"We believe Arden." Rydan's tone is firm. "She's the only one who's experienced the Savant's wrath firsthand. I doubt it's something she could forget, even if she wanted to."

I shoot him a quick smile as a silent thank you. Vira seems to take notice of our little moment because she instantly grabs his hand and inches closer to him. I meet her gaze only for a second, then turn it back to the group. "I'm almost certain it was the Caster."

"Clive Ridley." Cerylia frowns. "He stole Estelle's pocket watch."

"Which means he has full access to the Veil," Opal affirms, "including Midvale."

I can't help but glance at Rydan again. "That's how we stumbled upon this place to begin with . . . it must be."

Rydan drops Vira's hand, moving closer to me. "And why we were, more or less, *ejected* so suddenly." He rakes a hand through his hair. "Clive must have closed the portal right as we were about to meet Casimir."

I nod, the events of that day coming back to me. "So, he's been here before. And he came back—and will likely return, especially if he didn't find whatever it is he's looking for."

"But what would he be looking for?"

Haskell's question hangs heavy in the air. None of us have the answer. Not even the slightest clue.

"If we need to fortify the perimeter, we'll have to get the Archmage involved." I can tell by the way Cerylia looks at me that my suggestion might just be the very thing to push her over the edge. "I know you were successful once before, but this isn't Sardoria. And we're talking about *thousands* of people. Not to mention, we're in the Veil. I'm sure the Archmage has some protocol to follow, but how can she enforce it when she isn't even aware that Midvale's security has been threatened?"

Cerylia drums her fingers against the oblong table we're all sitting at. The fire roaring in the hearth behind her only emphasizes her frustration. "I'll speak with the Archmage."

"And in the meantime?" Haskell asks.

"We need to tell the others. Estelle, Avery . . ." I nearly choke out his name. "And Felix."

"I'll inform Estelle," Opal offers.

"And I'll tell Avery," Haskell says pointedly, even though he could very well tell Felix just as easily.

I glare at my brother. It's like the lords-damned rooming assignment all over again. "Right. I'll tell Felix," I submit.

"It's settled then," Cerylia says, rising from her chair. "Everyone is to return to their rooms until I discuss this with the Archmage and send word on what to do next. And stay paired up, would you? In case Clive makes an unexpected appearance. With two Caldari up against one Savant, we have much better odds."

My chest tightens as I realize what this means. *Looks like Felix has gone from uninvited to mandatory . . . for safety purposes.*

As if he can read my mind, Haskell winks at me. Rydan and Vira are first to leave the library, then Cerylia and Opal. I hang back, watching as my brother slithers over to where I'm standing. A smirk begins to wrinkle his face, but I put my hand up before it can spread any further. "Don't even start."

"Start what?' Haskell teases, elbowing me in the side.

I angle my head at him before rolling my eyes.

"Felix would rather hear it from you anyway—"

I throw my hands up and march away from him, not bothering to look back at the full-fledged grin that's surely plastered across his face.

✶ ✶ ✶

I've barely finished tidying up my room when there's a soft knock on the door. *Already?* I've hardly had time to process what's going on with the Savant, so to add the weird drama with Felix to the list? I was really hoping I'd have at least another hour. Or two. *Or longer.*

But no. Not when a lockdown's about to take effect.

Not when the fate of Midvale rests in our hands.

I straighten from my position over the bed, giving the sheets one final fluff before heading for the door. I take a deep breath, hoping it'll calm my nerves but, if anything, it only intensifies everything I'm already feeling.

Felix knows about my history with Rydan.

He knows that that connection is still strong.

But he also knows that *our* connection is strong, too—*was* strong, *is* strong? I really don't know anymore.

I open the door as casually as I can, turning away before we have the chance to make eye contact. "Come on in," I say with a flourish of my hand, already feeling ten levels of awkward. "Seems that little arrangement didn't last long, did it?"

"What's going on?"

The urgency in his voice has me whirling around to look at him. *So much for avoiding eye contact.* I'm immediately pulled into his deep chestnut gaze. "Haskell wasn't joking, was he?" I murmur.

He angles his head, clearly confused. "Come again?"

"Haskell didn't tell you anything? Just sent you over here?"

Felix nods. "Quite urgently."

It's then a wave of unease washes over me as an alarming thought enters my mind. *Is it possible I just let Clive into my room? That he's using his abilities and this is just some elaborate illusion?*

Without a second thought, I pull my chakrams from my sides and charge maybe-not-Felix until I've pushed him completely up against the wall, my blades crossed at his neck. With the right amount of pressure inwards, they'll slice right into his skin, decapitating him.

His eyes grow wide at the sudden shift in my demeanor, at the compromising position he's now in. Ever so slowly, he raises his hands in surrender. "Arden, what the hell is this?"

The way he says it, the calm in his voice—when it should be anything but—tells me that it likely *is* him and not the Caster, but I'm not entirely convinced.

"What did you gift me?"

"Arden . . ."

"Tell me. Now," I demand, leaning further into the blades. "Or I swear I'll keep pressing and won't stop." A trickle of blood slides down his neck. "What did you gift me?"

There's only lethal calm as he says, "A ship."

I nearly growl at the vagueness of his response. "Be more specific."

"A wooden carving. Of a ship."

I allow the words to register fully without breaking my stance—or my grip.

"You know, you could have just asked me to *show* you it was me."

It's then I feel his presence, overwhelming serenity amidst a sea of fury. How he isn't amplifying my rage is beyond me, but I suppose if the roles were reversed and *he* had chakrams held to *my* neck, I'd search far and wide for even the smallest morsel of calm.

I blow out a long breath before stepping away and lowering my weapons. "Neat trick."

A smile tugs at the corner of his mouth. "I could say the same to you." He presses off the wall and walks over to the bed to pet Juniper. I can't help but watch the way he moves, as if he's gliding across the floor, completely unrattled by the fact that I'd nearly executed him mere seconds ago.

I'm transfixed by my thoughts, absently watching as he scratches Juniper behind the ears, when he clears his throat. "Now that you've confirmed that I am who I say I am, can we get on with it?"

Oh. Right.

I join him on the edge of the bed, a short distance away. "I was in the lobby when I overheard Cerylia, Vira, and Haskell talking about summoning Xerin." The statement seems to give him pause, but only briefly. "Opal stopped them, which is another topic entirely, but it seems the Savant know about this place—and one of them has broken in, undetected."

Felix furrows his brows, but his confusion doesn't seem genuine. In fact, the news doesn't appear to rattle him in the slightest. "Which one?" he asks.

His reaction gives me pause. "The one they call the Caster. Clive."

He's rather quick to put two and two together. "Estelle's missing pocket watch."

"More like stolen."

He shoots me a tired look and it's then I realize just how weary he must be. "When was the last time you slept?"

"Admittedly?" he sighs. "It's been days."

My heart does that stupid pitter-patter thing. "Why?"

He raises his brows. "Do you really need to ask?"

I smirk. "I'm flattered."

"As you should be."

When he doesn't say anything else, I consider inching closer to him on the bed, but think better of it. We're still navigating this weird relationship spiral of friends-turned-lovers-turned-friends-again, so there's no need to amplify whatever it is we're both feeling—because if I had to guess, it'd be a whole lot of confusion and we already have enough of that to go around.

"I'll take first watch." I rise from the bed, making for the door.

Felix meets me halfway at a startling speed. Seems one of us was bound to close the distance—just not me. "I can stay up."

I give an adamant shake of my head. "There's no way in hell I'm letting you stand guard looking like that. You'll get us both killed."

There isn't so much as a hint of trepidation as he says, "You know I'd never let that happen."

The way he says it, with so much self-assurance, is enough to give me full body chills. I lower my head slightly, hoping he can't see the blush that's crawling across my cheeks. "I know. And *you* should know that I wouldn't either."

He presses his mouth in a firm line. "You're not going to budge on this, are you?"

I grin. "Not even a little."

"Three hours, that's all I need. You'll wake me then?"

He needs way more sleep than that, but I'm not about to argue. His eyes are drooping with each passing minute—the sooner he gets to sleep, the better. For the both of us.

I nod as convincingly as I can.

He narrows his eyes but doesn't say anything further.

I watch with satisfaction as he stalks toward the bed, nearly throwing the covers over his head.

"Goodnight, Felix," I coo.

Much to my delight, a snore is my only reply.

FELIX BARLOW

"I LIKE WHAT you've done with the place," Felix quips as he carries two mugs of peppermint tea to where Arden's perched by the door. "Can I have the name of your decorator?"

Arden rolls her eyes. "Ha-ha," she says, taking a sip from her mug. "I'm sure it looks exactly the same as it did before."

Felix lowers himself against the wall across from her, his tea sloshing over the edge. He props himself against it, trying to ignore the fixture on the wall that's now digging into his back. "How long was I out for?"

"Not long enough." A hint of pink graces her cheeks. "I didn't mean that how it sounded. It's just that I can tell you're tired and probably need a few days' worth of sleep before you'll even be remotely close to catching up."

"Can't argue there." He grips his mug tighter, allowing the warmth to seep into his chilled skin. "It's a good thing Midvale has an endless supply of peppermint tea."

"Especially with all the late nights we're about to have."

There isn't anything underlying her tone, but the way her voice trails off as she averts her eyes tells him her thoughts have also drifted to previous nights they'd spent together. And here he'd thought she'd be hard-pressed to forget he ever existed.

"Can I ask you something?"

Her head pops back up, almost as if she's surprised by the question. "Ask away."

"What do *you* think happened to your abilities?"

She blows out a long breath. "You and I both know that that's a loaded question, Felix."

"I know. But you've got the Archmage telling you one thing, Queen Jareth another, and now the Healers, whenever they finish with their research . . . but, to be frank, I'm not interested in what any of them have to say. I want to hear it from *you*."

Arden takes another slow sip of her tea, no doubt stewing over her answer. "I wish I could say, but everyone's voices have been so loud, they've seemed to overshadow my own."

"Do you believe the Mallum took your abilities?"

An adamant shake of her head. "No. Because I'm here right now and not lost in the Void like Braxton." Her voice cracks at the mention of her cousin. "And also because of everything we just witnessed in the infirmary."

Felix gives her a small smile. "Well, that's a start."

"Admittedly not a very big one."

He angles his head at her. "Do you think they've morphed?"

"I honestly don't know. Part of me would like to think so, but having little to no information about my parents really makes it tough to figure out."

"Have you asked Cerylia?"

Arden chews on her lower lip. "I've been meaning to, although I don't know how much insight she'll really be able to give. If she truly knew something, wouldn't she have said something by now? Especially if it was important?"

"One would like to think so." *So she hasn't spoken with her aunt yet.* Felix tries to hide his relief.

"What about you? Any thoughts?"

"About your abilities?" He tries not to sound caught off guard, even though that's exactly how he feels. "Much like Cerylia, don't you think I would have come to you if I knew anything?"

"One would like to think so," Arden echoes. "But you've been in the Caldari for much longer than I have. I just thought that *someone* would at least know *something*." She pauses for a minute. "What about Xerin?"

The grimace on his face is involuntarily. "What about him?"

"Could he have some insight?" Arden presses.

"I wouldn't count on it," Felix answers smoothly. "He may be wise, but he doesn't care to involve himself in others' business."

Arden arches a brow. "Is that so? Because I got quite the opposite impression."

Felix doesn't respond right away, his mind whirling as it attempts to steer the conversation in another direction—any direction but this one.

"Even if he could help, Xerin isn't here," he says nonchalantly. "Nor can I imagine him being too keen on helping. Your best bet is your aunt."

Part of what he's said seems to snag on something in her mind because she quickly asks, "What do you mean you can't imagine him being too keen on helping?"

"I just mean . . . that Xerin's only ever looked out for number one. Himself. I mean, he left his sister to fend for herself, rotting in Trendalath for all those years—"

That's quite enough, his mind scolds. *Whose side are you on, anyway?*

Arden studies him, confused. "I thought he didn't know where she was? I thought he'd been looking for her, searching high and low to no avail."

At least we're onto another topic. "Did Vira tell you this?"

She averts her gaze, cheeks reddening, refusing to answer the question. *Because it was Rydan she'd gotten the information from.*

Felix takes a steadying breath, hoping what he's about to say next will nip this entire conversation in the bud. "The only reason I brought any of this up was to get your take on it, to see how *you* feel about everything."

"How I feel?" Arden scoffs. "How I feel is confused. Defeated. Borderline hopeless."

Felix suddenly feels bad for asking the question to begin with. "Confused, I can understand. But defeated?" He shakes his head. "Absolutely not. Are you forgetting what you just did in there, in the infirmary? That certainly isn't defeat. And, if you ask me, it isn't hopeless either. In fact, at the risk of sounding cliché, you may be the only hope we have."

Arden smiles at the sentiment, as cheesy as it is, before realizing the context of his words might have a deeper meaning. But before she can clarify, there's a knock on the door.

"Arden? Are you in there?"

Haskell. "Yes, where else would I be?"

Her brother snorts. "And Felix?"

"Right where you told me to be."

"Good. Just stay where you are and await further instruction."

Felix glances at Arden apologetically. "Any idea when that will be?"

"Your guess is as good as mine."

Arden sighs as the sound of her brother's footsteps fade into the distance. "Looks like we need to come up with a way to kill some time."

Felix pushes himself up off the floor before extending his hand. "I have an idea. If you're up for it, that is." He makes sure to say it in such a way that she can't possibly misconstrue the intention behind his words.

Even so, she hesitates before meeting his grip, allowing herself to be pulled to her feet. "Let's hear it, then."

RYDAN HELSTROM

RYDAN WAITS FOR Vira to cross the threshold into their room before securing the door behind them. They'd walked the entire way without speaking and, by the looks of it, that trend is likely to continue. Vira collapses into an armchair near the hearth, not bothering to acknowledge him *or* the information she's now unmistakably aware of. Head in hand, she heaves a loud sigh.

Rydan is cautious as he approaches her. He takes a seat in the adjacent chair, the creaking and moaning of the leather the only sound in the silence. It's just enough to get them both chuckling, however minimal.

Rydan leans forward, then reaches out to her. She raises her head and offers him a small smile before taking his hand in hers.

"Want to talk about it?"

"I don't know." She shrugs her shoulders, then shakes her head. "But, if anything, I suppose I owe you an apology."

The sentiment rings true. Rydan squeezes her hand in response.

"I just can't believe . . . my brother . . ." Tears rim her eyes. "Why would he bring us all together just to tear us apart? Just to work with the *one person* who made all of our lives a living hell? After what that monster did to our mother—" She sucks in a sharp breath, not daring to finish the thought aloud. The pain contorting her features is palpable—and how he wishes he had answers, *something* to give her to ease her strife—but all he can offer her is a speck of comfort in the dismal silence.

They sit like that for what feels like hours before she pulls her hand from his and wipes her tear-stained cheeks.

"Want me to make you something?" he offers.

She glances at the fire, running a hand through her tousled waves, but doesn't say anything. He'd hardly noticed how much her hair's grown in the past few months, how the innocence in her features has sharpened ever since that fateful day in the Trendalath dungeons. She's every bit the person who'd saved his sanity down there, but there's an edge to her now. A wall around her heart.

"Why are you looking at me like that?"

Rydan's thoughts scatter as he realizes he's just been gawking at her. "I . . . well, I suppose it just feels like it's been a while since I've seen you. Since we've done this." He gestures to their surroundings.

"What? Sat by a fire?"

He smiles at her attempt to lighten the mood. "Yeah. Alone."

She nods in agreement. "Seems our training schedules run opposite one another."

"You sleep, I train. When you train, I'm asleep."

"Almost as if it were designed that way."

He raises a brow. "On purpose, you mean?"

She sighs. "I don't know. I'm exhausted."

"Understandable."

"Well, from what Cerylia's told us, it seems like our schedules will be lining up just fine for the foreseeable future."

He guffaws. "Lockdown will do that."

"Honestly, I'm more than okay with it. I need a break."

He wants to agree, but the thought of not helping Arden discover her abilities worries him—or perhaps it's something more than that. After the moments they've recently shared in the library, at Tap's . . . he's grown accustomed to her company, similar to the camaraderie they'd shared in the Cruex. And yes, accustomed to that spark as well . . .

"I'll get something started. Potatoes, maybe?"

Rydan's pulled from his daze as Vira pushes out of her chair and walks over to the corner of the kitchen. He glances at the door, suddenly feeling trapped. Exactly how long are they expected to be in here? How will the Archmage react to the news? That Midvale's newcomers, more or less, lured the enemy right to them?

He glances at the door once more, feeling the urge to leave. A thousand excuses fill his head—all of them lies. A lump forms in his throat, as if his body is rejecting the very idea of dishonor. He forces it down. Vira deserves so much better.

"Get that fire roaring, will you?" she calls from the kitchen.

This is his life. Potatoes and fires and lockdown.

Say what you will about the Cruex, but at least there'd been purpose. At least they'd been fighting for something— even if that something had been unjust. He heaves a loud sigh as he kneels by the fire and adjusts the wood, barehanded.

It's only temporary.

It's only temporary.

But just *how* temporary remains to be seen.

CERYLIA JARETH

CERYLIA'S BEEN DREADING this conversation for what feels like an eternity. She strolls down the hall that leads to the Archmage's office, purposely taking her time, even though the situation at hand calls for much greater urgency. She positions herself in front of the door, gathering the nerve to knock when, much to her surprise, it swings open. Cyfrin looks as put out as ever.

"Finally. There you are. I've been expecting you."

How that's even possible is beyond baffling, but she doesn't question the Archmage. Instead, she enters the room, turning to face Cyfrin with an expression she can only hope conveys the gravity of what she's about to say. "I'm afraid I come bearing unfortunate news."

The Archmage closes the door, then meets her in the center of the office. "I'm listening."

"I have reason to believe there are trespassers in Midvale."

Cyfrin raises a brow in disbelief. "While I appreciate the concern, Queen Jareth, I can assure you that the safety measures we have in place are rather extensive."

"I'm not doubting that at all," Cerylia replies. "But one of the Caldari is missing her pocket watch."

Cyfrin's face pales.

"We'd originally assumed it'd just been misplaced, but it seems . . . well, it seems it's been stolen."

"By whom?"

Cerylia winces as she says, "A Caster. Of King Tymond's Savant."

"I see." Cyfrin exhales slowly. "We haven't discovered a breach, but I'll get my cadre on it to investigate further."

"I'm afraid that won't be necessary because they're already here. They've *been* here."

Cyfrin seems to catch her meaning. "The lights."

Cerylia nods. "You and I both know it couldn't have been just a faulty wire."

The Archmage looks to the door, deep in thought. "You came here to propose a lockdown of Midvale."

"That I did."

Cyfrin sighs. "I can't say I'm surprised."

"Do you have the proper protocol in place?"

"Of course we do," she snaps. "We've just never had to use it. And certainly not to this scale."

"I'm here to help," Cerylia offers. "Anything you might need, please let me know." She begins to walk past the Archmage toward the door when Cyfrin puts an arm out, stopping her.

"You will remain here, with me."

"I'm sorry?" Cerylia asks, suddenly feeling blindsided. "You want me to *stay?*"

Cyfrin gives a grim nod. "If I'm not mistaken, you've had close encounters with both the Mallum and the Savant, have you not?"

"I have." A bleak admission.

"Then consider your knowledge invaluable to those of us, like myself, who've had no such encounters."

"But the Caldari, my niece, my nephew . . . I can't just leave them to—"

"To what?" Cyfrin raises a brow. "Fend for themselves?"

"Not all of them have had an encounter."

"And with you by my side, let's hope they never will."

Cerylia opens her mouth to protest further, but the look on the Archmage's face has her thinking twice.

"Think of it as an opportunity to redeem yourself." Her tone is cold, unfeeling. "Lords know Midvale's entitled to that much from you."

She has a point, one the queen can't argue. Cerylia swallows her pride, her voice strained. "As you wish. I will remain here, by your side, until the threat subsides."

DARIUS TYMOND

HIS PATIENCE IS wearing thin.

Darius storms down the corridor to the Curser's room, not bothering with pleasantries as he passes the guards. He reaches for the door handle, dismayed to find that it's locked. "Sir Graeme," he calls out, his voice brash. "A word?"

The rustling and subsequent swearing from behind the door indicates that the Savant is indeed there. Mere moments later, Landon flings the door open, his glasses crooked over his nose, papers strewn across every inch of the floor. "And to what do I owe this most inconvenient of disruptions?"

Darius bristles at his tone. "Status?"

Landon sighs. "The same as it was three hours ago." He waves to the mess obliterating his room. "I assure you, I'm working as fast as I can to find a solution. In fact, I think I was nearly there until . . ." His voice trails off, once again pointing to the unwelcome interruption.

"Continue," Darius orders, not wanting to waste any more time.

Landon just stares at him before bursting into a fit of raucous laughter. "Might I remind you that *nearly there* does not mean *all the way there.*"

"Regardless," Darius seethes, his hand pressed against the door, "tell me what you think you've uncovered."

Landon stands firm in the doorway before finally sighing and backing up a few steps. Darius enters the room, hastily shutting the door behind him. "Well?"

"Give me a second," Landon murmurs as he returns to the desk littered with tomes, scrolls, and wrinkled pieces of parchment. He begins rifling through them, swearing as he discards the pages he isn't looking for.

Impatiently, Darius watches as they fall to the floor, not bringing them any closer to the Curser's so-called "solution". The king is just seconds away from committing Landon to the Daegrum Chambers when, finally, he gets a reprieve.

"Here," Landon says breathlessly, clutching a half-scribbled sheet of parchment in his bony hands. "This is what I need to destroy the grid."

Darius snatches it from him. He blinks, not quite believing what he's seeing—that it took Landon this long to find information that's already common knowledge amongst illusié. "Your solution is . . . an Amplifier?"

Landon nods fervently, somehow looking even more disheveled than before. "Using an Amplifier during the cursing ritual will ensure that each of the crystals are properly converted—especially the obsidian."

"You're certain of this?"

"Yes."

Darius purses his lips in annoyance. "Seems you were *all the way there* with a solution after all."

Landon hesitates. "I didn't want to approach you until I had the name of an Amplifier in mind. Unfortunately, my illusié circle these days runs rather small—"

"Well then," Darius retorts, dropping the page to the floor, "I suppose it's a good thing I know exactly who we're looking for."

BRAXTON HORNSBY

BRAXTON SITS QUIETLY as the information he's just shared with Hanslow sinks in.

"Why didn't you mention anything about Xerin at the time?" The crushing disappointment in his voice is hard to miss. "I could have warned you, *helped* you—"

"I didn't know he was someone to be warned about."

The old man's expression softens. "As one of the eldest bloodlines in Aeridon's history, an interaction with the Greys is not to be taken lightly. It sounds like he knew exactly what he was doing at the time."

"The only question is *why*?" Braxton runs a hand along his jaw. "Why would he pretend to have joined forces with the Caldari only to turn his back on them?"

"Who says he has?"

"I saw him talking—rather discreetly, I might add—with my father," Braxton whispers. "He isn't to be trusted. In fact, I wouldn't be surprised if the two of them had planned and executed my escape together, only to recapture me as a prisoner of Trendalath."

"It's a power play." *When* Stanton had stepped back into the room and joined the conversation, Braxton doesn't know, but the point he's made is valid. "Xerin likely got information from you that Darius couldn't have due to your estranged relationship, hence his valiant 'rescue mission'. However, once that avenue was exhausted, Darius played the role of poor wounded father to perfection, using your mother's death as a way to manipulate a connection with you and glean the information he needed."

Braxton blinks, his voice near breaking. "Just a pawn."

Stanton sighs. "It may be a harsh truth, but it's the truth nonetheless."

"Have the others caught on?" Hanslow asks.

Braxton shakes his head glumly. "Doubtful."

"Which means as long as Xerin's around, your friends are in danger—Arden's in danger." Stanton lowers his gaze before lifting it to Hanslow. "If there was ever a time to leave the Medial, this is it."

Hanslow regards him with wide eyes. "The risks are astronomical."

"Even more so if we choose to stay and do nothing."

Braxton looks between them, hanging on their every word.

"It'll disrupt everything," Hanslow counters. "Midvale, the Veil, Aeridon . . . it'll all hang in the balance—"

"What other choice do we have?" Stanton challenges. "There's no mistaking the fact that a Tymond found his way to us after all this time. We have what we need."

"And if you're wrong?" Hanslow presses.

Stanton looks to Braxton, his eyes filled with determination. "For all our sakes, let's hope I'm not."

ARDEN ELIRI

MY ROOM IS not even remotely close to the size of the training room, but I'm impressed with what Felix has managed to put together. After pushing all of the furniture to the sides, we're left with ample space. What he plans to do with it is hard to say, but if it means even the slightest chance of discovering what my ability has morphed into, I'm all in.

I'm sitting in the middle of the perimeter he's created, watching as he carries over yet another large stack of books before setting them to the side. I angle my head, reading the spines, realizing just how many of them I've thumbed through, more than once. "Perhaps I should be the one picking these out?" I offer.

Felix grunts as he rounds a corner, reappearing shortly after with yet another stack weighing down his arms. "Just because you didn't find anything the first time around doesn't mean it isn't there." He drops the books with a deafening thud before slapping the title on top. "Plus, now you've got another set of eyes."

I scoff. "Mine work perfectly fine, thank you very much."

When he doesn't respond and heads back around the corner for what must be the fifth stack, I push myself to my feet and follow him. I reach him just in time, grabbing his arm to pull him away from the rows of texts. "You've chosen more than enough. Believe me."

He glances at the book that's currently in his other hand, then sighs before returning it to its spot on the shelf. "You might be right . . . but we don't know how long this lockdown will last."

"Exactly."

He raises a brow, realizing we're thinking two different things.

"If we need more reading material, lords have mercy, we know where to find it," I quip, pulling him away from the tomes. I point to the floor. "Sit."

For once, he doesn't protest. He sits cross-legged, setting his hands in his lap, looking up at me expectantly for my next instruction.

"Why can't you always be this obedient?" I say with a laugh, joining him on the floor.

"Because I'm not a dog, Arden."

"Aren't you, though?" I retort.

He glares at me, but it's borderline playful. "Well, now that I know how you really see me . . ."

"Oh, please," I say with a roll of my eyes. He goes to stand as if he's about to leave, but I pull him back down, the force of which causes us to tumble to the side. A surprised laugh escapes him until he's laying on his right shoulder, me on my left. Our eyes lock, my hand still resting on his forearm. I start to move it, but he shifts ever so slightly so that his right hand presses against mine, keeping it firmly in place.

"Stay," he says, his voice just above a whisper.

I soften at the command, instantaneously relaxing my hand under his. I nod, unsure as to what to say or do next.

Although a long silence stretches between us, it doesn't go without eye contact. He's holding my gaze as if his life depends on it—and that's when it hits me. That unmistakable feeling.

"I suppose you're right," Felix whispers. "Books can only teach us so much, only provide us with half the picture. The other half comes from experience . . . *lived* experience."

I keep my hand on his forearm even though I want to move it to his chest to see if his heart is racing as fast as mine is, but the next words out of his mouth stop me.

"Tell me what you feel."

FELIX BARLOW

IT'S DANGEROUS, THIS much he knows. Inviting her in again without knowing the full extent, the potential risk. The absolute destruction that could come from it all. But from destruction comes renewal. Rebirth.

Perhaps that's exactly what he needs . . .

What they *all* need.

"Tell me what you feel," he repeats.

Arden doesn't flinch at the commanding nature of his tone but, instead, closes her eyes. He can tell by the deep inhale she takes, the steady rise and fall of her chest, that she's focusing on just that.

"I feel . . . you." Her face scrunches, eyebrows drawing together. "But it's different. A layer that must have been hidden before."

Try layers. Plural.

"Conflict," she says assuredly. "Like there's a war waging within you. About what, I don't know."

Felix lowers his head, shaking it even though she can't see him. "What else?" he murmurs.

A shaky breath precedes the one word he'd hoped not to hear. "Guilt." Her eyes shoot open. "You know something. Something you're choosing not to share. Not only with me, but with the others." Her gaze narrows as she studies his face. "What are you hiding, Felix?"

"Hiding?" he asks. "Since when does feeling guilty coincide with having secrets?"

"You can't be serious," she scoffs. "Since the dawn of time."

"Guilt wears many different forms," he counters. "Words left unspoken. Actions never taken. A life only half lived—"

"Sounds more like regret to me."

He raises a brow. "Two sides of the same coin."

"Depending on how you look at it."

"How telling that your first instinct is deception." He sits up, leaving her no choice but to release his arm. "Perhaps your subconscious is trying to tell you something."

She mimics the movement, her expression shifting to one of concern. "Stop deflecting. You were the one who demanded that I tell you what I feel. *Twice.*"

"While that is indeed true, I don't remember telling you to make assumptions around said feelings."

She leans back on her heels, studying him. Finally, she says, "Why are you getting so defensive?"

"I'm not." He shrugs. "I'm simply explaining my viewpoint."

"Explaining?" she challenges. "Or justifying?"

He hesitates, giving her all the more reason to say, "Being defensive usually means you're hiding something. Which brings me back to my original question. What do you know, Felix?"

In hindsight, perhaps helping her understand her abilities wasn't such a good idea, but the less she knows, the less they both know—and that certainly doesn't help his case.

"I think I know what happened to your abilities," he says a little too quickly, hoping she'll settle for a half truth.

She narrows her eyes. "Be more specific. Because we already know that they've likely morphed. Are you saying that you know what they've morphed into?"

He sighs. "I have an inkling. But I didn't want to say anything until I knew for sure. I didn't want to lead you down a path that would take you nowhere," he explains, anticipating her response.

"Felix, an inkling is the closest I've gotten. It's the only thing we have to go off of."

"But if I'm wrong . . ."

"If you're wrong, then we're back to square one, which is exactly where we are now." She reaches for his hand, taking it in his. "Please. You know as well as I do that time is a luxury we don't have. Especially with the Caster having breached the walls of Midvale."

This is it. The moment he could choose to lead her astray or set her down the very path where her destiny awaits. But how to tell her without revealing too much? Like he'd said, it's just an inkling . . .

"I've only ever heard of one other illusié having this ability, so it's a long shot. But I think you may be what's called a Channeler."

And there it is. The actual truth for once.

No turning back now.

"A Channeler." He can tell by the way she says it that she's trying to comprehend the full meaning, the complexity of it. She whispers the word again, still unsure as to what to make of it.

"A Channeler is someone who can channel the abilities of other illusié and use said abilities for a limited amount of time." He pauses, waiting for her reaction, but her face is blank. Clearly still processing. "It isn't permanent by any means. Think of it as temporary access to all illusié abilities, so long as it's within proximity of your location."

"So I have to be near another illusié? Physically?"

He nods. "Which explains . . ."

". . . why it feels like *I'm* the one who's amplifying when I'm near you. I've been channeling your amplification abilities." She shakes her head slowly, stunned. "Holy shit."

"And it's clear you already know how to do it, how to channel. It comes so . . . naturally to you."

"I wasn't even trying." She lowers her gaze to her hands, looking damn near ashamed.

He lifts her chin with his hand. "I know. Can't you see how powerful that is? Imagine what you'll be able to do now that you know."

A heavy breath whooshes out of her. "Well, we don't really *know*. Like you said, this is just an inkling." She chews on her bottom lip, thinking. "That other person you mentioned . . . the one other who is also a Channeler? Do you think they could help us?"

The question he'd feared. Felix doesn't dare break eye contact, doesn't dare reveal what he knows as he says, "I'm afraid not. That's more of a legend than anything else."

Arden slumps in defeat, not pressing further. "So I'm somehow supposed to just . . . figure this out?"

Felix offers a consolatory grin. "Hey, look on the bright side. What better place to be than Midvale? Someone here is bound to know something."

Arden glances at the door despondently. "That's a promising thought, except for the fact that that someone is out there and we're locked in here for lords know how long."

"Have a little faith, Eliri." He winks. "In the meantime, why not find a way to confirm our theory?"

"You mean practice channeling amplification? On what? Who will be on the receiving end?"

"Who says it has to be a who?" He hops to his feet, offering her a hand. "The great thing about being a novice is that we're starting from scratch. In many ways, there are no rules. No boundaries. No limitations."

She stares at his hand but doesn't take it.

"What, like you have something better to do?"

"I suppose not." Exasperated, she heaves a loud sigh before reaching for his outstretched hand. "Take it away, Barlow."

RYDAN HELSTROM

IF IT WEREN'T for the punishingly intricate board game they'd discovered in one of the cabinets, he'd certainly have lost his mind by now. The setup alone had taken nearly half an hour, but they'd managed to get all the pieces in their proper places. Eyes narrowed, mouth pressed into a firm line, Vira's calculating her next move. He's never met anyone who's taken a game so seriously.

Rydan leans back against the seat of the armchair, uncrossing his legs before kicking them out on the floor. Vira doesn't so much as stir at the movement, her focus completely occupied by the game at hand. Little does she know, Rydan's already played through the various moves available to her and, regardless of what she chooses, the outlook's pretty grim. He doesn't have the heart to tell her that, though.

After another few minutes of unrelenting focus (and no decision), she finally glances up from the board, defeat in her eyes. "I thought this was supposed to be fun."

"It is," Rydan says with a shrug, surveying the board yet again. "Until you made that last bonehead move that put you in the position you're in now."

She gapes at him. "My choices were limited."

"And now they're not."

"Yeah, but . . . I've gone through all the scenarios thrice over." She sighs. "You see what I'm seeing, right?"

"I do," he says with a nod. "Regardless, you've still got to make a move."

Another sigh, heavier this time. "Fine." She begrudgingly moves one of the pieces. "Just know that I'm not too keen on making a move that'll inevitably lead to my demise."

"We can always play again," Rydan offers, moving his piece to block hers. "Although I can't guarantee you'll win."

Vira doesn't respond as she observes the board, desperately looking for a way to shift the odds back in her favor. Finally accepting defeat, she takes her turn, leading them down a trajectory of one more move each, but she never gets to take hers because his move ends it all.

Game over.

Vira frowns through her congratulations. She goes to clean up the board when Rydan reaches his hand out to stop her. "You sure you don't want to play again? I mean, we've got nothing but time."

By the way she shakes her head, he can tell that she's already on another thought plane entirely. He clears his pieces to the side of the board, watching her closely. "Want to talk about it?"

A hint of a smile tugs at her mouth. "How did you know?"

"Because I know you." The game pieces clatter as they hit the bottom of the box. "I know that look."

"I wasn't aware I was giving one."

He places the lid onto the box before shoving it to the side. "So, is that a yes or no?"

She chews on the inside of her cheek, debating. "At least that was a decent distraction."

He doesn't even have to ask but does anyway. Anything to get her talking, to open up. "From what?"

She blows out a long breath. "My brother. It just . . . it doesn't make sense."

Rydan gives a silent nod, not wanting to further derail her train of thought.

"I mean, I know he isn't around much. Comes and goes as he pleases. Keeps to himself mostly. Doesn't really let anyone in, doesn't let anyone get too close. So, from that perspective, it makes perfect sense. But what if . . . he just needs someone to talk to? Someone he trusts. We all need that, right?"

"Sure," Rydan says, wondering where this conversation is headed. "We all need connection."

"Queen Jareth wanted me to summon him until"—she gestures at their current situation—"well, until all this."

"You're not thinking of contacting him, are you?"

"Would it be so terrible if I was?"

What he wants to tell her is that yes, contacting Xerin would be putting not only them, but *all* of Midvale in danger. As it stands, there's enough to worry about with the current lockdown.

"The only problem is . . . I'd need a way out of here. A pocket watch. And seeing as Haskell has been making his rounds to ensure that we're all safely tucked inside our rooms, I doubt he'd be willing to go against orders," she thinks aloud. "Now, *Arden*, on the other hand . . ."

Oh, no she doesn't. He refuses to drag Arden into this.

"Do you think you could . . . ask her?"

Rydan looks at Vira, dumbfounded. "And how am I supposed to do that? We're supposed to be locked in our rooms, remember?"

"Don't do that," Vira says, narrowing her eyes.

"Do what?"

"Act like you aren't capable. We broke out of Trendalath, remember? You're an assassin, for crying out loud. Sneaking around is kind of your thing."

He tries to ignore the dual meaning of the statement, refusing to let it sting. "Might I remind you that we had help when we broke out of Trendalath. The help of the very people you're now wanting to put at risk."

"I knew you wouldn't understand. How could you? You don't have any siblings."

"That I know of."

A long silence stretches between them, the insensitivity of the remark lingering in the air like an unwanted guest.

"I'm sorry, I didn't mean . . ."

Rydan waves her apology away. "You know what I think? I think you should sleep on it."

Vira considers his proposal, weighing her options.

"Sometimes, in the heat of the moment, we make decisions that aren't for the greater good. Especially when our emotions are heightened, as they should be when it comes to a family member."

"My only family member," Vira whispers. "Xerin's all I have left."

Rydan places a hand on hers. "Promise me you won't do anything tonight?"

She hesitates, eyeing the door to their room. Finally, she says, "I promise."

"Good," Rydan says, patting the top of her hand. "Now let's get some rest."

"You know, I was actually thinking I'm ready for round two." She pulls the board game into reach, shaking it with a mischievous glint in her eyes. "Are you up for getting your ass kicked?"

He grins. "You're on."

CERYLIA JARETH

CERYLIA FISTS HER hand and raises it in the air as she rounds a corner, indicating to the cadre to proceed with caution. They've been searching the grounds for what feels like an eternity, but the reality of the matter is that it's only been a couple of days. She isn't sure what they expect to find today that they didn't find yesterday, but with the Archmage breathing down their necks, there's no questioning her strategy, no matter how futile it may seem. Why Cyfrin wanted her by her side stumps Cerylia, but if it'll keep Midvale—and, more importantly, the Caldari—safe, who's she to complain?

"Clear," Cerylia barks, sounding like one of her guards back in Sardoria. "Just like every other hallway we've covered thus far," she murmurs.

Having stationed herself in the back of the group, it takes a few moments for the Archmage to join her. "Where to next?"

Cerylia regards her with incredulous eyes. "As I've mentioned before, you're a much better fit for leading the charge," she prompts.

"I respectfully disagree."

Cerylia scowls, reeling in her tone as she says, "I may have attended Midvale as a prior student, but *you* are the Archmage, the very heartbeat of this institution. I can assure you that if we have any hope of catching the intruder, it'll be by your guidance."

"Did I ask for justification?"

Cerylia bites her tongue, knowing that if she responds, it'll only be to lash out at this infuriating woman. Instead, she takes the dignified route and simply shakes her head.

"Onward," Cyfrin orders, lifting her chin at the corridor ahead. "We've still got at least seven more floors to cover."

It's nearing midnight, making the reality of that statement all the more taxing. Cerylia turns away from the Archmage before she can catch her seething and continues down the hall. The thud of the cadres' boots sound in time behind her as if they were moving as one person, one unit. They reach the end of the hall and start down the next, but two additional turns into different corridors reveals absolutely nothing. Just as she'd suspected.

Waste of time is the only phrase worth thinking at this juncture, but it certainly isn't helping diminish her frustration. She *should* be focusing her efforts on something that'll actually be useful, like regaining her extracting abilities, but instead she's rounding corners, looking for a threat that's dwindling with each futile step. That is, until a clang echoes at the end of the hall.

Cerylia stops dead in her tracks, signaling to the others to do the same. A few seconds pass with no movement to accompany the sound. Longsword in hand, she advances toward the source of the noise. She doesn't bother to look back and see if the cadre is following her . . . this is the most action they've seen in days. If she has to take it on solo, she will.

A shadow emerges, causing her to lift her sword higher, readying to strike, when a familiar voice says, "Lower your weapon. It's only me."

Cerylia halts in her pursuit, surprised to see that the shadow belongs to none other than Cyrus—and in his hands he carries a staff. *King Tymond's* staff.

"Identify yourself," Cyfrin demands, pushing her way to the front. "By order of the Archmage."

"He's not our intruder," Cerylia says, stepping in front of Cyrus to block him from harm. "He's here to see me."

The Archmage gives her a disapproving stare. "And why is this the first time I'm hearing about it?"

"Because I'm King Tymond's advisor."

Cerylia turns over her shoulder and widens her eyes at him, hoping her expression alone will shut him up before he says anything else incriminating.

"I hope, for your sake, that the next thing out of your mouth gives me one good reason not to detain you this instant," the Archmage hisses.

"Must be my lucky day then because I'm holding it." Cyrus taps Cerylia on the shoulder before stepping in front of her, raising the staff so that it's at eye level. "King Tymond's staff complete with"—he pauses, pulling a small circular object from his pocket—"a speculor I intentionally planted."

The Archmage looks between Cerylia and her co-conspirator. She squeezes the bridge of her nose, then blows out a long sigh. "Neither of those things mean anything to me."

"Well, they should," Cyrus says, standing his ground. "And they will once you see what the speculor holds."

Cerylia leans in closer. "We got something?" She says it low enough so that only he can hear her.

Cyrus gives a slight nod before holding each item out to the Archmage. "So, what'll it be?"

Cyfrin studies him, thinking through her options.

Cerylia waits with bated breath, as does the rest of the hall.

Finally, after much deliberation, the Archmage comes to a decision. "You two," she says, pointing to her and Cyrus, "come with me, to my office. I didn't have these cheval glasses constructed for nothing." She pauses as she deliberates her next set of orders. "As for the rest of you, keep searching the halls. Finish the rounds on the floors we haven't covered, then report back. Understood?"

The cadre nods in unison, murmuring their agreement before opening the portal to the next floor.

Cyfrin takes a step forward, plucking the speculor from Cyrus's grasp. "Follow me."

DARIUS TYMOND

DARIUS WATCHES FROM the safety of the castle as Clive enters Midvale once more, this time accompanied by none other than Landon Graeme, the Savant's Curser. Even though they'd reviewed their strategy numerous times the night prior, his faith in the proper execution of said plan is waning. There are so many moving pieces: entering Midvale undetected, discreetly capturing the Amplifier, returning to the Vaults to destroy the crystals powering the grid . . . what happens after that—whether his Savant make it out alive—is none of his concern.

Or so he's trying to convince himself.

The illusion Clive has cast is rather intricate. Even with the lockdown, Lane had greeted what appeared to be two illusié newcomers at the doors. She hadn't gotten far in her line of questioning, though, as Landon had thrown a paralysis curse her way. It'd taken effect instantly and, with the doors unlocked, had granted them access to the building. Witnessing the two of them drag her body into a supply closet had given him immense pleasure. She'd gotten away from him once unscathed, but not this time.

The next person to approach them is Casimir, to which Landon repeats the paralysis curse and the dragging of the body to the same supply closet. Darius surmises this means they have their two impersonation targets. Clive casts another illusion around them, this time turning himself into an exact replica of Casimir, Landon into Lane.

There's an edge to the Curser's voice as he says, "Why do I always get the short end of the stick?"

"You should be grateful," Clive says, rounding the front desk to confirm where Felix is residing. "I'm the one who has to do all the talking."

Landon follows him. "Looks like they've paired up." He grimaces at the femininity of his voice before pointing to the map. "He's staying with Arden."

Clive grins. "Even better."

Darius sits back in his chair, releasing a breath as the two men head for the portal that leads to Arden's floor. So far, so good. Everything's going off without a hitch. They arrive at her quarters shortly after and knock. There's a rustling behind the door, followed by a familiar female voice.

"Casimir?" Arden says, looking out the peephole. "Is everything all right?"

"I'm afraid not," Clive responds, his voice sounding older, more seasoned. "The Archmage has requested that you come to her office immediately. She sent us to escort you, given the current status of things." He elbows Landon-masquerading-as-Lane in the arm.

"Right, yes, it's rather urgent," Landon quips. "She's also requested that you bring your weapons."

Clive shoots a steely look at his partner but doesn't say anything. Scolding him would only give away that they aren't who they say they are. Unfortunately, it seems Arden's already caught on.

"Why send the two of you and not her cadre?"

"They've been assigned other tasks pertaining to the lockdown."

A bout of silence as she no doubt observes them from behind the closed door. "So, you're traipsing around Midvale during a lockdown without the protection of a guard *and* without weapons of your own?"

Shit. Darius shakes his head at the exchange. Leave it to Clive to forego the smaller details. Rightly so, his casting abilities are all he's ever needed to protect himself, but Casimir and Lane? They'd certainly be armed.

"Enough of this," Landon mutters as he steps back and braces himself. "We don't need her, at least not right now."

Clive's about to protest when Landon sends a curse straight through the door. A thud sounds from the other side, indicating that Arden has indeed been hit. Additional footsteps sound, followed by shouting. The door swings open to reveal a fuming Felix. "What the fuck, Casimir?"

What can only be fear darkens his eyes as he realizes his mistake, but it's too late. Clive knocks the Amplifier over the head, just as Landon is about to send forth another curse.

"Save it for the grid," Clive admonishes while catching Felix's unconscious body as it falls to the side.

"What about her?" Landon tilts his head at Arden. "You want to just leave her?"

Clive looks around the room at his options. "Station her in the bed," he orders. "Make it look like she's sleeping."

"Already halfway there," he says, dragging her body across the room. He lays Arden on her side, head facing away from the door, before covering her with the sheets. Ever the perfectionist, he fluffs her pillow.

"Are you finished or are you going to tuck her in, too?"

"Of course not," the Curser scoffs.

"Well, come on, then," Clive says hastily. "We need to get to the Vaults before he wakes up."

"Which I would have had complete control over if you'd let me do what I do best," Landon mutters as he follows Clive out the door.

"Too risky. We couldn't jeopardize his ability to amplify. Otherwise this entire operation would be a bust."

"Who says his abilities won't be jeopardized after knocking him unconscious?"

Clive's about to knock *him* unconscious if he doesn't shut the hell up. "Can we just get going? We're wasting time."

For once, Darius is inclined to agree. Sitting at the edge of his seat, the king watches as the two Savant make for the Vaults with their Amplifier in tow.

BRAXTON HORNSBY

THE GRIM MANNER in which Hanslow presents Braxton with a vial is enough to make him think twice about what he's agreed to do. He takes the small glass bulb from the old man, turning it over in his hands. *This . . .* is his ticket out of here? For some reason, he'd expected something grander.

"When was the last time you ate?"

"Breakfast."

Hanslow looks at Stanton to confirm. "He didn't join me for lunch, if that's what you're asking."

Hanslow nods approvingly. "Best to drink this on a semi-empty stomach." He glances to Braxton's sides. "And the crest?"

Braxton points to a nearby chair. "Right there."

Hanslow nods again, rubbing his hands together vigorously as he begins to pace. "Let's go over this once more, shall we?"

From behind him, Stanton groans. "I'm pretty sure it's drilled into him at this point."

Hanslow waves the comment away as if it were a pesky fly buzzing by his ear. "What you're holding is the *only* vial of mugwort and skullcap we have on the premises. It took months to grow herbs like those in conditions like these."

"You've made it rather clear that this is our one and only shot," Stanton chimes in. "As if the boy isn't already nervous enough . . ."

"Pipe down back there, would you?" Hanslow scolds from over his shoulder before bringing his attention back to Braxton. "Now, once you drink this tonic, it'll work rather quickly—within seconds. You'll need to have a firm grip on the crest as the tonic registers your heat signature. It'll pick up on the crest, on illusié, and will transfer you back to the original location of the crest."

"We may as well just throw him into the lion's den at this point," Stanton murmurs. "For all we know, he could end up in Trendalath or worse, back in the Void."

"Is that true?" Braxton asks. "Could I get stuck in the Void again?"

"While anything *is* possible, you need not worry. That crest could not have originated in the Void. Seeing as it's of illusié origin, it must have been created in Aeridon. Now, *where* in Aeridon is hard to say; but I trust that you'll be resourceful enough to find your way to Lirath Cave?"

Braxton nods, patting the roll of parchment tucked in his back pocket. "As long as this map you gave me is accurate."

"Painstakingly so," Stanton says, removing himself from the kitchen table to join them at the hearth. "Once you've found the hidden entrance near Lirath Cave, you'll be able to access my study and open the portal that leads here, to the Medial, allowing both myself and Hanslow to return to Aeridon."

Braxton nods, making as many mental notes as possible so as to not forget a single detail. "And the key to open said portal is hidden within a globe in your study?"

"The one and only."

"And I'm to place this key into the indentation on one of the bookshelves?"

"Precisely."

Braxton chews on his lower lip. "What if the key isn't in the globe? What if someone moved it? Or took it?"

"Possible, but unlikely. That study hasn't seen many visitors."

The response puts Braxton somewhat at ease, until another thought sends him spiraling again. "What if, somehow, your study no longer exists? Or the entrance has been made unreachable?"

Stanton gives him a sad, yet reassuring smile. "If that *does* happen to be the case, at least you'll have gotten out. You'll be able to find the others, tell them what you know—"

Braxton stares at the two men in disbelief. "I'd come back for you, you know. *We* . . . we all would. It may take months, years even, to figure out exactly how, but we wouldn't just leave you here."

"While we appreciate the sentiment," Stanton says, bringing a hand to his chest, "what we said earlier still stands. That, in coming here, we'd already submitted to our fate long before your arrival."

"What Stanton's trying to say," Hanslow says hurriedly, "is that we made peace with our decision long ago. If we happen to return to Aeridon, that would be a pleasantly unexpected outcome. But if we don't . . . well, we've accepted that outcome as well."

"If you think Arden won't do anything and everything it takes to see her father again . . ."

Stanton smiles, blinking back tears. "There is no doubt in my mind that the two of you will do everything in your power to see this through. But do not be blinded by what is out of your control. Promise me that."

Braxton nods. "You have my word."

Stanton takes a few steps forward to retrieve the crest before handing it to Braxton. He pats the boy on the shoulder but doesn't say anything further.

Braxton raises the vial in a toast before bringing it to his mouth. "I'll see you on the other side."

RYDAN HELSTROM

RYDAN STARTLES AWAKE to an empty bed—and sheer panic. He looks around the room, hoping Vira's just using the washroom or warming a kettle for tea. But the room is silent, save for his footsteps, as he darts across it.

"Vira!" he shouts, knowing full well that she isn't here.

He rakes a hand through his hair, stopping at the nape of his neck. What had she said during their last conversation? Something about wanting to contact Xerin—and the how, *the how* . . . was with a pocket watch.

Arden's pocket watch.

"Damnit, Vira." He swears under his breath, not even bothering to change out of his pajamas as he makes for the door, trying to recall exactly where Arden's room is located. He doesn't get far, though, because, in a surprisingly fortunate turn of events, he flings the door open to find Vira standing on the other side. His relief is instantly replaced with concern when he realizes she's panting, completely out of breath.

Face flushed, she grabs hold of Rydan's arms and yanks him into the hall. "Something's wrong," she says, eyes darting every which way. "You need to come with me."

Rydan digs his heels in, wanting more of an explanation. "Where?"

"To Arden's room. And you can save me the lecture because I already know what you're going to say. It doesn't change the fact that you need to come with me." She glances at his hands. "If it comes to it, you should be able to ignite the door down, right?"

Rydan lifts a brow in genuine concern. "Why would I have to do that? Vira, what's going on?"

"We're wasting time," she says, dragging him along. "Arden isn't answering the door. Neither is Felix."

Rydan quickens his stride. "Maybe they went somewhere?"

"During a lockdown?" Vira scoffs.

"Well, *you* did. Who's to say they wouldn't?"

"Doubtful, given how protective Felix is over Arden and her safety."

Like he needed the reminder.

"At the very least, he would have answered. But he didn't. Oh, and that's the other thing . . . it's completely silent on the other side of the door."

"That could be because it's the middle of the night and all the *sane* people are sleeping."

Vira whirls around. "Are you going to take this seriously or not? My intuition is telling me that something isn't right, and it's *especially* because Midvale's on lockdown that I believe this is worth looking into. Not to mention, I wouldn't be able to forgive myself if I were to turn a blind eye. And neither would you."

When they arrive at Arden's door, Vira knocks to prove her point. Just as she'd stated, no one answers. She knocks again, harder this time, and even goes so far as to shout their names. "Arden? Felix? Are you in there? It's Vira!"

More silence. But not just any silence . . .

It's eerie, unnerving. Definitely a cause for concern.

"Light it up," Vira commands, stepping away from the door.

Rydan whips his head toward her. "How about instead of destroying private property, we just stop by the front desk and ask Lane for the master key?"

She grits her teeth. "What part of *there isn't time* aren't you getting?"

"We don't know—"

"Rydan, just shut up and do it!" she shrieks. It's a sound he's never heard from her before—and hopes to never hear again.

"Fine," he mutters, focusing his energy into his hands. They heat up almost instantaneously, flames dancing at his fingertips. He directs the blaze at the door handle, wondering just how furious the Archmage will be once she finds out.

The door handle melts along with the mechanism keeping it locked. Rydan pushes the door open with his foot, ushering Vira inside. They nearly stumble over one another as their eyes adjust to the darkness of the room.

"There," Vira whispers, pointing at the bed.

From where he's standing, he can see a clear lump underneath the sheets. "Like I said before, she's probably just asleep," he hisses.

"Then where's Felix?"

Even though the thought of Felix and Arden sharing a bed is enough to make his stomach roil, he manages to keep his tone even as he says, "Let's focus on one thing at a time."

He takes a few steps toward the bed before accidentally bumping into it. The wooden frame shakes, but Arden doesn't move. From their Cruex days, he knows she isn't a heavy sleeper, so the movement certainly should have woken her. So why didn't it?

"Arden," he whispers as he sits on the edge of the sheets. Gently, he shakes her shoulder before saying her name again. When she doesn't respond, he tightens his grip and shakes a little harder. "Arden, wakc up."

She doesn't move. Doesn't even flinch.

Vira leans in to check her pulse. "She's still breathing."

Rydan shakes her shoulder once more. "Arden." When there's still no response, he carefully lifts one of her eyelids, then the other, surprised to find that both pupils are dilated, irises darting back and forth.

"She seems to be conscious, but unresponsive," Vira says.

"How is that even possible?"

Slowly, Vira shakes her head. "The only time I've seen something even remotely close to this was when . . ." Her words falter, as if she doesn't want to speak them aloud.

"Was *when*, Vira?"

Her voice breaks as she answers, "A paralysis curse."

"The Savant," Rydan starts, following her train of thought. "They have a Curser in their ranks."

"The Savant has infiltrated Midvale, then," Vira says glumly. She turns her attention back to Arden. "We need to get her a tonic—and quick."

"Where are we going to find that on such short notice?"

"Luckily we know someone who can make such things on the spot," Vira says, already heading for the door. "Fellow Ignitor and our very own herbal enthusiast."

Of course. Avery.

ARDEN ELIRI

I DON'T KNOW where I am, but it feels familiar. That liminal space between dreaming and waking. A space I don't get to visit often enough. Always something waiting in the wings, always on to the next . . .

But not here. There is no "next". Nothing waiting for me.

It's peaceful and unbothered. Utterly serene.

Although a touch of sadness lingers.

I don't know why.

Waterfalls cascade all around me, journeying down mountainsides. I reach my hand into one, wanting to feel the crisp water on my skin, but a voice stops me.

Not here, it echoes in my mind. *You're not really here.*

"Of course I am," I say out loud, my voice breaking the hollow silence. I wait for a response, but there isn't one. I shrug, reaching out to touch the water once more when a force stronger than a storm wind knocks me backward and off my feet. "What the hell!" I shout, looking around for the culprit, but the voice only repeats itself, this time more harshly.

Not. Here.

I bring my hands together, brushing dirt from my palms, when something in the distance stops me. The waterfall flows into a river and floating atop it is a wooden ship. Logic tells me that its size doesn't fit the landscape, that it belongs on a larger body of water like an ocean—but that isn't what's concerning me. It drifts closer, and I realize it's almost an exact replica of the one I own. The one I was gifted.

From Felix.

Blurred events begin paving their way through my memory, mere fragments of a timeline. They're chaotic. Out of order. Impossible to piece together in my current state.

"Where is Felix?" I ask aloud.

Not here, unsurprisingly, is the only response I get.

Right. Not here. Because I can't be here if I was somewhere else before this . . . but where? I must be asleep, must be dreaming, but this doesn't feel like a dream. It feels lucid, yet surreal and improbable at the same time.

What had happened?

A fog settles in between my memory and reality. Again, I gaze at the ship in the distance, trying to connect the dots.

Perhaps Felix is on the ship? No, impossible.

Felix isn't here. *I'm* not here.

I worry I'm suffering from amnesia. Could that be why I don't remember anything, *can't* remember anything?

I refocus on the ship. Felix and I were . . . together before this. Yes, that feels right. But *where* were we? What were we doing? Why am I here without him?

I try not to panic as I continue to come up short with logical answers. Nothing makes sense. There's no sequence of events, no order, nothing for me to grasp onto. As soon as I do, it slips away . . . until I look at that ship again. Every time I *think* I'm starting to remember, I end up arriving at the same disjointed conclusion. It's like a never-ending circle.

But then, there's something new. It isn't a memory. Or a fragment. It's a . . . *taste.* Pungent and foul. I gag, unsure as to what's causing my reaction, seeing as I'm not eating or drinking anything. My eyes water, blurring my vision but not the fact that the landscape around me is dissipating. The ship, the river, the waterfalls, the mountainsides . . .

A new sensation grips me.

I'm being pulled, but to where?

Where is there to go?

Knowing that it's futile to fight, I relax into the upward motion. Into the unknown.

FELIX BARLOW

THE SOUND OF whirring jolts Felix to his senses. His first instinct is to shield his eyes from the brightness surrounding him but, in trying to do so, he realizes his hands are bound. His vision being accosted certainly isn't helping the raging headache that's beginning to form.

"He's awake," a voice says from his left.

"About time," another voice echoes.

It takes him a minute to recall where he is, what happened, why he's here . . .

Damn Savant.

Whatever they have planned can't be good.

He squints as a copper-headed man comes into view, immediately remembering that he'd been with Arden when they'd unexpectedly barged in. "Where is she?"

"Where's who?" a coy smile tugs at the Savant's mouth.

"You know who," he growls. It takes every ounce of control not to spit in his sneering face.

"Arden?" Clive taunts. "She'll wake up . . . eventually."

Felix glances at the man standing next to him, realizing who he is. The Savant's Curser. *Great.*

"I told you," Clive says, clicking his tongue against the roof of his mouth. "It's a shame you didn't heed my warning."

Felix glares at him, his rage cresting like a wave. "If you think I'm going to help you with whatever it is you have planned, you're more delusional than I gave you credit for."

Clive takes a step closer so that he's mere inches from the Amplifier's face. "Perhaps you didn't hear me correctly. I said that Arden will wake up *eventually.* If you refuse, we'll make sure that that isn't the case."

Which implies they've used a paralysis curse.

Felix can only hope that *someone* has reached her room by now and is tending to Arden before she's too far gone. But if not . . . well, the quicker he can get out of here, the faster he can rush to her aid. Which leaves him with only one choice.

"So?" Clive presses. "What'll it be?"

"That depends. What do you need?"

Clive claps his hands together with glee before motioning to the massive grid before him. "Any idea what this is?"

Felix shrugs. "Nope. Never seen it before."

"It's a crystalline power grid. I'll give you one guess as to what it's powering."

"Midvale," Felix says, wanting him to hurry up and get on with it.

"Yes and no. This grid powers the entire Veil—and everything in between," Clive explains, making a grandiose gesture at the beaming lights surrounding them. "*You're* here to help our Curser destroy it."

Felix stares at him, slack jawed. "You want me to amplify the curse that'll be put on the crystals?"

"Precisely."

Felix looks to Landon. The same level of terror is reflected in the Curser's eyes. "You're aware that this could kill us, right?"

Landon casts his gaze toward the floor. "It's the only way we can ensure the curse holds for the required amount of time."

"And once the grid is down . . . then what?"

"The protective shield disappears, meaning there's nowhere for you—or any other illusié—to hide," Clive jeers.

So Xerin can finish his work.

Felix swallows the lump in his throat. "This might serve as a timely reminder that *you* are also illusié." He angles his head at Landon. "As are you."

"Illusié under the protection of King Tymond," Landon counters. "How you must wish you could say the same."

How little they know. Mere pawns. But he needn't say more. Assuming they've been ordered by King Tymond to destroy the grid, Xerin must have also had his hand in the decision to do so. Destroying the grid could have its benefits, at least in the meantime.

Felix straightens, hoping his intuition is right about this. "Tell me what you need me to do."

CERYLIA JARETH

CERYLIA STUDIES THE ordinary-looking metallic-framed mirror the Archmage rolls out of an alcove behind her desk. "What is this called again?"

"It's a cheval glass," Cyfrin answers curtly. "Because the springs are located outside the Veil along with our one and only Extractor"—she gives Cerylia a pointed look—"I needed a way to view the contents, a way that doesn't involve leaving the grounds or depending on someone else's abilities."

"A smart move," Cerylia says, trying to hide the contempt in her voice.

"Those are the only kinds of moves we make in Midvale."

Cerylia doesn't respond, watching in silence as Cyfrin readies the mirror. Once it's properly positioned for everyone to see, Cyfrin lifts the speculor so that it's directly across from the small indentation in the frame of the mirror. Slowly, she releases her grip. The speculor hovers in mid-air until it's pulled into the frame's empty space by some invisible force. What they'd all come to witness after that had left them completely and utterly speechless.

King Tymond accessing the jaded spring.

Calling forth the Mallum.

Speaking with it, and it understanding him.

Not only that . . . but *responding* to him.

"So, the Mallum is a . . . *sentient* being?" Cerylia asks, unable to hide the shock in her voice.

"It would appear so," Cyrus says, rubbing his jaw, "which also raises more questions than it does answers."

"Tymond's connection with the Mallum seems to indicate a sort of . . . infatuation," the Archmage muses. "I don't know whether to be concerned or intrigued."

"The ring," Cerylia says suddenly. "It not only summons the Mallum—it also unlocks the gates to the jaded spring."

"And this," Cyrus adds, raising the staff with both hands, "is how he's able to *communicate* with it, for lack of a better word."

"But why would he want to?"

The Archmage looks at the queen, eyes flaring with annoyance. "Infatuation. As I just stated."

Cerylia shakes her head. "That doesn't make sense. The Mallum may show signs of sentience, but it isn't a *person*, with a life and a history and—"

"Perhaps we're overlooking a fundamental possibility," Cyfrin interrupts. "One that I'd hoped wasn't possible."

A wordless exchange passes between the Archmage and the queen. Cyrus looks to each of them, impatiently waiting for their theory.

Cerylia blows out a long breath before saying, "Soul magick."

Cyrus guffaws. "You can't be serious. No one, in the history of illusié, has been successful in even *attempting* such an endeavor. It's wildly dangerous, unpredictable, and downright foolish."

"Then how do you explain what we just saw?" Cerylia presses. "The Mallum shows signs of sentience. It has some level of cognitive ability. It can *feel.*"

"It can *feel?*" Cyrus scoffs. "I think that's taking it a little far, don't you?"

"If you're not going to be helpful," the Archmage warns, "I'm going to have to ask you to leave."

Cyrus stares at her in disbelief. "Was putting my life on the line and bringing the staff directly to you not helpful? Because I can leave and take the staff with me. Just say the word."

"Enough," Cerylia snaps. "No one is going anywhere."

"I wouldn't be so sure about that," Cyrus says, his gaze cast down at his hand. "Look."

Cerylia hears it before she sees it. *Tick, tick, tick.*

Cyfrin rushes to her desk, rifling through one of the drawers before pulling out a pocket watch. It's ticking, just like Cyrus's. "They did it," she whispers. "They managed to destroy the grid."

"Which means . . . what exactly?" Cyrus presses.

"That we're no longer safe here," Cerylia says, the words barely a brush of air. "The Veil has officially been taken down."

DARIUS TYMOND

BY SOME MIRACLE, their efforts to dismantle the Veil's energy source had gone exactly as planned. He'd had the King's Guard on stand-by and, as soon as the grid had powered down, he'd given his troops the all-clear. Having already set sail, they'll be approaching the Isle of Lonia any minute now. Darius, on the other hand, has other means of transportation.

Just one of the many perks of knowing a Shaper.

Right on time, a falcon swoops into the king's chambers, a flash of golden light following.

"I see you got my message," Darius says as he pulls his robes over his shoulders. "My fleet is on their way to Orihia as we speak."

"I must admit, I'm impressed," Xerin says with a fiendish grin. "The Savant is proving to be worthwhile after all."

"As I've stated before, sparing them will only make us stronger in the end. Between the Mallum and the Savant, we'll be unstoppable." Darius revels in the thought. "It's all finally coming together."

"Yes. Well, this is only the first step. Let's see how the rest of it plays out," Xerin suggests as he reaches the door and opens it. "The Veil may be down, but I'm sure Midvale isn't without its contingencies—not with Archmage Galdor in charge."

Darius attempts to bite back his retort, but the urge is too strong. "Without the protection of the Veil, illusié is entirely exposed. Regardless of contingencies, they have nowhere to go, nowhere to hide. This is what we've been waiting for. I suggest we not squander our opportunity."

Xerin bristles at his tone. "Then I suggest you finish whatever it is you're doing here and meet me in the courtyard. Unless you'd rather find your own way to Orihia."

There isn't time for Darius to respond as Xerin stalks out the door, not bothering to close it behind him. Perhaps his next recruit for the Savant should be a Shaper so he won't have to deal with Xerin's shit anymore.

All in due time, he tells himself as he adjusts the amethyst ring—and that time is nearer than he thinks.

BRAXTON HORNSBY

WATER LAPPING AT his face isn't the worst way to wake up. Braxton's eyes flutter open as another small wave crashes into his chin, splashing into his nose and eyes. He coughs, sitting upright on the shore of a freshwater spring, much like the one he and Lane had witnessed Darius entering near Volkharn.

The crest sits idly by but within reach. He crawls over to it, his clothes sticking to his body in all the wrong places, before grabbing it and hugging it to his chest. *He'd made it.*

Where exactly remains to be seen, but he's conscious, breathing, and no longer trapped in the Void, the Veil, or anywhere in between. He pushes himself to his feet, looking at his surroundings for clues as to where he may have landed. If the claw marks on the walls are any indication, he certainly isn't in Lirath Cave—far from it, actually. But he *is* in a cave, no less.

He draws closer to one of the walls, running his index finger along the smooth indentation. It isn't the mark of a bear, but something much, *much* larger . . .

The crest falls from his grip, causing quite the echo in the vast chamber, but with one distinction. It isn't hollow. Braxton turns in a slow circle until he finds exactly what he's looking for: an exit. But not just any exit . . . *a death drop*. He glances over the cliffside, toeing the edge of the massive plunge, wondering how anyone—or *anything*, for that matter—could climb this high. Based on his observations, there's no clear path, no steady incline up this mountain; rather, it's steep, heavily wooded, and mostly hidden. A single creature comes to mind, one that wouldn't need to climb because it could swoop right in. A creature large enough to leave claw marks of that depth and size.

A dragon.

Not to mention, a freshwater spring is the perfect source of water and, based on his view of the horizon, the ocean isn't too far from here. Between that and the dense forest below, there's plenty of opportunity to catch fresh game. A dragon's paradise.

His mother had told him stories of the winged creatures, where they'd originated from. From the details he can recall, that place is nearly identical to this one, which can only mean one thing. He's in Drakken Isle.

Thereby the crest . . . was forged in Drakken Isle.

With this knowledge, finding his way to Lirath Cave *should* be simple—if he weren't literally stuck in a mountaintop cavern with no way down. He takes a few steps back from the cliffside, assessing his options. If only he possessed Xerin's ability to shape or Vira's ability to summon, but no, he's no longer illusié—powerless and at the mercy of one of the most feral creatures in Aeridon.

A draft sweeps into the cavern, his damp clothes doing little in the way of warmth. If he's going to survive this, he needs to be smart. Fortunately, shelter is a given, as is a supply of fresh water. "Food and warmth," he murmurs, beginning his search. He removes his clothes and lays them flat across a large boulder at the entrance to dry. By some miracle, strewn across various stretches of the cavern are tree branches. He gathers them in a bundle before finding a spot to set up camp—near the water, but hidden just enough in case one of the dragons decides to pay a visit. To hope for such a thing might make him insane, but how else is he to eat? Or get out of here?

He's in the process of creating a makeshift firepit when a loud roar sounds nearby. It fills the cavern, embedding itself into the walls. Braxton shrinks back into the boulder, suddenly feeling vulnerable and exposed. He tries to formulate some sort of plan but really, what is there to do in a situation like this except sit and wait? The impending confrontation is inevitable . . . and entirely out of his control.

ARDEN ELIRI

I NEARLY COUGH up a lung as I come back to, glad to be surrounded by familiar faces.

Avery. Vira. Rydan.

"See? Like I said, just under five minutes for the tonic to take effect," Avery boasts.

Rydan shoulders his way past the fellow Ignitor, brows drawn with concern. "Arden, are you okay? What happened?"

I open my mouth to respond, but the taste coating my tongue is so foul that I start gagging. I clutch my throat, trying to swallow, but it only makes things worse.

"Oh, right," Avery says. "Tastes like shit, huh?" He hurries across the room and pours a fresh glass of water from one of the pitchers. "Here, this should help."

"You didn't think to have that prepared ahead of time?"

Avery hands me the glass all the while shooting daggers at Rydan. "I was in a bit of a rush, thanks to you. Herbal tonics are known to be pungent—something you should already know from transporting here."

Seeing that I'm struggling to bring myself upright, Vira props some pillows behind me, scowling as Avery and Rydan continue to squabble. "Would you two stop and just let her talk?"

I give her a gracious smile before downing the entire glass of water. It's only as I'm looking at the three of them that I realize Felix is missing. The memory comes flooding back.

"They took Felix," I say, my voice cracking. "The Savant, I mean. The Caster and . . ."

"The Curser," Avery finishes. "That was a nasty paralysis curse, by the way. He definitely did a number on you. It took almost triple the normal amount of herbs to make an effective tonic."

"Thank you," I say, "even if it did taste horrendous."

Avery shrugs. "Just the nature of the beast."

"Okay, so the Savant took Felix . . . how? And, more importantly, why?" Rydan presses, clearly wanting more information.

"The Savant showed up at our door, masquerading as Casimir and Lane." As soon as I say it, I realize that the two of them have likely suffered the same fate. "We need to find them immediately. Avery, can you whip up a few more tonics? I'd be surprised if they weren't also victims of the same paralysis curse."

"On it," Avery says, heading for the door. "Vira, meet me in the lobby in twenty and we'll start looking for them."

She shakes her head. "I'm going now. We shouldn't waste any time."

"Agreed," Rydan says, his face still clouded with worry. "I'll join you later. I'm going to accompany Arden for a bit and make sure she's regained full mobility."

"You can't," I say quickly. "What if the Archmage doesn't know? You need to find her and inform her as soon as possible."

Rydan levels a steely look at me. "I'm not leaving you here alone. Not with those two lunatics freely roaming Midvale."

I raise a brow. "You forget who you're speaking to."

"I know exactly who I'm speaking to—*and* what you're capable of," Rydan counters. "But I refuse to leave you here alone sustaining injuries from the influence of a paralysis curse."

"Do I look paralyzed to you?" I wiggle my fingers for emphasis. "The tonic worked. You need to find the Archmage. Now. Cerylia, too. You should probably gather the others while you're at it."

"Like I said," he repeats, gritting his teeth, "I'm not leaving you here alone. However, seeing as you're so adamant in advocating for yourself, let's get moving." He pulls me upright only to reveal just how shaky my legs are—and how full of shit I am. "Just as I suspected. You can hardly stand."

"Just . . . give me a minute," I mutter, yanking my arm from his grip. In doing so, I nearly knock myself off balance, only proving his point further.

He sighs as he rakes a hand through his hair. "Avery and Vira are perfectly capable of handling this. For now, we need to be patient and wait."

For once, I don't argue.

The look on my face must have him feeling all kinds of guilty because the urgency in his voice suddenly dissipates.

"Do you have any idea as to why they'd take Felix? What they'd need him for?"

I blow out a long breath. "I've been asking myself the same question."

Rydan drops his shoulders in disappointment. "Felix is smart," he says, although the reassurance in his tone is jaded. "I'm sure he'll do everything in his power to stop the Savant or, at the very least, hinder them."

I nod unconvincingly, trying to ignore the chill that's lodging in my chest. Whatever the Savant want with Felix isn't nearly as concerning as what they'll want with *me* once they learn what I'm capable of . . . which, as it turns out, is something only Felix and I know at the present moment.

"We need to get you some sustenance. A meal is in order," Rydan offers, breaking my train of thought. "I'll see what I can find."

I force a smile as he leaves the bedside to start rummaging through the kitchen cabinets, even though we both know it's going to take a hell of a lot more than a single meal to help me regain my strength.

FELIX BARLOW

AMPLIFYING THE GRID may as well be a death wish. The rhythmic sway beneath him indicates that he's currently on the move, but not of his own accord. He's being carried. A slight turn of his head dashes his hopes of it being a fellow Caldari. He'd recognize that unruly head of hair anywhere. It's the Savant's Caster. He must have fallen unconscious after amplifying the curse on the crystals—an expenditure of energy he never could have prepared for.

Metal clanks between his wrists, and he doesn't so much as need to open his eyes to confirm that his hands are bound once again. Not that it matters in the slightest. His abilities are completely spent.

What illusion Clive has cast to get them back through Midvale's halls and into the lobby is beyond him but, in no time at all, they've reached the massive double doors and are pushing through them. His head weighing a ton, Felix strains his neck, lifting it as much as he can manage. Arden's name forms on his lips. *Is she okay? Is she still under the paralysis curse?*

So many questions, yet no voice to speak them with.

He uses what little energy he has to knock his metal bindings against the Savant's mid-back, but his plea for attention goes unnoticed. A grunt is the only reply as the Caster continues walking. The view of the doors grows distant, his salvation along with it.

"Release me," he orders, refusing to give in to the feeling of helplessness.

"Why would I do that?" the Caster retorts.

"You did what you came here to do. You no longer have use for me. I'll only slow you down."

Clive scoffs. "We're moving along just fine."

If these were normal circumstances, Felix would have no problem taking the Caster down, the brunt of his weight and all. But with his abilities depleted and energy completely drained, he may as well be a sack of potatoes—which is exactly how the Caster is carrying him.

Felix wets his cracked lips, his voice hoarse as he asks, "What more could you need from me?"

"That isn't up to me, mate," Clive says as he adjusts the position of his shoulder. "But I'll bet you can guess whose it is."

As if on cue, a menacing laugh sounds from the end of the bridge. While Felix's interactions with the king have been few and far between, there's no mistaking that laugh. It's the sound of someone who's won . . . who intends to *continue* winning.

"Where do you want him?" Clive asks as they approach.

"He's bound?"

"He is."

"Here's as good a place as any."

Before Felix can fully comprehend the king's response, Clive hoists his body from his shoulder onto the unforgiving ground below. Felix grunts, dirt spewing from his mouth before being pulled to his knees by the King's Guard. His eyes flick to the robed man before him.

"You've served us well," Darius says with an approving nod. "If it weren't for you, I wouldn't be standing here right now."

Felix scowls. "It certainly wasn't by choice."

"No?" Darius angles his head, gleefully accepting the challenge. "According to a reliable source, you've kept one foot in our business and are soon to reap the rewards. You wouldn't call that a choice?"

"To willingly bring you to Midvale while it stands defenseless?" Felix bares his teeth. "No—no, I would not call that a choice."

"Then you must be blind to your own actions, Sir Barlow, because everything you've said—everything you've *done*—has led you straight here. Including this paltry act to buy your friends more time."

He doesn't bother to hide the coy smile that's tugging at the corner of his mouth. "It worked, didn't it?"

The king purses his lips. "As you'll soon discover, it isn't nearly enough," Darius says as he brings his hands together, the amethyst ring glowing in the dim cavern light. "I'll make sure your friends know who to thank for putting me in such a foul mood." Black mist swirls around him, the King's Guard retreating a step in the Mallum's wake. "I won't stop until every last ounce of illusié is contained." He looks to Felix, eyes shadowed. "Not to worry. I'll save you for last."

Felix can only gulp as the formidable mist sweeps across the bridge and advances to the doors of Midvale.

RYDAN HELSTROM

RYDAN CAN'T HELP but grimace as he watches Arden attempt to eat. Not only had the paralysis done a number on her mobility, it'd also affected her ability to keep anything down. Water? Fine. But anything food-related?

Disastrous.

"We need to get going," she croaks, placing a hand on her chest. "The others are probably waiting for us."

Rydan refills her glass of water. "We're not going anywhere until you can keep something down for longer than thirty seconds."

"I am," she counters, raising the glass of water. "Fluids."

"Nice try." Rydan sighs. "While hydration is necessary, so is sustenance." He angles his head at the half-eaten sandwich he'd made and the untouched fruit on her plate.

"I know I may not look it, but I'm already feeling better, stronger." She hops up from the chair, then paces back and forth across the room.

While he's somewhat impressed, he doesn't want to admit it and encourage her even more, so he merely raises a brow in response.

She grunts, joining him back at the table. "I need you to trust me when I say that I'm okay and that I *will be* okay. I'm worried that if we don't leave soon—"

A whoosh followed by a flash of green light interrupts her train of thought as Haskell appears in the middle of the living room.

"Ever heard of knocking?" Arden jokes.

"Given what you've just been through, would you have answered?" her brother retorts, rushing over to her. "Vira told me everything. I came as fast as I could."

Arden jumps to her feet, pulling her brother into a firm embrace. "What about Casimir and Lane?"

A shadow falls over Haskell's face. "The lobby's currently off limits."

Now it's Rydan's turn to ask questions. He rises to his feet. "What's happened?" He studies the Transporter's face with sheer intensity. "What aren't we aware of?"

"That's precisely why I came to get you . . . to transport you to the Archmage's office, where the rest of the Caldari are waiting."

A chill runs down Rydan's spine. "He's here, isn't he? King Tymond."

Haskell only lowers his head.

"This is all our fault. We brought them straight here," Arden whispers, mortified. "Tymond, his Savant, the King's Guard . . . the Mallum."

Haskell nods his head. "It seems they needed Felix in order to dismantle the grid that powers the Veil—"

"Rendering us completely and utterly exposed," Rydan finishes.

"If we're going to save as many illusié as we can from the Mallum's fate, then we need to go. Right now."

Arden shudders, already green in the face. "Well, if this isn't poor timing . . ."

"Where's Avery and his tonics when you need them?" Rydan jokes, although he's half serious.

Haskell grins, digging in his pocket before producing two vials. "Fortunately," he says with a wink, "I've got you covered."

CERYLIA JARETH

INSTANT RELIEF WASHES over Cerylia as Haskell appears in the middle of the Archmage's office with Arden at his side. Rydan flanks him on the left, all color leeched from his face. Even so, his expression remains steadfast. Cerylia scans the room, doing a quick count in her head.

Who's missing?

Avery. Lane. Felix.

The hope in Arden's face comes crashing down as she, too, looks around the room at her fellow Caldari.

"Seeing as we're all assembled—"

"We are not," Cerylia interrupts.

Annoyed, the Archmage angles her head at the queen. "I assume the others will join us in due time." She flicks her gaze to Haskell in silent order to retrieve the missing Caldari.

"I can't make any promises," he grunts, "but I'll report back with whatever I happen to find."

"No," Cerylia says firmly. "We need you here, for this discussion. The others will have to find their way to us in another fashion."

"I don't think anyone else will be joining us anytime soon." With all eyes pointed at her, Arden lowers her gaze to the floor. "The fact of the matter is the Savant is here, as is King Tymond." She nearly chokes on the formality, the inherent respect imbued in such a title—one Darius Tymond certainly does not deserve. Cerylia can feel the disgust radiating from her as if it were her own. "Felix was taken captive. As for the others . . . well, my instincts tell me it'd be wise to proceed without them." The harshness in her tone causes unease to settle across the room, to which she quickly adds, "At least for the time being." It does little to soften the blow.

The Archmage nods in understanding. "I think we're in a stronger position than we realize. Just look around this room."

"And?" Vira presses, clearly not loving the idea of leaving her childhood friend alone to defend himself.

"If I'm not mistaken, everyone here has dealt with King Tymond in one form or another? And the Savant? The Mallum?"

The Caldari murmur their agreement except for Vira.

"A narrow victory, if you ask me."

The Archmage locks eyes with the Summoner. "But a victory nonetheless."

"So what are our options?" Estelle asks. "We can't hide in here forever."

"We're not hiding, we're strategizing," Haskell says. "Speaking of strategizing, how many Transporters are currently in Midvale? If I can round them up, perhaps we can get as many illusié out of here as possible."

"That could work," Vira agrees. "I can also summon whatever creatures we need for our escape—"

"While I appreciate those thought-provoking solutions, neither will be necessary," Cyfrin says. "With the grid down, nowhere is safe. Not Midvale, not Orihia . . . Aeridon may as well be a black hole for illusié."

"At least we'd be dispersed," Cerylia counters, "making the Mallum's job more difficult and more time-consuming."

"It's a double-edged sword," Opal says. "Dispersing illusié is only a temporary solution. We're stronger together—and together, we can fight."

"But can we win?" All eyes turn to Rydan. "In theory, we know what we're up against. But the reality? Well, the reality is that we'll lose. Not just our abilities, but our lives."

"Maybe it isn't the Mallum we should be focusing on," Arden says, brows furrowed, "but the person wielding it."

"Tymond," Rydan murmurs. "And that damn ring he wears."

Cerylia scoffs. "You'll have to pry it from his cold, dead hands."

"I'd be lying if I said that isn't something I've dreamed about ever since fleeing Trendalath," Arden retorts. "Hell, even before then."

Rydan nods. "You aren't the only one."

Without warning, a resounding shriek echoes in the halls, followed by another and another, signaling only one thing: Midvale is officially under attack. The entire room appears rattled by the sound except for the Archmage. With bated breath, they await her guidance.

"So, we're agreed, then," the Archmage declares. "We stay and fight."

"To the end." Cerylia steps forward, speaking for the group as she says, "We are at your disposal, Archmage." Her gaze travels around the room, each Caldari nodding in firm agreement. "Whatever you need."

DARIUS TYMOND

WITH THE KING'S GUARD stationed near
the entry doors, Darius sets the Mallum free to roam the
grounds of Midvale. Who would have thought the lobby would
have so many unsuspecting bystanders? Grinning, he follows
the trajectory of the entity as it rips through the halls of the
institution, absorbing ability after illusié ability.

Most of the unfortunate souls who find themselves in the
path of the Mallum are eager to fight back . . . only to discover
that their efforts are futile. It's a swift surrender, the look of
devastation on their faces apparent as they're forced to give
up the gifts they were born with.

Gifts *he* should have had all along.

Where it wasn't before, with the Mallum, this is now
entirely possible. And within reach.

Darius turns his attention back to the frenzied sight before him. Down they go, falling like dominoes, each illusié more helpless than the last when, suddenly, a wall of flame shoots across his path, briefly separating him from the Mallum.

No doubt the work of an Ignitor.

Darius stops in his tracks, hoping that the perpetrator is one ex-Cruex, Rydan Helstrom, but is dismayed to find that it's no one special—just a young man with olive eyes and auburn hair and, apparently, a penchant for defeat. But it's who steps in front of the Ignitor, in foolish defense, that ultimately makes the situation worth his while.

Lane bares her teeth at the king as animals come rushing into view. Although the beasts can't physically alter the state of the Mallum, what with their sharp claws and biting canines, they prove to be a potent distraction. Lane's antics allow for enough time to escape through a portal that must lead to Midvale's additional floors.

The rage that surges through him is surprising and unexpected but, seeing as she'd escaped with Braxton in the tunnels in a similar fashion, he supposes it shouldn't be. Whether she realizes it or not, she's just provided him with some vital information—information he'd deduced but hadn't confirmed. If Lane is here, Braxton must be here as well.

She's just made herself his number one target.

And as long as he finds her, he'll find the others as well.

The Caldari don't stand a chance.

Although the beaming portal beckons, it's the desk situated to his left that wins his attention. He pauses mid-step, not wanting to waste any time. The knowledge that the portal could take him to one of hundreds of floors is overwhelming in and of itself. Add the fact that he's unfamiliar with the landscape and that puts him at even more of a disadvantage. Perhaps the Caldari are in a single wing of Midvale, all stationed together, like lambs to the slaughter.

Now wouldn't that be something?

His best bet is to rummage through the drawers of the desk in hopes of finding a map of Midvale's current residents. It doesn't take much digging, however, because it's on his second try that a yellow orb floats out. Much to his surprise and delight, it doesn't seem to be locked or inaccessible. A map of Midvale is revealed.

One name sticks out to him immediately.

Arden Eliri.

According to the map, she's in the northeastern wing, chambers three through seven, along with fellow ex-Cruex, Rydan Helstrom.

Darius takes a mental snapshot of the location of their rooms before readying himself to direct the Mallum, the Savant, and the King's Guard when another thought occurs to him. He refers back to the map, searching endlessly for the Archmage's quarters.

Call it a hunch, but wouldn't the commanding officer gather as many in her ranks as possible to discuss their strategy moving forward? Especially with something as dangerous as the Mallum ravaging the premises?

Yes, that's where he'll go first—with knowledge of the northeastern wing tucked securely in his back pocket.

BRAXTON HORNSBY

TIME PASSES IN a blur of sleep, hunger, and confusion. Braxton's starting to think that perhaps this cave is destitute, no longer a refuge for dragonkind, but a sad, abandoned hole in the side of a mountain. If it weren't, surely one of the majestic creatures would have flown in by now, but the treetops remain ever so still, the skies empty, save for the stars that make their appearance at night. While it's better than being in the Void, it isn't by much. Thinking straight hasn't come easy either, especially paired with a grumbling stomach, so any solutions to leave the cavern—without leading to his demise—are difficult to come by.

He's about to settle in for the night when a loud noise grabs his attention. Startled but curious, he creeps to the edge of the cave. The starlight is just bright enough to bring things into view, but the source of the noise remains hidden in the night. What he'd heard had more likely than not been a large bird or a bat—not a dragon. What any other winged animal would be doing this high up in the mountains at this time of night is a mystery to him, but perhaps there are other creatures as elusive as the dragon that he knows nothing about.

Disheartened, he trudges back over to his makeshift bed, the rumbling of his stomach near deafening, when, suddenly, he feels a giant rush of air. There's another noise, louder this time, as the sound of flapping wings make themselves known.

Definitely a dragon.

Feeling the need to take cover and hide, Braxton rolls behind a boulder, pressing himself against it as if it were a lifeline. He isn't prepared for this. How does one confront a dragon without being burned to a crisp, brutally slaughtered, or eaten alive? He's debating the endless number of outcomes, none of them good, when something entirely unexpected happens.

He hears a laugh.

Feeling as though his ears are deceiving him, he slowly peeks out from behind the boulder to see not one, but *two* familiar faces riding atop what is indeed a dragon.

"We can see you, you know," Hanslow says as he slides down the beast's side. "And Goldie here can certainly smell you."

His cover blown, Braxton pushes himself upright, not quite believing his eyes. "How did you find me?"

Stanton gives Goldie a pat on the back of the neck, her metallic scales gleaming even in the dim light of the cave. "Most people don't know this, but dragons are a lot like bloodhounds. With your scent lingering on the tonic bottle, Goldie here was able to track you down rather quickly."

Braxton stares at him, dumbfounded. "How did you escape the Medial?"

"Before I answer such a loaded question, I suppose I should preface by saying that we come bearing both good news and bad news."

Bag in hand, Hanslow stalks over to Braxton's campsite, shaking his head as he observes the meager setup. "It appears we've arrived just in time." He turns, shooting the Caldari a sidelong glance. "When was the last time you ate?"

Braxton tries not to let his embarrassment get the better of him, but he can feel his cheeks flush with color. "I haven't eaten since I arrived."

Hanslow looks him up and down, clicking his tongue against the roof of his mouth. "I could have guessed as much. Fortunately, we also come bearing gifts." He holds up the bag for emphasis. "The largest hare we could find."

Braxton nods in appreciation, his mouth watering at the sight. "Here, let me help—"

"No, no," Hanslow insists, holding a hand up. "Conserve your energy. This won't take long."

"Hopefully not as long as it took you to catch it," Stanton says as he gracefully dismounts the dragon. "Otherwise we'll be here all night." He gives Braxton a wink before walking over and clapping a hand on his shoulder.

"Honestly, I don't care how long it takes, I'm just glad to be in the company of someone other than myself. Which brings me back to my original question . . ."

"Ah, yes. How we arrived here." Stanton furrows his brows. "The good news is we were able to leave the Medial due to the grid going down. The bad news is . . . the grid is down."

"The grid? What grid?"

"The crystalline grid that powers all sites constructed by illusié. The Veil, the Void, the Medial, Midvale—"

"Orihia," Braxton whispers, suddenly feeling very excited by the prospects this news brings. "Orihia is powered by the crystalline grid, too, I take it?"

"Indeed, it is."

"I don't know what could be bad about this. Ever since losing my deviating abilities to the Mallum, I haven't been able to travel anywhere with the Caldari. What's worse, I ended up in the Void, so this is welcome news."

"But, from what I understand, your friends—including my son and daughter—are currently in the Veil. At Midvale. And if there isn't anything keeping non-illusié out . . ."

"Then that means anyone can get in." Braxton swallows the lump that's forming in his throat. "Including my father."

Stanton gives him a solemn nod. "And the Mallum."

Braxton's blood chills. "They're in danger. We have to go to them straight away."

"Dinner is served!" Hanslow calls from the other side of the cave.

Stanton pays him no mind. "Do you still have the crescent fire in your possession?"

"I do." Braxton hurries over to the campsite, pulling the crest from behind where Hanslow's sitting.

"Good," Stanton says. He follows Braxton's lead, bagging up the cooked rabbit, despite Hanslow's silent protests. "We'll be taking this to-go." He motions toward the dragon, giving Braxton a wink. "After you."

ARDEN ELIRI

I SLIP THE chakrams into their holsters, my breath catching at the familiar feeling of gearing up for what's likely to be my most important mission yet. I close my eyes as I fasten my hair into a single braid at the nape of my neck, my fingers working deftly like so many times before.

I've faced the Mallum.

On more than one occasion.

And I've lived to tell the tale.

Why would this time be any different?

Because Tymond wants you dead, a cruel inner voice whispers. He wants us *all* dead.

The thought lingering, I finish securing my weaponry—a couple of daggers in each boot, for good measure—before slinking toward the door. I press my ear against it, expecting to hear something out of the ordinary, but only silence greets me. Normal in most cases, except for the fact that there's a madman roaming the halls.

Correction—mad*men.*

I listen by the door for a few more minutes before deeming it safe to leave the confines of my room. My first instinct is to find Rydan and pair up, but something stops that thought process in its tracks. Two familiar faces stand before me, ones I'd sincerely hoped to never see again.

Certainly not under these conditions.

Ezra Denholm and Percival Garrick.

Two of my least favorite Cruex members.

A wolfish grin crosses Ezra's face the moment he lays eyes on me. "Arden Eliri," he says, his tone dripping with derision. "We've been looking for you."

Memories of sparring Ezra in the bullpen surface, particularly the brutality with which he'd come after me. Internal misogyny at its finest. I'd never gotten along with him, never felt the pull to listen to him, even when Tymond had appointed him captain of our ranks. The assignment was laughable and he knew it. I've only ever been the one to see through him—which has made him despise me all the more.

"As Aeridon's elite assassins, it seems to have taken you a while," I prod, wanting to get under his skin. "I'm sure that didn't please His Majesty in the slightest. Do I sense trouble in paradise?"

"Shut your mouth, traitor scum," he snarls, hand reaching for his serrated scimitar. "Unless you'd like a matching wound to go with the original."

Instinctively, my hand goes to my left tricep, at the scar his cowardly attack had left behind.

His cobalt eyes flash with something lethal. "So you *do* remember."

"Your penchant for foul play?" I nod. "Like it was yesterday. You know, it takes a true coward to wield their weapon after being defeated in the ring. And by a *girl*, no less."

He narrows his eyes, seething. "If it were foul play, King Tymond would have called it. But he didn't."

"It's like you two were made for each other." I spit at his feet, even though he's standing a good distance down the hall. "Which will make it all the more satisfying to bring him your head when I'm finished with you."

Clearly the third wheel, Percival looks between us before stating the obvious. "I never would have guessed we used to stand together, *fight* together . . . as allies."

I turn my gaze to him. "Perhaps I should take care of you first. That way, I can fully savor the moment your partner's heart stops beating."

Percival draws his glaive in defense. "I'd like to see you try."

I reach behind me, fingers gripping the handles of my chakrams. "Perhaps it'd be wise to take you both out simultaneously. Two birds with one stone and all that." I grin, waiting for them to make the first move.

And, just as I assumed they would, they do.

Ezra charges first, his stocky build blocking my view of Percival, who's surely just steps behind him. Predictable as ever, Ezra brings his blade down in an attempt to match my original wound by slicing my right arm, but I dodge the attack, whirling around him so that my elbow drives into the back of his neck. He stumbles, nearly falling to his knees, then turns to look at me with a baffled expression. I may not be actively practicing as an assassin, but that doesn't mean I've forgotten. It also doesn't mean I've squandered my unique skillset. On the contrary, it's amazing how muscle memory returns, making me even sharper than before.

Seeing his comrade close to defeat so early on must spark something in Percival because he comes at me with a vengeance. His attacks are unhinged and much less predictable than Ezra's, and as I parry each one, I can't help but grin. I've always loved a challenge. That hasn't changed.

"You didn't deserve to be with us then and you don't deserve to be with us now," Percival growls, backing away momentarily to catch his breath. "You're lucky we tolerated you for as long as we did."

"You and I both well know that *I* was the one doing the tolerating," I counter. "Being stuck with you lot was, in all honesty, rather embarrassing. Just look at you now." I click my tongue against the roof of my mouth in disdain. "You're breathless, out of shape, and in way over your head."

From behind me, Ezra growls. I can sense his attack before he has the opportunity to strike true. Another failed attempt has him seeing red as he goes on a similar striking spree as Percival, except this time, the lowly Cruex joins in. It's times like these where I'm thankful I chose a dual-weapon to master all those years ago. Not only are my chakrams fun to wield—they're practical, too.

Percival makes another snide comment as he lunges for my throat and it's then I realize that I'm growing tired of the back and forth. When something's no longer a challenge, it's time to end it. I loop a chakram over and around the back of my head, a move that leaves Percival confused and throws him off his game. It lasts long enough for me to kick Ezra right in the kneecap before decapitating the unsuspecting Cruex. Percival's head lands with a sickening thud, his blonde head of hair covered in crimson. His headless body collapses to the ground in a heap of useless limbs.

Ezra cries out as his comrade's head rolls right in front of him, amber eyes still open and staring into the abyss. He bares his teeth, glaring at me, but doesn't rise.

"Get on your feet," I order.

Ezra hisses but doesn't move.

"Stand up and fight me!" I yell, suddenly needing the adrenaline rush that comes with exacting such revenge. "Or does the great Ezra Denholm surrender?"

He scoffs, pushing himself to his feet. "Know thy opponent."

I know him better than he thinks. The snake that he is goes for the low blow and aims for my Achilles heel, but not before I stomp on his hand, causing his blade to clatter to the floor. I'm not usually one to beat a man while he's down but that last attempt has me reeling. It was desperate, cowardly, and wildly unsuccessful.

Throwing one of my chakrams at his feet, I use my free hand to pull him up by the front of his uniform—the same uniform I used to wear with pride. He squirms, trying to get away, but he isn't fast enough. I slice his left tricep and if the yelp that follows is any indication, it's a deep cut.

"Well, would you look at that?" I deadpan. "We match."

Before he can respond with another snarky comment, my blade comes crashing down directly in the center of his skull, splitting it clean in half. Blood pools at my feet, staining the carpet crimson. Something feral washes over me as I bend down and swipe my index finger across the growing stain, then smear the sticky substance onto my cheeks as if it were warpaint. As tempting as it is to bag their heads and take them with me, I know there isn't time.

Two down, countless more to go.

༄ ༄ ༄

It's all a blur.

I rip through the halls, determined to take out as many of Tymond's men as humanly possible. Not once have I relied on my illusié abilities, only my physical prowess. It feels good to get back to my roots, even if those roots originated in malevolence. Turmoil, destruction, and death—all at the hands of the Cruex. All at the hands of the man who shaped them . . . who shaped *me*.

I'm passing by another string of the Mallum's victims when I hear it: a bloodcurdling scream. Following the direction of the sound, I dash down the hall, veering right, then left, before spotting shadows lurking at the end of the corridor. I draw in a breath, positioning myself in an alcove that gives very little visibility of whatever's heading toward me.

My hearing becomes my saving grace.

More than one pair of footsteps grows louder and more defined as they approach, the present chill in the air unmistakable. I've felt this sensation before—the eerie, spine-tingling awareness that something is about to go horribly wrong. That I'll be at the center of it.

I remain hidden, unseen, my back flush against the wall of the alcove. A dense mist appears, snaking along the corridor like a deadly vine, searching for its next unsuspecting victim. If only it *were* a vine, I could sever it with the blade of my chakram, but my weapons are useless in this scenario—my magick even more so.

But where the Mallum goes, Darius follows.

This is my chance.

I pull my chakrams from their holsters, crossing my arms over my chest as I wait in the wings for the footsteps to reach me. They're slow, calculated . . . familiar.

I steady my breathing, my muscles tensing for the upcoming attack. *I strike to kill,* I remind myself.

Ruthless.

Brutal.

Just the way he'd taught me.

It ends here. Whether it's Tymond, his Savant, the King's Guard, I will not stop until every last one of them is slain. And when I finally pry that ring from the king's cold, dead hands, I'll ensure the Mallum never sees the light of day again. Illusié will be safe. Furthermore, it'll be celebrated. And Aeridon will know harmony once again.

A gold glimmer catches my eye as it passes by on a head of white. *Tymond.* As much as I want to knock that stupid crown from his undeserving head, I know that the purpose of this blow is to kill. I leap from the shadows, airborne, a mere blur of limbs slicing straight across the king's chest. I allow my sudden burst of momentum to carry me across the hall. I roll, landing diagonally on my knees in a crouched position. The king halts in his tracks, hands reaching for the red that's now blooming across his chest. I pant as I watch in satisfaction, briefly wishing I'd opted for the neck instead, when I notice that something is very, *very* wrong with this picture. Not only is he alone—no King's Guard or Savant in sight—but something else is missing . . .

My eyes dart to his hands. To his left, to his right, then back again. To where the ring should be.

Where the fuck is it?

Panic sets in as I realize the gravity of the situation.

That wasn't the king wasn't the king wasn't the king—

If I weren't already on my knees, I'd have dropped to them.

What have I done?

The illusion around me falters, giving way to reality.

How could I have been so careless?

Of course Darius wouldn't be walking the halls alone.

Of course he'd be surrounded by the King's Guard.

Clive snickers.

No.

The face of the person I'd just assassinated appears in front of me.

Shaggy auburn hair I'd run my fingers through.

Midnight-colored eyes I'd stared into countless times.

Cheeks I'd caressed, lips I'd pulled toward my own.

My stomach clenches and turns, bile rising in my throat as Felix's gaze locks on mine. The corner of his mouth twitches in shock, but his eyes grow lighter—weightless, even—as if to comfort me . . . as if to say that what I'd just done is okay.

But it isn't. Far from it.

A sound I didn't know I could make wrenches free from my throat. Felix falls to his knees, his bound wrists clutching his chest, before collapsing sideways onto the floor. In that moment, I don't care if the Mallum exists or not, if it's behind me, waiting to pull what last bit of illusié I have left—

Because all I see is red.

I lunge for Clive, knowing full well he's probably just going to cast another illusion around me, which is exactly what he does. But not before I see a flash of green light and

my brother, saint that he is, grabbing Felix's slain body and
disappearing from sight.

FELIX BARLOW

HE'D SEEN IT coming and yet he'd been powerless to stop it. It was almost his undoing, seeing the sheer agony on her face as she'd realized what she'd done, who she'd sliced with such deadly precision.

In those final moments where they'd locked eyes, he'd wanted nothing more than to assure her that it was okay. To reach out, pull her into a comforting embrace, and whisper that death by her hand is the only way he'd want to go.

But he hadn't gotten the chance. She hadn't come to him. Understandably so, white-hot rage had consumed her.

"Don't you give up on me yet," a gruff voice says as he's carried down a familiar corridor. Haskell shoulders his way into the doors leading to the infirmary, calling frantically for a Healer, but there isn't one in sight. Felix can feel the blood oozing down his chest, his heart pumping in sporadic bursts.

His vision begins to fade in and out. One minute he's hot, the next, cold. He isn't going to make it. It's a stark realization. He's going to die in Midvale, but at least he won't die a prisoner—he'll die in the arms of a friend.

He opens his mouth to speak, to tell Arden's brother not to waste his energy or his time on the inevitable, but Haskell shakes his head. "You bastard, don't you dare."

"Tell her—"

"Don't," Haskell says through labored breaths as he picks up the pace down another hall, winding toward another corridor. "Just hang on."

How he wants to. Just for a little while longer. If only to see her face one last time. To say goodbye.

Instead, he feels his grip loosen, the color draining from his face. His chest shudders, heart slowing to a stop, a final breath leaving his lips. His eyes drift close, mind blank, as he starts to fall deeper and deeper into a forever sleep . . .

The last thing he expects to see is a flash of golden light and those unnerving crimson eyes.

Do you have the information I seek? Xerin's voice floats across his mind.

What does it matter? Felix questions through the tether. *I'm as good as dead, but at least I'm finally free of this contract.*

A low rumble of laughter. *You and I both know you won't leave Arden suffering with the guilt of killing you. You grew too attached . . . I warned you.*

Felix doesn't have a response. The truth is hard to hear.

I'm the only one who can save you now. I'll ask once more . . . do you have the information I seek?

How? Felix questions, hating himself for even considering striking another deal with the Grey clan. *I'm already dead.*

Soul magick, Xerin hisses. *Your body may have shut down, but your consciousness hasn't. How else would you explain this conversation?*

It's his only bargaining chip, sharing the information he possesses. If he doesn't, it'll cost him his life.

You'll bring me back? Free and clear of all obligations?

I will.

I have your word?

You have my word.

Although it's growing murky, Felix reaches into the depths of his mind, pulling each delicate thread until it's at the forefront.

As we suspected, Arden is a Channeler through and through. I witnessed her ability in person—felt it, too. She may be inexperienced at wielding it, but full development is on the horizon.

Is that all? Xerin's tone indicates that he's unimpressed.

The other spring, the one where the crescent fire was forged . . . it's in Drakken Isle. Felix pauses, unsure if revealing more information is in his best interest.

Your source?

Templar Odell, the Archmage's second-in-command.

Very well, Xerin responds, sounding pleased. *Your service is appreciated, Sir Barlow.*

Now, about bringing me back—

As I said before, you have my word, Xerin interrupts, his voice growing sinister. *I'll bring you back . . . when the time is right.*

CERYLIA JARETH

IT'S A GOOD thing the Archmage had permitted the queen to briefly return to her chambers, even if just to gather a few belongings, because if she'd been forced to stay a moment longer, she wouldn't have been stopped by Haskell—carrying a fallen Caldari—in the hall.

"We're losing him," Haskell pants, blood streaking his chest and forearms. "We need to act quickly. The Healers have fled the infirmary." He glances behind the queen, no doubt expecting Opal to be there.

"She's with the Archmage," Cerylia says, answering his unspoken question. "How did this happen?"

Haskell sighs as Cerylia ushers him into the room, carefully laying Felix on the couch near the hearth. "I don't know. All I heard was Arden scream, so I transported as quickly as I could—"

"Is she alive?"

"Yes. Very much alive . . . and furious." Haskell leans over the back of the couch, hands shaking as he checks Felix's pulse. "Given the current situation, I'm thinking Opal might be our only option."

Cerylia weighs the suggestion—the pros, as well as the many, many cons. "You might be right. However, if we're going to invert time, we need to go back to *before* the grid is taken down. It's the only way to ensure that all illusié remain safe, to stop the attack before it even has the chance to begin." She chews on her bottom lip, deep in thought. "But," she continues, "we cannot guarantee that things won't turn out differently . . . worse, somehow."

"Hard to imagine them getting much worse, being under attack by the one entity that can completely wipe our kind from existence."

"Indeed, it is a rather grim outcome, especially for Felix here." She eyes the door, knowing she may very well be sending Haskell to his death. "Are you equipped to find Opal, to bring her back here without hesitation?"

"Correct me if I'm wrong, but transporting seems like the most logical way to go. And the quickest."

Cerylia gives him a firm nod. "I'll look after Felix." *And come up with a Plan B,* she adds silently.

Haskell leaves as quickly as he'd arrived but before Cerylia can consider their predicament further, there's a knock on her door. She's about to ask who it is when none other than the Archmage's voice sounds from the other side. It's odd, seeing as Cerylia told her she'd return in a short while, but perhaps she'd taken too long. Archmage Galdor is nothing if not impatient.

Upon opening the door, Cyfrin sweeps by her, acting as if knowledge of Felix's situation had already found its way to her. She makes for the couch, looking the Caldari over, assessing the damage.

"I take it you ran into Haskell on your way here?" Cerylia questions.

"Hmm?" Cyfrin gives the queen a blank stare. It's unnerving . . . and out of character.

"About Felix," Cerylia says cautiously. "Haskell must have told you."

"In passing, yes," the Archmage muses, checking for a pulse. "But it certainly isn't the only reason I'm here." She turns over a shoulder, locking eyes with the queen. "Does this look familiar?"

Cerylia tries not to gape at the item she produces from the pocket of her cloak: the key from the Vaults. The very key she'd stolen to open the locked door located just steps away from where they stand . . . where she'd taken something that does not belong to her.

Cerylia gulps, hating the feeling of being caught red-handed. "Curiosity got the better of me," she admits, knowing better than to feign ignorance. "I can assure you, I only had the best of intentions—"

"Is that what you call taking the soul gem? The best of intentions?"

Cerylia casts her gaze toward the ground, cheeks burning with humiliation. "I thought, in a time of crisis, it'd be worth having immediate access to it."

"That it would," Cyfrin agrees, "but did you ever consider that perhaps it was placed behind a locked door for a reason?"

It feels like a rhetorical question, but the expectant look on Cyfrin's face indicates she's waiting on an answer.

"I'd be happy to return it, if that's what you're getting at."

"On the contrary," the Archmage replies. "I'd say it's about time you put your extracting abilities to good use—and what better way to do that than by saving a Caldari?"

Catching her meaning, Cerylia glances at Felix, eyes growing wide. "You want me to extract Felix's very life force and place it into the soul gem?"

"You and I both know he isn't going to make it otherwise."

"But Opal—"

"Do you really think she's going to risk inverting time to save him?" the Archmage scoffs. "If I've come to understand correctly, the girl refuses to jeopardize our timeline."

"And for good reason," Cerylia counters, coming to Opal's defense. "Inverting changes the very fabric of our reality." As soon as the words leave her mouth, she realizes what she has to do. Opal isn't going to fix this. No one is.

Because no one can . . . except for her.

"Well?" the Archmage presses. "The longer we wait, the more at risk we are of losing him entirely. His pulse is already weak, his breathing shallow—"

Cerylia bites her lower lip. "I fear I'm not practiced enough."

"That's why I'm here," Cyfrin assures. "To guide you through it."

For some reason, the Archmage's presence is jarring enough, but Cerylia's in no position to turn down the offer. If she's going to save Felix via soul magick, she needs all the help she can get.

"Do you have the gem?"

Cerylia nods, producing the palm-sized crystal from the inner pocket of her robe. "It hasn't left my person since I discovered it."

"Come," Cyfrin urges, moving closer to the couch. "Stand here and with the soul gem cupped in both hands, focus on the subject's heartbeat."

Her use of the term *the subject* to describe a previously living, breathing human being is unsettling, but Cerylia follows the instruction.

"Breathe," Cyfrin says before slowly counting. "One. Two. Three."

Cerylia takes a few deep inhales and exhales. With each deepening breath, she zones in on Felix's life essence: the rise and fall of his chest, the pulse of his heart, the blood coursing through his veins. She's not sure if she's imagining it but, after a few minutes of intense focus, a tiny orb of blue light leaves the Caldari's lips. At the same time, his chest falls, the pumping of his veins goes still, and his heartbeat halts.

"Very good," Cyfrin applauds. "Now pull it to you—to the gem."

Like an invisible rope, Cerylia draws the orb to her. The gem begins to vibrate in her hands before turning the same color as the orb, a deep ocean blue. Within seconds, the two collide, causing a sort of ripple effect to take place inside the crystallized structure.

"Fascinating," Cerylia breathes, holding the gem up to eye level.

"You must be quick to seal it," Cyfrin orders, "before anything has the chance to contaminate it . . . before it can draw any more energy from you."

Cerylia regards her with a blank stare. "Seal it? How?"

"By using Jera, the rune for harvest." With her index finger, Cyfrin draws the shape of two arrows parallel one another, their points facing opposite directions, in the air.

Cerylia mimics the motion, doing so just inches above the soul gem until the blue light dissipates, winking out entirely, leaving the original gem in its wake.

"Well done." Cyfrin heaves a loud sigh of relief. "Seems you're more practiced than you believed yourself to be."

"Seems so." Cerylia glances at the corpse on her couch, grimacing. "What do we do about that?"

Cyfrin waves a dismissive hand in the air. "Not to worry, my people will attend to that."

She's about to ask for clarification when an unusual sensation hits her. Without warning, her eyes grow heavy, her body feeling like lead. Suddenly, it's a struggle to remain upright, to remain *conscious*. "Something isn't right . . ." The words come out slurred, her vision blurring.

"Yes, well, as you feared, that would be the extraction taking its toll on someone who is, indeed, less practiced."

Given her current state, Cerylia can't tell if she's just imagining things, but the Archmage's voice is sounding a lot less like Cyfrin's and a lot more like Xerin's. Even through her hazy vision, she can see the Shaper morph from one form into another.

When she'd fallen to her knees, she doesn't know, but Xerin meets her there, kneeling so that they're eye-level. He drops his gaze to the soul gem in her outstretched palm before snatching it from her hand. "It's been a pleasure working with you, Queen Jareth. Truly remarkable to see you in action."

She knew it. Something had been off, but doubt had clouded her intuition. Mouth agape, Cerylia searches for a retort but comes up empty. So tired . . . she's so, *so* tired . . .

"May your sleep be fit for a queen," Xerin says before leaving her side. "However short the remainder of your reign."

Cerylia can only watch, helpless, as he leaves the room before drifting into darkness.

DARIUS TYMOND

THE ARCHMAGE'S CADRE had put up a decent fight, but their physical prowess was no match for the Cruex, the King's Guard, even the Savant. Illusié could only get them so far. With the grid acting as a barrier for so many years, Midvale's residents had relied solely on their abilities without a second thought. A weak contingency plan.

Now they lay slaughtered on the ground, but not before the Mallum took what was necessary from them, draining their abilities first, then their souls. The Archmage's wide eyes stare up at him, lifeless yet still somehow full of disdain.

"Was that really necessary?"

Darius turns to face the voice, realizing that Opal Marston, the Caldari's Inverter, had been lurking in the shadows the entire time. *A valuable asset,* Xerin had assured him—she's someone they could trust. But with the way she's standing there, looking him up and down as if he's pure evil, Darius feels like she's anything but.

"Unless you'd prefer to be next, I'd watch the next thing that comes out of your mouth." The Mallum floats behind him, hovering but not advancing.

"An empty threat," she says, stepping into view, "but I admire your resolve." She looks to the Archmage, immobile on the floor, as well as the other members of the cadre scattered about the room. "Pity that they can't serve you the way they served her. Didn't even give them a chance."

"On the contrary, they *are* serving me and will continue to do so until the end of time." He looks to the Mallum, eyes shining with triumph. "The cycle is almost complete—"

"Whatever he's promised you is a fallacy," Opal says, circling one of the desks. "You *can* see that, can't you?"

Darius tightens the grip on his ring, trying not to be coerced by what she's seen, what she knows.

"I was so, so close to unraveling that final thread, to uncovering the truth that's plagued us all for decades," she hisses. "But *you*, in your selfish quest for power and glory, destroyed the one thing I could use, the one thing that could get me there."

The grid, Darius realizes.

"He's had us all fooled," Opal shrieks, bordering on hysterical. "And I was *this* close—"

Darius takes a step back as she reaches for the most unlikely of weapons—a quill—and lunges at him. It's almost laughable, the contempt on her face, the feather fluttering in the air, but before he can decide on a defense, a mass suddenly appears in front of him, driving a dagger straight into the girl's heart.

Opal stills, eyes flashing with shock at the perpetrator. She takes a shuddering breath before falling to the floor.

Xerin turns to face the king. "That's quite enough of that, wouldn't you agree?"

RYDAN HELSTROM

WHAT HE'S WITNESSING is something out of a nightmare—and that's saying something for a former assassin. Bodies line the halls of Midvale, complexions pallid and wrinkled from meeting their cruel fate with the Mallum. He's witnessed death before, by his own hands in the Cruex, as well as in Lonia when he and Avery had come across the fallen illusié, but this . . . this is just sickening.

Little does he know, something even more horrific lies just around the corner. The faces of those he'd fought side by side with in the Cruex lay motionless in the hall. He comes across Ezra first and even though the stocky brute had sliced him up pretty badly in more than one sparring session, he certainly didn't deserve to go out like this.

His eyes trace the fatal wound, instantly recognizing the weapon it belongs to. A chakram—Arden's chakram, no less.

On the other side of the hall, he finds Percival, who's seemingly met the same fate. Rydan hangs his head, squeezing his eyes shut at the camaraderie he'd shared with Percival in the halls of Trendalath castle. He'd been a kiss-ass, sure, but he'd been one of the good ones. Talented as hell, too.

But Arden had been the outcast, the odd woman out. Literally. It isn't at all surprising that she could—and did—take their lives without a second thought. Honestly, he would have, too, with how they'd treated her.

Arden may be callous when it comes to killing, but she isn't heartless—although, as he continues down the corridors, passing by more of the fallen Cruex, he's beginning to wonder if he's had her pegged wrong all along. At the going rate, there won't be anyone left among Tymond's ranks. The thought should liberate him but, surprisingly, it saddens him. Those in the Cruex were no different than he and Arden—just misguided souls who were thrown into a volatile situation with no way out. They'd made the best of it because they'd had to.

Who's to say that, given the chance, Percival and Ezra wouldn't have turned out to be kind, gentle, possibly even upstanding citizens of Aeridon? That they wouldn't grow to accept and appreciate illusié like he had? It's no longer an option, seeing as they'd been robbed of the opportunity by someone he's cared for since day one. How to reconcile that knowledge with his feelings will take time.

With each step he takes down the corridor, one thing becomes obstinately clear: that Arden is blinded by her emotions. Rage, vengeance, enjoyment . . . it doesn't matter. He's the only one who can get through to her. Rydan picks up the pace, determined to reach her in time before it's too late— before the damage she causes is irreparable.

ARDEN ELIRI

Even so, I press on. I've searched Midvale's halls far and wide, killing any who cross my path bearing the Trendalath insignia. With every slice of my blade, Felix's face darts across my mind. *Where did Haskell take him? Did they make it to the infirmary in time? Is it possible he could be healed by the very hands that had killed him? Would he even want to be?*

Fallen illusié and Trendalath soldiers lay all around me, discarded like yesterday's trash. King Tymond sure has been busy and, from the looks of it, mostly successful. But that'll all stop once I get that ring. I'm so focused on this singular goal that I don't even realize the room I've just wandered into is the Archmage's office. Her body is the first one I fix my gaze upon, her eyes wide open in a dead stare at the ceiling above.

"Shit," I murmur, returning to some semblance of emotional normalcy after an endless string of rage-killing. I kneel beside the elderly woman, gently brushing my fingertips against her eyelids to close them for her eternal rest. I scan the rest of the room, not recognizing anyone else until . . .

Splayed silver hair.

Blood-stained porcelain skin.

Hands clutching the dagger embedded in her chest.

Opal.

I go to her and check for a pulse, but there isn't one.

Even though I've had my issues with Opal, that doesn't mean I wanted her dead. I hang my head, feeling the sudden weight of losing two Caldari, the Archmage—and likely many more.

I have to stop him, to stop this . . .

My gaze lands on the Archmage again, the stark difference between her and Opal's death growing clearer with each passing second. In fact, upon looking around the room, I realize that she's the only one with a dagger in her chest—which tells me that it wasn't the Mallum who took Opal's life.

She could have fixed this, prevented it even.

She could have inverted time.

Someone wanted to snuff out that possibility entirely.

I take a closer look at the dagger, at the emblazoned handle. Blood-red rubies adorn the sides, shimmering in response to the light shifting as I move from side to side. The sight instantly brings Xerin to mind, but he isn't here . . .

That I know of.

I scan the room for my aunt, feeling both relieved and anxious when I can't find her. If Xerin *is* here, if he did this to Opal like I think he did, then Queen Jareth is in danger—likely even his next target. But if she isn't here, in the Archmage's office, then where is she?

A flash of green light reflects off the surface in front of me, causing me to whirl around and rush over to my brother. "Haskell, thank the lords you're here," I pant. My guilt only climbs when I notice that the Amplifier isn't with him. "Where's Felix? Did you make it to the infirmary in time?"

"That's precisely why I'm here." He surveys the massacre in the room with solemn eyes, swearing once he sees Opal among the fallen. "Is she—?"

"I'm afraid so." I glance over my shoulder at the Inverter, then back at my brother. "As for Felix?" I press, knowing that he must have heard me the first time around.

Haskell runs a hand along his jaw before shaking his head. "We were going to ask Opal to invert time, to take us back to before the Savant powered down the grid." Defeat lines his eyes. "I'm sorry, Arden."

What he means to say is that he's sorry that it's *my* fault Felix is dead—that I'll have to live with this guilt for the rest of my life. My heart shatters all over again and I have to bite the inside of my cheek to keep the tears from streaming down my face.

"It was the Caster," I explain, my voice cracking. "An illusion. I thought it was Darius walking down the hall—"

Haskell inches closer, placing his hands atop my shoulders before pressing his forehead to mine. "I believe you. I always have and I always will." When he pulls back, I can see the tears clouding his eyes. "As much as I hate to say it, we can't worry about that right now. We need a Plan B—"

"Cerylia isn't here," I interrupt. "And I have reason to believe that Xerin was partly, if not fully, responsible for

Opal's death. I'm concerned that he might target our aunt next."

"That'd have to be mighty swift work, seeing as I just left her in her chambers."

"You *what?*"

"She's with Felix. I brought him there. It was her idea to find Opal, to invert time to try to save him and prevent all of this from happening in the first place."

Dread curls in my stomach. "We need to go to her, now."

"You don't have to tell me twice." He takes my hand, readying to transport.

I take a deep inhale, closing my eyes as the familiar sensation of catapulting through space overwhelms me. The nausea isn't too bad this time around and, when I open my eyes, we're in the entryway to Cerylia and Opal's shared chamber.

"They were right in here—" Haskell takes off past the open door, veering right.

I follow, not sure what I'm expecting to find, but it certainly isn't Cerylia lying face down on the floor. I dart over to her and help my brother gently flip her body so that she's slightly inclined on her back. "She's still breathing," I affirm as I observe the rise and fall of her chest. But when I look up at Haskell, I notice he's distracted by something behind me.

"He was right there." Haskell leaves the queen's side, stalking over to the couch near the hearth. "Right here," he says, pointing to the cushions. "This is where I left him. I'm sure of it."

I say aloud what we're both thinking. "Xerin."

"We have to warn the others," my brother says as he starts to pace the length of the couch. "What I don't understand is *why* Xerin would do something like this. I mean, what's his motive? His end game?"

Still kneeling, I look to my unconscious aunt. "I think our best shot at understanding anything at this point is to find a way to wake her up. We need to know what happened here."

As soon as I say it, the queen begins to stir.

"Get some water and a cold towel," I order my brother, slowly helping her sit upright as she comes back to. "And something to eat, if you can manage."

"Avery's prepared some extra tonics. They're in our room."

Before I can even look up to respond, he disappears only to reappear again seconds later, vial in hand.

"Lords that was fast," I comment.

He grins, then uncorks the vial and brings it to Cerylia's mouth. She still isn't fully coherent, so I lean her back to help the tonic go down. If the pungent aroma wasn't enough, the taste is sure to have her waking up in no time.

Like clockwork, she gasps, sucking down air as if it's her first time breathing. I move my hand vertically along her upper back in the hopes that it'll soothe her.

"Haskell?" she sputters before turning to face me, eyes wide. "Arden?"

"We don't have much time," I tell her. "I need to know if Xerin was here. Did he do this to you?"

Recognition briefly illuminates her face, but it's quickly replaced by a look of pure disgust. "He used me," she chokes, still catching her breath. She glances at the couch, no doubt looking for Felix. "He has the soul gem—*Felix's* soul gem."

"What do you mean?" I press.

She regards me with a somber expression.

We aren't at all prepared for what she's about to say next.

❧ ❧ ❧

I'm in the process of comprehending Xerin's audacity—and the fact that Felix might still be alive—when an earth-shattering roar shakes the walls around us. The three of us exchange glances before joining hands. There's no mistaking what kind of creature it belongs to. It has to be a dragon. Perhaps it's an evacuation plan the Archmage had laid out before meeting her demise?

"Are you sure you feel well enough to transport?" Haskell asks our aunt.

"Honestly," she says with a sigh, "what choice do I have?"

Haskell shrugs, looking to me for confirmation. I nod and he transports us to the lobby mere seconds later. I'm surprised to see that, somehow, we're the last to arrive amongst the group. I'm simultaneously relieved and gutted to see that the only people missing are Felix and Opal. The Mallum hasn't quite gotten its claws into the Caldari as a whole—at least, not yet. I'm determined to keep it that way.

I race to the double doors to join my ranks. It feels like the longest stretch I've ever run in my life. I clasp a hand over Rydan's shoulder as I reach them, peering out the door to see what they're all staring at. Yes, there is indeed a dragon outside Midvale's walls, its giant claws nearly severing the bridge's entrance to the school, but that isn't nearly as important as who's riding atop it. As if I haven't already cried enough today, tears sting the corners of my eyes as the rider in the back dismounts the dragon, his platinum hair a beacon in the dark.

My cousin, Braxton . . . is alive.

BRAXTON HORNSBY

HIS SPIRITS LIFT the minute Arden comes into view, her hair whipping wildly behind her as she sprints across the bridge to greet him in what is possibly the sincerest embrace of his existence. The group follows her lead, leaving behind the screams, terror, and havoc wreaking Midvale Arcane Haven.

"It's really you," Arden says, squeezing his shoulders as she takes a step back to look at him. "You're okay."

Braxton takes in the sight of her, the blood streaked across her face, her clothes, her hands. "Yes, I am, but more importantly, are you?" He glances at the school. "What the hell is going on in there?"

Before she can respond, Lane comes barreling into view, wrapping her arms around his neck in a near-suffocating grip. "Braxton! Lords, I'm so sorry," she whispers, the weight of her guilt hanging heavy in the air. "I should have known better, should have realized what would happen if we attempted traveling through the Veil." Her body shakes as she pulls away from him. "We've been trying to reach you, trying to do everything we can using Midvale's resources to rescue you." Her gaze wanders to the dragon, to the two riders still mounted atop it. "But it seems you had some help in another manner."

Braxton watches as Arden tracks the same path. Confusion clouds her expression at first, but it's quickly replaced by clarity. Her eyes shine with disbelief.

"Dad?" she whispers incredulously.

CERYLIA JARETH

BEFORE SHE CAN fully process the overwhelming miracle that's just occurred, the ground begins to shake. What feels like an electric shockwave tears across the bridge. All eyes turn to the doors of Midvale, to the Trendalath presence now standing there, guarding it as if it were their own. King Tymond makes his way front and center, his Savant flanking him on either side, the Mallum hovering above like an overprotective mother.

And that's when she sees him.

Xerin.

To her left, she can hear Vira suck in a breath, no doubt having difficulty believing her eyes. Arden takes a step forward to mark her ground, but Cerylia crosses her niece's path, shielding her from whatever reckless thoughts she's convinced herself to act on. The queen gives her a knowing look as she continues onward with Cyrus in tow. The irony isn't lost on her.

One of their own, each turned against the other.

If only it were a bargaining chip of sorts.

Thankfully, she's got another one up her sleeve.

"By order of the Archmage's Second, we demand that you leave Midvale at once." Her voice booms across the bridge, echoing in the now silent cavern.

Darius scoffs. "I take it that that's you?"

Cerylia advances, but doesn't deign to respond.

"Well, I suppose I should be the one to inform you that whoever *was* her second is now her first." Malice gleams in the king's eyes. "Your Archmage is no longer with us."

Something Arden and Haskell failed to mention. The news stops Cerylia in her tracks. Even though her breath catches, her composure remains that of a regal queen—of royalty. "Then by *my* order, I demand that you leave at once." She's mere steps away now, essentially putting herself in the line of fire.

The king's blatant ignorance of her demands only angers her further, even more so as he shifts his attention to Cyrus. "You always were a traitor."

The accusation doesn't rattle the advisor in the slightest. "I go where I'm needed. Unlike some, I know my place."

Darius snarls. "Pity. You chose the wrong side." He looks to Xerin. "We have what we came here for. Burn it to the ground."

Knowing there are still hundreds, if not thousands of illusié inside, Cerylia raises a hand in the air, palm open. "A moment of your time may have you considering otherwise."

"What could you possibly have to offer me—?"

Cerylia reaches into the back of her cloak to reveal something that Darius knows all too well and has certainly been missing for quite some time.

The staff.

His only line of communication to the Mallum.

He blanches at the sight of it, at the realization of what Cyrus has done; the betrayal that's taken place right underneath his nose.

It's the ultimate bargaining chip.

She's got him. This ends now.

But Cerylia's smug smile fades as she watches Xerin lean in and whisper something into the king's ear. The color that had leeched from his face returns. "And if we refuse to leave?"

"The staff will be destroyed."

Now it's Xerin's turn to speak. "And how are you planning to do that?" He approaches Cerylia with lethal calm, shadows flickering in his eyes. "The staff is illusié-made after all."

Something she hadn't considered until this moment. It occurs to her that they could make a trade—the staff for the soul gem—but then they'd be back to square one. The balance of power would shift out of their favor.

I'm sorry, Felix.

Tongue-tied, she grasps for the right thing to say when Stanton appears by her side with exactly that. "We can and will destroy it because we have, in our possession, the crescent fire."

Xerin's demeanor changes instantly, his eyes widening as if he's just seen a ghost. "Impossible," he whispers without elaborating further.

From the back of the group, Braxton pushes his way forward, crest raised in the air. "I believe this belongs to you," he says, handing it to Rydan. "It seems we have everything we need to obliterate the staff, that ring, and your precious Mallum."

"So, here's what's going to happen," Stanton says. "You're going to retreat, as your queen commands, and leave Midvale fully intact. Darius will renounce his throne so that Aeridon and *all* of its inhabitants will know peace once more. There will be no further injury or death. Is that understood?"

At a loss for words, Darius looks to Xerin, panic written all over his face.

"Understood," Xerin says coolly, unable to hide his smirk. "But, as I'm sure you recall, I was never one to do things your way, now was I?"

ARDEN ELIRI

I CAN SENSE it before it happens. The exorbitant accumulation of power. The build-up of something nameless. Untamed. Dangerous. What it is, I don't know, but I know we can't stay here a moment longer. The thrumming in my ears, neck, and chest grow more pronounced in desperate warning.

He's distracting us.

From behind Xerin, behind Darius, behind what's left of the Cruex and the King's Guard, I can feel them. The Savant. Amassing their abilities. I'm instantly taken to my time in the Daegrum Chambers. A shiver snakes its way down my spine.

"Everyone, mount!" I scream, pulling on limb after limb in an effort to get the Caldari away from the middle of the bridge and toward the dragon. "Get out of here—now!"

One by one, stares of confusion greet me, but no one so much as questions the instruction. The utter terror and desperation in my voice should be enough to make even the most stubborn person listen and, thankfully, it does.

If they leave now, they can make it out in time. If they leave now, no one else has to die . . . My use of *they* only confirms what I already know. That I won't be going with them. If I can feel what they're about to do, surely I can stop it. Surely I can do *something*.

I glance at the dragon, noticing that everyone's on board except for two people. My brother. And my dad.

I can feel Haskell's eyes on me as I turn my gaze to Midvale, to the fallen illusié inside. To the Archmage. And Opal. And Felix, wherever his body may be. This is not the death they deserve, to be reduced to a pile of rubble and ash underneath Aeridon's surface, never to see the light of day again. They deserve so much more. We all do.

"Take them where it's safe," I tell my brother.

His eyes brim with tears, but he doesn't argue. "Give 'em hell, sis." He lowers a quick kiss to my forehead and gives our father a hug before whispering something inaudible into his ear. A flash of green light follows, and I can only hope that he has enough time—that we're able to *give* him enough time—to retrieve as many bodies as he can.

I stand my ground in the middle of the bridge, waiting for my father to join the others, but he remains rooted in place, right behind me. I can hear Rydan frantically shouting my name as the dragon lifts off, its wings creating a powerful gust of wind.

"You should be with them!" I yell to my father through the flying dirt and debris. "Go! Please!"

He shakes his head, the picture of calm. "I've waited my whole life for this, kid."

I have no idea to what he's referring, but there isn't time for clarification.

He braces himself, shouting, "Send it all to the Mallum! It's our only option!" An arm extends toward me, along with an indigo tether of light. It wraps around my chest, encircling my arms and hands in a magnificent display of energy. I focus my attention on the Mallum, not entirely sure what to expect— but just as the Caldari had trusted me in those final fleeting moments, I'm choosing to trust my father.

It's then I feel it.

All of it.

Fire, wind, water, earth, lightning—the ability to conjure the elements.

Strength in numbers—the ability to multiply.

Lethal enchantment, daring allure—the ability to curse.

Illusion, fantasy, façade—the ability to cast.

And the darkness deeply entwining them all.

Not only do I feel their presence radiating in every fiber of my being, but that I, too, somehow possess these abilities; that I could wield them if I so choose . . .

Is this my morphed ability?

To wield not just one, but all illusié abilities?

To essentially *be* the Mallum but in human form?

A Channeler, Felix had said.

The tether connecting me to my father grows denser, thicker, harder to see through. It's all-consuming, this rush of power, this thirst to have it all . . . to keep it all for myself.

My father's plea echoes in my mind. *Send it all to the Mallum! It's our only option!*

But what if it isn't?

What if I could possess the abilities of the entire Savant? Who would *King* Tymond be without them?

Nothing. No one.

I refuse to give him more power.

Not while he still wears that lords-damned ring.

I break my focus from the Mallum, instead turning it inward on myself. *I* possess these abilities now, *I* can harness them whenever and however I choose . . .

I could gather even more, maybe even find a Necromancer, then bring Felix back, and Opal, and the Archmage, and anyone else we've lost—

Suddenly, the tether binding me to my father snaps. The surge of power goes with it, ripping every ability I've just accumulated from my grasp. The euphoria I'd felt just moments ago fades, leaving me feeling hollow and depleted.

I fall to my knees, gasping for air.

Even in my vulnerable state, I notice both Xerin and Darius are no longer standing at Midvale's doors; but the Savant, what's left of the Cruex, and the King's Guard have all been left behind, their bodies slain by some seemingly invisible force across the last half of the bridge.

I look behind me, to my left, to where my father had just stood. He's crumpled on the ground with his back to me, a shell of the man I'd just met. I crawl to him on weak hands and knees, praying that he's still breathing, that he's still alive.

That I didn't somehow just kill him.

I turn him on his side, searching for signs of life. Seeing his face instantly takes me back to Lirath Cave, when I'd first found the photo of him—my only proof that I'd ever had parents, had a father. The relief, joy, anger, and longing I'd felt simultaneously knowing that he existed, yet never knowing if we'd have the chance to meet. But we did, in the here and now. And I'd squandered it.

Even more crushing is the realization that he's the only person who could tell me about my mother. At the freshwater spring, I'd seen her in a memory before I was even born and, since then, my curiosity has only heightened. What really happened to her? Did she die at the hands of the Savant like I'd been led to believe? And why did they leave me with the Tymonds? Do they know what I've turned into? The monster their choice had created?

I squeeze my eyes shut, trying to control my spiraling thoughts, but the effort is futile. I never wanted this. I only ever wanted normal. A childhood with a mother, father, and brother. Instead, I was afflicted with abandonment issues and a rigorous upbringing to boot.

The quintessential daughter? Wouldn't know her.

But the ruthless assassin? I know her all too well.

I sit idly by my unresponsive father, the surrounding silence threatening to swallow me whole. He doesn't move for what feels like an unbearably long time. I'm on the verge of tears when, by some miracle, his chest shudders. I wait for his eyes to open, to look at me so that I can apologize profusely for the selfish, power-hungry decision I'd almost made, but that opportunity doesn't come.

Time ticks by ever so slowly and when Haskell finds me, I'm nothing more than a mess of tears and a tangle of limbs thrown over my father's slowly decaying body. The look on his face says it all.

What the hell happened here?

But he doesn't speak the words.

Instead, he gently lifts me up and places me over one shoulder, then picks up our father and cradles him as if he were a small child. He takes a deep breath as he prepares to transport us away from the wreckage of Midvale. Through my tear-streaked gaze and the gap underneath his arm, I catch a glimpse of my father's ashen face.

Of the man who had only just met me and trusted me enough not to run, but to put himself in harm's way instead.

Of the man who'd put his abilities—*his life*—on the line.

Of the man who could have taught me everything I'd ever need to know about my newfound abilities.

I fear I may have just killed the one person who was capable of giving me the very answers I've been searching for.

ACKNOWLEDGMENTS

This book was drafted during a time in my life when *everything* was changing. I reunited with my soulmate after 8 years apart, we moved in together, got engaged and married, and then I gave birth to our baby girl. I must say, writing a book while pregnant is no easy feat! It was definitely a challenge and took longer than usual, but this just goes to show what happens when we're willing to show ourselves grace. Regardless of the deadlines I had for myself, the book still got drafted, edited, and is now published for the world to read. This time in my life has only reinforced the saying "honor the season you're in". I'm proud to say that, with this particular project, I did just that!

First and foremost, I'd like to thank the Divine Feminine, namely the Goddess Brigid, for keeping the creative spark alive during a time I felt the most exhausted and least motivated. Learning to flow with my energy has been the greatest gift as I've relinquished the self-induced pressure I used to place on myself to "get things done".

To M.O.: my husband, my soulmate, my pea—I always hoped that, one day, I'd be able to write you into my acknowledgments… so to say this moment is surreal is an understatement. You were the first person outside of my family to know about my love for writing and my dream of becoming an author. I'm so grateful we found our way back to one another. I couldn't have asked for a better, more caring, more supportive partner in this lifetime. Thank you for making me a mama and for showing me what love is supposed to look like every single day. I'm so lucky to have you. I love you, to whatever end.

To my sweet Ivy girl—You're only one month old as I'm writing this and time feels like it's going by *way* too fast. I wrote this book while you were in the womb and finished it after you were born so, in many ways, this book is just as much yours as it is mine. You've been the best writing buddy I could ask for. Your little coos while sleeping on my chest as I type away are something I know I'll come to miss. I can't wait to watch you grow and learn about all the things that light you up. You bring so much joy to my life. Mama loves you so much!

To Anna Vera, for being the voice of truth and reason in a world that can feel overly curated at times. I thank my lucky stars every day that we hopped on that Skype call ten years ago. Who knew I would have gotten a best friend out of something so simple? I love you, bb!

To my sister, Erin, for nerding out with me on all the bookish things, especially anything Harry Potter related. In case you didn't already know, our theme park adventures are some of my favorite memories we've made together. And no secret here, but I'd say we're way overdue for a visit to Hogwarts! I love you, sister!

To my Mom, for always keeping the line of communication open, no matter the topic. Thank you for always being so supportive and for nurturing my creative energy when I was a kid. It looks like all those years of folding and stapling computer paper together to make my "chapter books" finally added up to something. I love you!

To my Dad, for always being there "behind-the-scenes" of some of my hardest days and most trying experiences, and for offering support most daughters could only dream of. I hope you know just how much you're appreciated because it's *a lot*. I love you!

To the incredibly talented cartographer, Deven Rue, for bringing The Lands of Aeridon to life, and to the cover designers at Damonza who continuously stun me with their artistry and professionalism. Thank you for being such a pleasure to work with!

To my furbabies—you are simply the best. The snuggles, the loves, the zoomies, the belly and ear rubs… I don't know how I got so lucky to deserve such sweet little companions. I remember the first time I read about spirit animals and nothing has ever rang more true. I love you more than life itself, my sweet, sweet, girls!

And finally, to my YouTube fam, readers, and fans—you are all just so lovely. Seriously. Thanks for sticking with me, especially during these huge life changes. It still baffles me that there are people out there who care enough to follow along on this wildly unpredictable journey of creativity. You guys rock. Write on, beautiful people!

Don't miss the sixth and final
installment in the *Shadow Crown* series:

MIDNIGHT

REIGN

TURN THE PAGE FOR A SNEAK
PEEK OF CHAPTER ONE

ARDEN ELIRI

EMBERS LICK THE sides of the pyres in honor of our fallen Caldari.

Opal Marston.

Felix Barlow.

Except, unlike Opal, Felix's body still hasn't been recovered. Nor has the soul gem Cerylia informed us of.

Angry tears prick my eyes as I recall the events from Midvale—how I'd foolishly and mistakenly murdered the man I'd shared a bed with. The way he'd looked at me as the light had left his eyes, the last thing he'd ever see . . . *me*. Betraying him in the worst way possible. Heat builds within my body, a stark contrast to the snow falling around me.

Having known them the longest, Estelle stands on the dais, delivering her eulogy. How desperately I want to listen to her beautifully curated words, but there's only one repeating in my mind over and over again. *Murderer.*

The irony isn't lost on me—attending my victim's funeral. It hadn't been intentional. Quite the opposite in fact. When I'd brought my blade down upon his chest, I'd done so because it'd been Darius I'd hoped to strike down. That's who I'd seen, thanks to the immaculate work of the Caster. In more ways than one, he's just as at fault as I am for Felix's death. Not that it matters to him in the slightest.

Why should it?

I'm briefly pulled out of my guilt-induced thought spiral as Estelle finishes her speech and leaves her post at the dais. The flames dance against a backdrop of snow-capped mountains and, if it weren't for the morose setting of a funeral, the view would be one I could look at for hours on end. I lift my gaze to the mid-afternoon sky, catching Rydan's stare along the way. He mouths a question we both already know the answer to.

Are you okay?

No. Absolutely fucking not.

If there's one thing giving me any glimmer of hope, it's that, before his untimely death, Felix's soul was extracted and placed inside a soul gem by none other than my aunt. How the soul gem came to be in her possession is, quite frankly, a mystery to me, but what isn't a mystery is who has it now.

Xerin Grey.

Seeing him at Midvale, standing side by side with Darius, was enough to make my stomach turn. Trusting him hadn't come easy and I suppose now, in hindsight, that was for a reason. Despite his sister's many defenses in his favor, the look of disgust on her face that day had said it all. As much as we might think we know someone, all we ever really see is the surface—what *they* want us to see. Xerin expertly hid behind a cleverly constructed mask, one we all failed to recognize.

Even those closest to him.

The fire is still burning bright when I realize I'm the last one standing outside. When everyone had left and returned indoors, I haven't the slightest clue. I shiver as the chill evening air wraps itself around me, the lights to Sardoria castle flickering in the near distance. I gaze at the setting sun, dreading the next visit that's about to take place: to the infirmary to see my father. Not that he can actually *see* me, since he's still unresponsive.

Yet another reminder of how badly I've fucked up.

At least he's still breathing, still has a pulse.

The reminder does little in the way of consolation, yet I've told it to myself every night since arriving here.

I sigh, leaving the pyres behind as I head toward Sardoria castle. I'd much prefer to visit my father alone this evening, but Haskell is hell-bent on making sure that doesn't happen. Not because he doesn't trust me, but because he wants to be there for me and for our father. I find his persistence in the matter both incredibly endearing and downright infuriating.

I've only made it a few steps inside the castle walls when my brother appears seemingly out of nowhere. "Is it that time already?"

I give him a dubious look. "It would appear so, seeing as you're lurking in the shadows, waiting for me."

He brings a hand to his chest in mock offense. "That would imply that I have nothing better to do."

"Than visit our father?" I shoot back.

He narrows his eyes, then says, "Touché."

We begin to climb the stairs to the fourth floor, walking in silence as we have every night prior. There comes a point in every family when all there is to say has been said and all that's left to do is sit with your own thoughts, no matter how awkward or inconvenient. Luckily with Haskell, it's never been either.

The fourth floor is quiet, save for the bell tower chiming in the distance. How it's already midnight is beyond me. I glance at Haskell, knowing he's thinking the same thing.

"I'm surprised you haven't asked for an update on my travels." He waggles his brows at me. "Then again, I suppose there's nothing new to report."

"Figures." I sigh. "Although, if I were Darius and Xerin, I wouldn't want to be found either."

"Certainly not with the current condition of their ranks being nonexistent and all."

I make a sharp left down the hall that leads to the infirmary. "I wouldn't exactly say *nonexistent*. I'm sure there's still a Savant or two out there somewhere."

"Did we not witness the same obliteration at Midvale?"

"We did." I pause. "But if Xerin and Darius were able to escape, who's to say a few of the others didn't as well?"

"But you saw the bodies—"

"It's not like I was keeping track," I counter. "I was a bit preoccupied." *With our dying father*, I want to add, but decide against it. I push open the door to the infirmary, its familiar creak both welcoming and looming. At first glance, it seems all of the Healers have retired for the evening, as should be expected seeing as it's so late—but then I hear the clinking of glass vials. In the far back corner, I can see the shadow of a woman behind a curtain. There's some rustling, the knocking of wooden trays, and the opening and closing of cabinets before she draws the curtain back and steps out from the workstation. Our sudden presence must come as a shock because she nearly drops the tray she's carrying.

"Lords, I didn't hear you come in," she says with a nervous smile. "You gave me quite a fright." She shuffles a few of the fallen items around on the tray before returning her attention to us.

There's something about the way she looks at me that sets me on edge. There's a hint of recognition in her gaze, but I'm certain I've never met this woman before in my life.

"I'm Edith," she goes on to say as she adjusts a gold pendant that's looped around her neck. "I take it you're here to see our one and only patient."

I lock eyes with her, trying not to be distracted by the intricate design of her necklace, but it's hard not to take notice. It must have cost a fortune. She toys with it again before saying, "A wedding gift. From my husband."

"You must be new," I say, bringing the focus back on her. "We've been here every night to see our father and not once have we seen you attend to him." I angle my head at his bed across the room.

Edith hesitates. "I'm not new, no, but this *is* my first night shift in the infirmary." She crosses the room, making sure to take a path that comes nowhere near Haskell or me.

I follow her warily, motioning for my brother to trail behind me. I can't help but notice the small metal tin in the center of the tray. "What's that?"

Edith looks from me to the tin, then wets her lips. "A healing salve. My own recipe." She removes the lid, dipping her ring finger into the yellow balm before gently working it into each of my father's temples. "It's primarily used to stimulate the mind, although it's particularly effective on victims of the casting variety." She purses her lips, shaking her head before adding, "Disillusionment is nasty business and can take months, if not years, to fully restore one's faculties, as well as overall sense of reality."

Having been a victim of the Caster's attacks more than once, the statement should give me cause for concern, but it actually does the opposite. I've got a pretty good grip on reality, as unfortunate as it may be.

"We didn't see the other Healers use a salve," Haskell notes.

"Perhaps they should have," she retorts. "His progress would be much further along." Edith leans back to assess her work before adding some of the salve to his lips.

I study her closely—the wrinkles lining her eyes and mouth, the strands of gray poking through waves of chestnut, the way her shoulders hunch even when she's standing upright—and realize that she's likely more seasoned in her profession than I've given her credit for.

"What's your prognosis?" I demand.

She regards me with inquiring eyes, no doubt making her own judgment about me. "It'll take time, but eventually, he'll wake."

It isn't what the other Healers have said—far from it, actually. Their outlook on the matter has been rather grim, but Edith doesn't need to know that. Something tells me it wouldn't affect her belief in the matter anyway.

"How long?" Haskell asks, taking the next question right out of my mouth.

Edith shakes her head. "It's hard to say."

"Ballpark it," I challenge.

She narrows her eyes, irked by my tone. "No longer than two months, no earlier than two weeks."

She says it with such conviction that I find myself questioning if such a timeline truly is plausible. "And this healing salve of your own making . . . it'll do the trick?"

She pockets the tin with a hasty nod. "As long as it's administered daily in the proper quantity, preferably at night." Her eyes dart around the room as if she expects an interruption of some sort. "If for any reason I'm not here or happen to be reassigned to another shift, you must see to it that the patient receives the proper dosage."

The statement lacks confidence and the way her voice falters near the end makes the conviction I felt just moments prior disappear altogether. I exchange a wordless glance with my brother, but he doesn't seem to pick up on the uncertainty I'm feeling. "Who do we speak with about having you as our father's primary Healer?"

My mouth drops open. He can't be serious.

There's a brief glimmer of victory in the old woman's eyes, but, based on this interaction alone, I'm guessing she wouldn't be caught dead beaming with such pride. "You are Queen Jareth's niece and nephew, are you not?"

"We are."

"I have it on good authority that as long as you request such a thing, it will be so."

Before I can voice my growing concern, my brother says, "Consider it done. We'll see you tomorrow evening, Edith."

She grins with satisfaction. "I look forward to it."

Haskell gives Edith a small wave before abruptly grabbing my arm to lead me out of the infirmary.

"What was that all about?" I hiss.

He waits until we've cleared the doorway before asking, "How do you mean?"

"You heard the other Healers," I huff as I tear my arm from his grip. "We have four other opinions that say the chances of our father ever waking up are slim to none."

He stares at me in disbelief. "And now we have one that says otherwise—*and* with a time frame, no less. Two to eight weeks is promising."

"It may not be realistic, Haskell." I hate the doubt that's crept into my voice, but I can't shake the bad feeling I have about Edith.

"It has to be." His breath shudders. "He has to wake up."

And that's when it becomes clear to me. He's desperate. Desperate for answers, for results, for *hope* . . .

"I know." I sigh, feeling a wave of guilt all over again. "But we need to prepare for the possibility that this might be it. That we met *and* said good-bye to our father in nearly the same breath."

"I can't accept that." He shakes his head before turning a lethal gaze on me. "And you shouldn't either."

The shame I feel is near suffocating as he stalks down the hall without another word. I swallow the lump forming in my throat as I glance back at the door to the infirmary. *This has to work.* Because if it doesn't, I'll never be able to forgive myself for what I've done. And I have a sinking feeling that my brother won't either.

Kristen Martin is the International Amazon Bestselling Indie Author of the YA science fiction trilogy, THE ALPHA DRIVE, the YA dark fantasy series, SHADOW CROWN, the metaphysical standalone, BEYOND THE STARS AND SHADOWS, and personal development books SOULFLOW and BE YOUR OWN #GOALS. A writing coach and creative entrepreneur, Kristen is also an avid YouTuber with hundreds of videos offering writing advice and inspiration for creatives and aspiring authors everywhere. She currently resides in Texas with her husband and their six kids.

STAY CONNECTED:

www.kristenmartinbooks.com

www.youtube.com/authorkristenmartinbooks

www.facebook.com/authorkristenmartin

Instagram @authorkristenmartin

TikTok @authorkristenmartin